# Two Lives,
# One Heart

# Two Lives, One Heart

# Barbara Lynn Murphy

Desert Palm Press

# Two Lives, One Heart

By Barbara Lynn Murphy

ISBN (book) 9781954213579
ISBN (epub) 9781954213586

Desert Palm Press
1961 Main Street, Suite 220
Watsonville, California 95076
www.desertpalmpress.com

Editor: Toni Kelley
Cover Design: Mich Brodeur eeboxWORX

Printed in the United States of America
First Edition January 2023

# Acknowledgements

When I started this project, I expected to do what I've always done in the past—write a few paragraphs, only to have the creativity fade and the story abandoned. I'm not sure what forces in the universe kept the words flowing this time, but whatever it was, I'm grateful for it. Maybe it was the pandemic and my need to find some outlet to push away sadness and despair. Maybe it was the lightbulb that finally burned brightly over my head, telling me to rethink *how* I write. But whatever it was/is, I'm trying not to question it for fear that the words that have now become so plentiful in my head will suddenly vanish through some unknown vortex.

Lee Fitzsimmons and Desert Palm Press, thank you for taking a chance on me. As a debut novelist, I appreciate your confidence in this story more than I can say. You knew it needed work, but you saw through its imperfections and gave me the chance to make it better. Thank you from the bottom of my heart.

Toni Kelley, your editing expertise has improved this story tenfold and made me a better writer in the process. I'm eternally grateful.

Michelle Brodeur, thank you for your lovely cover design and for tolerating my constant requests for "just one more thing...."

# Dedication

To my wife, Nancy, for her unwavering support.

# Chapter One

## JOSIE 1998

JOSIE MOLINA PUT DOWN her pen, locked the screen on her computer, and stood up to make her way toward the fifth-floor conference room. In her normal focused and rushed fashion, she exited her office and bumped into Amanda Rathburn, who seemed to be headed toward the very same room. Amanda was armed with a box of donuts in one hand and a Filofax in the other, looking very much like the executive she was. Josie did a double-take and rechecked her calendar. Yes, it was Tuesday at ten o'clock, and yes, she had reserved the room for her weekly staff meeting. *Her* staff meeting. Josie managed a group of software developers. Amanda, however, was a VP, meaning she was Josie's boss' boss. Josie's team was too far down on the organizational chart for a VP to attend their meeting. A sense of panic set in. *This can't be good.*

"Hi, Josie," Amanda said as she made her way to the seat at the head of the conference table. Josie did another double-take. She had no idea Amanda Rathburn knew she was alive, much less her name.

"Hi, Ms. Rathburn. I'm sorry. I thought I had this room reserved at this time. I must be mistaken." Josie again rechecked her calendar, still wondering if she was in the right place at the right time.

"Please, call me Amanda. And no, you are not mistaken. I'm crashing your meeting."

"Oh, okay," Josie said, trying not to convey panic in her voice. Vice presidents don't attend staff meetings on this level unless it's to deliver bad news. Josie sat across from Amanda, mentally scratching her head, searching for a reason Amanda would be there. She calculated her financial situation, assuming her staff and possibly herself were getting fired. Actually, in their world, they wouldn't say 'fired'. That was too harsh. They would be 'RIF'd, which meant 'reduction in force,' a fancy corporate way of saying fired. As each of her team members trailed into the room, Josie could see Amanda's presence unnerved the otherwise informal group, most of whom were more than just a little bit frightened of her.

A quick glance around the room confirmed what Josie already suspected. Tension and panic were the themes among her staff, donuts or no donuts. At fifty-five years old, Josie had good reason to be alarmed. Getting another job at this age was not an easy task. In fact, it might be damned near impossible. She closed her eyes and drew in a deep calming breath. When she opened them, she found her gaze locked with Amanda Rathburn's. Amanda silently mouthed the words *don't worry*. Josie breathed a sigh of great relief, but now curiosity filled the space that unease had previously held.

Amanda checked to see if everyone was present, picked up her notes, and started the meeting. "Good morning. First, let me say you can all relax. I am here bearing donuts—not bad news." A collective sigh of relief echoed around the conference table. "Instead, I have an opportunity for some lucky person in the group. The principal of the elementary school down the street phoned me today. She and I have been friends for ages, so I guess she decided it was time to hit me up for a favor. They're having a career day and want an IT professional to come in and talk to the kids about careers in technology. So, I thought I'd scout around for volunteers. It's a short session with the kids to talk about what you do and why it might be interesting for them to get more involved in when they get older. So, who's it going to be?"

The entire team lowered their eyes and skulked into their faux-leather chairs. Suddenly, each staff member had something interesting, if not pressing, to read on their notepads in front of them. Not one person raised their hand. If they could have magically disappeared, each and every one of them would have done so.

"Your enthusiasm is overwhelming," Amanda said with as much sarcasm as she could muster. She took a moment to glance around the table two or three times before finally focusing on Josie. There was no escaping her now. Josie stiffened and waited. "Josie, how about you? I've been told you've done many presentations to other groups who often act like children. What's one more?" The whole traitorous group whooped and clapped their hands in agreement, proving Amanda's 'child-like staff' point. Yes, her team was sometimes known for their first-grade demeanor—it made for a fun work environment—but Josie was not so sure she wanted that on display here in front of Amanda. As the laughter died down, Josie contemplated the ramifications of saying *no* to the VP. It didn't take more than a few seconds for her to realize one does not refuse once the boss has proverbially tapped you on the shoulder. They called that career suicide. Josie knew how to avoid that. She had been playing this game long enough to understand the rules.

She reached up and tucked a lock of her shoulder-length brown hair behind her ear. "Sure, I'd be happy to go. Sounds like fun." *Not*.

Amanda smiled, and everyone, including Josie, knew she wasn't buying it. "Your acting skills may need a little bit of work. How 'bout we send you to an acting class some other time, huh? For now, just think of it as a way to get out of the office for a few hours. Maybe that will make it a more palatable adventure." The group snickered again. Perhaps they'd underestimated this VP, who suddenly seemed to have both a personality *and* a sense of humor.

After the meeting, the group dispersed to their assigned areas. Amanda stayed behind to give Josie the pertinent details. Amanda grabbed a donut from the center of the conference table, pulled the itinerary from her folio, and pushed it across the table toward Josie. "They set it up for the end of the day so any kids who stay for after-care can ask questions. So, you might want to prepare for their interrogation." Amanda flashed a quirky smile.

"How old are these kids?" Josie asked.

"I think they put you into a second-grade class. I don't know— seven, maybe?"

"A little young for a technology talk, don't you think?"

"Not these days. My kid is six and probably knows more than I do. So, bring your A-game, Molina."

Josie tilted her head in pleasant surprise to hear her VP call her by her last name, especially in such a familiar way, almost as if they were friends. She felt a jolt of excitement at the possibility of getting on the good side of Amanda and all the opportunities that might afford her.

"Are you going to be there?" Josie asked, not sure if she was hoping for a yes or a no.

"Nope. You're on your own. I'm sure I'll hear from the principal afterward, though."

"So, when is this presentation?" Josie inquired.

"Tomorrow."

"Oh, great. Thanks for giving me so much time to prepare." Josie smiled, hoping the reciprocated familiarity wasn't overstepping.

"My pleasure. Any chance I get to keep you all on your toes gives me a little thrill." Amanda laughed, grabbed her Filofax and another donut, then left the room. Josie cursed under her breath, not only for the less than twenty-four-hour notice to prepare for this gig but because Amanda was about a hundred pounds and had just reached for her second donut. *Bitch.*

# Chapter Two

## JOSIE 1998

JOSIE STOOD IN HER walk-in closet staring at her wardrobe. What does one wear to talk to seven-year-olds? When you work in IT, every day of the week is casual Friday. Unfortunately, that meant her options for appropriate attire were severely limited. Jeans and a t-shirt would not cut it, so she had to get creative. She didn't wear skirts or dresses—those didn't exist in this closet—but she managed to throw together a nice pair of black slacks and a lavender button-down dress shirt, giving her at least a somewhat professional image. She even added some jewelry for good measure.

* * * *

Josie pulled her Toyota into the school parking lot and realized she was twenty minutes early as per usual. Josie slow-walked into the office and introduced herself to the receptionist.

"Good afternoon. I'm looking for Principal Armstrong. My name is Josephine Molina, and I believe she is expecting me."

The receptionist picked up her phone to buzz Mrs. Armstrong, who came out into the lobby to greet her. They retreated into her office, both taking a seat at her conference table.

"Ms. Molina. So nice to meet you. Amanda buzzed me yesterday to let me know she had chosen the best person for the job here today. These kids of ours can be tough sometimes." Principal Armstrong smiled.

"Please, call me Josie."

"Thank you. I'm Susan."

"Don't worry. I've come armed and ready for them to challenge me. Here's a copy of the topics I plan to discuss." Josie pulled her agenda out of her bag, then slid it across the table. "I've tried to pick out some interesting tidbits of information for them. Let's hope I've chosen wisely."

Susan looked over the outline, nodding her head in agreement. "I like how you've covered the 'world-wide web' and what you think it's going to be like when they grow up. That will definitely catch their attention." She continued reading, then took her glasses off to indicate she was finished. "I think you've done a great job with this. Let's get their teacher in here, and we can brief her on your plans." Mrs. Armstrong picked up her phone and dialed three numbers. Josie could hear the phone ringing in the reception area outside the door. "Francine, can you please send someone to get Mrs. McCann from the teachers' lounge and ask her to come to my office? Thank you."

A moment later, a brief knock on the door signaled the teacher's arrival, and she entered without waiting for Susan to answer. Josie stood as the principal introduced her. "Ms. Molina, this is Mrs. Patricia McCann. Patricia, this is Josephine Molina, the guest speaker we talked about yesterday." As Josie reached her hand out to shake the teacher's hand, her eyes locked with the most vibrant blue-gray eyes she'd ever seen. The woman had gorgeous wavy blond hair that reached to just below her collarbone. Adorable freckles peppered her porcelain skin, revealing a hint of Irish heritage. Best of all, she had a smile with delightful dimples. Josie stared for what was probably a second too long while she recalled what Susan had said a moment ago. Mrs. Dammit. She snapped herself out of it just in time to commence with the introductory pleasantries.

"Mrs. McCann. It's great to meet you. I understand I'll be talking to your class today. I'm really looking forward to it."

"It's great to meet you too, but I'll be honest—I expected a young, nerdy kind of guy with a pocket protector in his shirt. You are a pleasant surprise."

Josie laughed a little awkwardly. "Yeah, we have a few of those, but they'll let an old dinosaur like me into technology every once in a while." She flashed a big smile, hoping her sarcasm would be well received.

Mrs. McCann lowered her head in embarrassment, her face turning a lovely shade of pink, making her freckles stand out. "Sorry. I didn't mean that you..."

Josie waved her hands in a 'no big deal' gesture and said, "Please. No apology is necessary. I'm just messing with you. I hope that's okay. It's a bad habit of mine." Josie smiled at her, hoping they hadn't gotten off on the wrong foot.

"Then we will get along just fine," Mrs. McCann said. Josie breathed an inner sigh of relief. "I hope my kids don't give you too much trouble. Either they'll ask a thousand questions, or they'll ask none. It could go either way, depending on the day. But I have a feeling you will be able to handle them."

"If they ask no questions, I'm going to assume I'm not engaging enough for them, and they just want me to hurry up and finish so they can get home in time for milk and cookies. So let's hope that's not the case, as tempting as milk and cookies may be."

"Well, like I said, my money's on you over the milk and cookies," Mrs. McCann said as she smiled and winked at Josie. The look from Mrs. McCann gave Josie the impression she may be interested in more than just the subject at hand, and Josie felt a familiar tingle down her spine. The trusty "gaydar" bells rang in Josie's head, but she was afraid to pay too much attention to them. She'd been wrong before. Besides, married women raised a big red flag. Nothing good ever came from getting involved with a straight woman with a husband. A lesson Josie had learned the hard way.

* * * *

As they entered the classroom, Josie noticed the room, decorated in typical second-grade style, with alphabet letters on the walls and flowers cut from construction paper. There was a distinct smell of Elmer's glue in the air. She smiled as she briefly—but fondly—flashed back to her own second-grade classroom.

The presentation went surprisingly well, and almost all of the kids asked questions about what cool stuff they could do with computers. Josie got them incredibly excited when she talked about things to come in the next few years. It was 1998, and technology was booming. It would likely be the center of everything by the time these kids grew up. It was best to get them involved while they were young. After answering each question, Josie glanced at the back of the room where Mrs. McCann sat. She tried to read the expression on the teacher's face. Given the kids' enthusiasm and participation, Josie felt confident the teacher was pleased with how her students were responding, but beyond that, Josie was having a tough time reading her.

After class was dismissed, Mrs. McCann walked up to meet Josie at the front of the room. She sat on one of the desks and motioned for Josie to do the same. "Wow. Well done. My kids haven't been that engaged since we had a magician in here, and he made me disappear in front of their eyes."

Josie felt a rush of heat rise from her neck to her cheeks. "They were an easy audience," she said, downplaying her performance.

"Easy? You obviously haven't spent much time with seven-year-olds, have you? They are unusually harsh critics and they have no filter whatsoever. They have no problem telling you that you suck if you suck."

"Then I guess I didn't suck," Josie said, with modesty and just a hint of self-satisfaction.

"No, you didn't. Not by a long shot. I was very impressed." Mrs. McCann flashed a smile, and Josie seized the opportunity to look her straight in the eye.

"Good. It was you I was trying to impress the most," Josie admitted.

"Me? Why?"

"Well, forgive me for saying so, but you have a bit of a poker face."

"So I've been told."

"I knew if I got *any* positive facial expressions from you, I was probably doing okay."

"I didn't know I was your target audience. I'm flattered." It was her turn to blush.

Josie suddenly felt embarrassed. What was she doing? This was a straight married woman, and shamelessly flirting with her was not in her best interest. By the time this day was over, she would need to wrap a rubber band around her wrist to snap forcefully as reinforcement of the mantra—*move along, Josie. This woman is not on your team.*

"So, Mrs. McCann, I appreciate…"

"Please call me Patricia. Or Trish. We don't need to stand on ceremony, do we, Josephine?"

"Um, er, well…no, of course not. Please, call me Josie. Only my mother called me Josephine."

"Josie. I like that." Trish's dimpled smile was beguiling. Josie tilted her head in a gesture of both confusion and intrigue. She could swear this woman was flirting with her!

"Listen, Josie. It's been a long day, and my kids were on my very last nerve until you came along. Would you like to join me for a drink? I could use a nice glass of wine and some adult conversation."

Josie's heart skipped a beat. "Um, sure. Yeah. That sounds great." Josie tried to hide her enthusiasm at the prospect of spending a few hours looking into those mesmerizing eyes. "Let me just get my things from the principal's office."

Trish stood, and Josie noticed for the first time that Trish was a couple of inches taller than her. Josie herself was only five-feet-four inches, and since she always considered herself short, she was typically *not* attracted to women who were shorter than she was. The list of things to like about this woman continued to grow. "Great. I'll meet you in the parking lot. I'm thinking of wine and a bite to eat at the bistro down the street. Sound good?"

"Sounds perfect." Josie left to collect her things. *Did she just ask me out? Where is that rubber band when I need it?*

* * * *

They drove to the restaurant in separate cars and regrouped in the parking lot of Tatianna's Italian Bistro. The aroma of fresh bread and garlic hung in the air. They sat in the small waiting area until their table was ready. Trish leaned into Josie and confessed she was a notorious people watcher. As each new person came into the restaurant, she concocted stories about them based solely on their attire and expressions. One guy was cheating on his wife, and the woman was both his secretary and his lover. Another lady was a closet alcoholic since she had downed three vodka tonics in less than five minutes. The bratty kids running around the waiting area must belong to the haggard couple in the corner, who looked like they would rather be at the dentist having a root canal than here with their kids. Josie and Trish giggled like schoolgirls as they spun their tall tales, each fabrication more interesting and outlandish than the last.

Once they were seated at their table, the Merlot flowed, and the conversation became less and less formal with each glass. With liquid courage fueling her curiosity, Josie began digging deeper with more personal questions.

"So, Patricia…"

"Trish."

"Right. Trish. Is there a husband at home that normally provides you with adult conversation? Or perhaps you have a house full of small and sometimes unruly children, and that's why you needed the adult beverages before going home?"

"Neither. I'm divorced. No kids. And since I'm fifty-four, I'm quite certain there will be no kids in my future."

"Ah, I see. So, you just haven't dropped the 'Mrs.' from your name yet? Stop me if I get too personal."

"I don't mind. As a teacher, I've found the 'Mrs.' title seems to carry more weight with the parents. So I just kept it, but as it happens, McCann is also my maiden name. I married a guy who was also a McCann. No relation, obviously—there are about ninety million

McCanns in the world. I feel slightly guilty about the deception with the parents, but not enough to change it."

"Well, that's convenient. You managed to avoid that dreaded trip to the DMV to change your driver's license."

"Yeah, it made for an easy transition into married life. The monograms all remained the same. Too bad that was the easiest part. It was all downhill from there."

"Hmmm. I don't know you very well, but I have to say if the fact that you didn't have to change your name was the easiest part of getting married, that's probably not a good sign. Do you have that many monograms?" Josie flashed her most playful looking smile.

"Nope. Not a good sign."

"I'm sorry to hear that."

"Don't be. It all worked out for the best. I think I'm better alone anyway. And no, I was joking about the monograms. Does anyone still do that anymore?" Trish asked. "Anyway, how about you? Husband? Kids? Sorry, but turnabout is fair play."

"Indeed, it is. There is neither."

"Never?" Trish asked, pleased with the answer to her first question.

"Nope." Josie shook her head, causing her a slight twinge of dizziness. Perhaps from the exquisite woman seated in front of her.

"Care to elaborate? Just haven't met the right guy? Enjoy playing the field? Lesbian?"

Josie was taken aback. "Wow—you are *direct*, aren't you?" She smiled at Trish.

"Yep. Sorry."

"Don't be. I like it. It's the latter." Josie waited for a reaction. There was *always* a reaction, one way or another. She just hoped she wasn't about to get a lecture from someone she barely knew about how she would burn in hell for her sins.

"Cool."

*Okay. That went well.*

"Cool? That's not usually the response I get. Instead, people say things like, 'you just haven't had sex with the right guy', or 'you should repent and ask God's forgiveness'."

Trish took another large swig of wine. "What the hell do I know about what God wants? To each her own, as far as I'm concerned. What you do in your bedroom is your business and no one else's."

"A very enlightened attitude. It's refreshing. Thanks."

"You don't have to thank me. In fact, I should thank you for being honest with me. It's probably not easy. People suck sometimes."

"Yeah, they sure do, but some people surprise you." Josie gazed intently into those blue-gray eyes and smiled, biting her bottom lip. *Oh boy. I'm in trouble.*

"I'm not gay," Trish announced only slightly defiantly.

"I didn't think you were. Don't worry. You can relax. I'm not going to hit on you."

"Why not? Am I not attractive enough for you?" Trish gave Josie a playful look of hurt and disappointment.

*What is she trying to do to me?* Josie thought.

"You just told me you weren't gay!" Josie thought she saw a sparkle in those sinfully tantalizing eyes.

"I'm not, but it's still nice to be considered." Trish batted her eyelashes.

"Consider yourself considered. Definitely considered. To answer your previous question, I think you are quite beautiful. However, given the 'I'm not gay' admission and my previous experience with straight women, I will keep my considerations to myself from this point forward."

Trish leaned in and said, "Tell me about these experiences with straight women."

"Why?"

"Because I want to know what kind of havoc we wreak."

"I can see I have my hands full with you, don't I?" Josie caught Trish's gaze with her own. *This woman is confusing. Playfully confusing.*

"You sound like my ex-husband. He always told me I was a handful."

"Did he mean it as a compliment?"

"Oh, no. He did not. Do you?"

"Maybe. I quite like a challenge."

"You are changing the subject by flirting with me. Straight women—come on, spill it."

"Why do I get the feeling you will be taking notes so you will know how to drive me crazy." Josie felt a rush of tingling heat radiate throughout her body.

"That's an excellent idea." A grin reminiscent of the cat that swallowed the canary appeared on Trish's face.

"Okay. Here's the thing. Many women from our generation felt they had no choice but to get married when they were younger. They have their kids, their big houses, their husbands who dote on them—you know, it's all very 'Stepford Wife-ish'—but it's not enough. They realize as they get older, they've been lying to themselves about what they really want. Then, when they wake up and discover they have more days behind them than ahead of them, they finally figure out they've only been hurting themselves. Even though that realization is as clear as day, most women still can't muster the courage to take that next step. They are too afraid of the chaos it will cause for their family. So, they dabble. And speaking for myself, I do not dabble. I'm all gay, all the time. Hence, the havoc. I do not want to fall for a woman who can't speak her truth because I'll be the one who will end up with a broken heart. So even though I have a *massive* crush on you, you're off-limits and, therefore safe from my consideration and advances. Havoc." Josie sat back, satisfied with her explanation.

Trish took another sip of wine and stared at Josie, contemplating her reply.

"Speechless?" Josie asked gleefully.

Trish paused for a moment, then said, "A little, yes. I'm sorry you've had that experience."

"As you can see, I've survived it quite nicely. I'm happily single. It's my dog and me, and I'm good with that. Max is too, I think. He's my dog, in case you were wondering."

"Yeah, I got that. Maybe you can add a friend—*just* a friend—to that equation? Assuming Max will approve, of course."

"He's a golden retriever. They are very agreeable. I think he'll be fine." Josie raised her glass and clinked it with Trish's. "And I'd like that too. Having a teacher for a friend is a good idea. Smart women keep me on my toes, and you never know when that might come in handy."

# Chapter Three

## JOSIE 1998

JOSIE AND TRISH MADE adult beverages at Tatianna's a Friday night habit. Their conversations were quick-witted, intelligent, sarcastic, and fun—exactly the way Josie liked it. She tried to keep from flirting, although she found it nearly impossible. Trish was just so damned attractive, both physically and otherwise. For six consecutive Fridays, Josie came home from the bar, sat on the floor, and cuddled Max. She would quickly remind herself straight, formerly married women were not to be considered, no matter how adorable the dimples. Max groaned and rolled over for a belly rub in what Josie could only interpret as agreement, so she put it out of her mind. At least until the following Friday. For her part, Trish still maintained she was straight, and that while she enjoyed the banter with a bit of sexual tension, it was a non-starter for her.

"I'm not saying it wouldn't be fun to experiment in bed with a woman," Trish said one evening as if it was no big deal. Josie's eyes widened, and she covered her mouth to keep from spitting out her wine.

"Oh, really? This is a new and exciting revelation. Have you ever experimented?" Josie asked, leaning in anxiously awaiting the answer like an impatient child. "No," Trish replied. "I'm sorry to disappoint you," she said, making a fake pouty face.

"Have you had the opportunity? Or the desire?" Josie asked with slightly less enthusiasm. Knowing Trish had thought about it was almost as intriguing as acting on it.

Trish sat back as if she was having an internal debate as to how much she wanted to reveal. "Yes, before I was married. I met a woman in college, and we became close. She kissed me one day out of the blue. Well...if I'm honest about it, maybe it wasn't really out of the blue. I probably could have taken her to bed, but I didn't." Trish waved her arm trying to downplay the event as if it held little importance to her.

"Why not? Were you attracted to her?"

"I was, but you know how it was back then. It was a shameful thing, and maybe I just didn't have the guts to pursue it. I guess I wasn't strong enough." Trish looked down at her drink, avoiding Josie's gaze.

"This sounds very much like my 'Why straight women wreak havoc' story, don't you think?"

"It does," Trish agreed, somewhat reluctantly.

"The only reason you didn't is because of how it was back then?"

"Yes. I guess that's true because, thinking back on it, I realize I wanted to. I found her very sexy, but I couldn't do it. Our friendship kind of fell apart after that. In hindsight, I think she may have been in love with me. She was a lovely woman, kind and funny, and I certainly enjoyed spending time with her. After all was said and done, I regretted losing our friendship. I still regret it." She stared off into the mirrored wall behind Josie, the sadness in Trish's expression becoming obvious.

"I'm sorry. Looking back, do you think maybe you were in love with her?"

"This is starting to feel like a therapy session." Trish began to fidget nervously, tension replacing her formerly relaxed state.

"Well then, maybe it's time for you to have a breakthrough, because I couldn't help but notice you didn't answer the question." Josie put her hand on top of Trish's, prompting Trish to meet her eye to eye. "Are you afraid that if you suddenly admit to being attracted to women, I'm going to pounce on you?"

"Are you?" Trish asked. She put her hands up on her cheeks in an exaggerated 'oh my' gesture, *pretending* to be uncomfortable if the answer was yes.

"No. Well, at least...not here. Not tonight." Josie sat back, putting her arm on the back of her chair. "You'd require a *lot* of thought before I would dive into *that* particular pool. Crush or no crush."

"I don't know if that is a compliment or an insult," Trish said.

"It's neither. It's just a statement of fact. And you still haven't answered me."

"I think maybe I was in love with her," Trish confessed.

"What was her name?" Josie tilted her head as she asked.

"Why?"

"Because when I hear interesting stories that someone I care about tells, it often helps to have names. Nameless people have less meaning, and something tells me this woman does *not* fall into that category."

"Her name was Andrea. Are you saying you care about me?" Trish looked both puzzled and intrigued.

Josie leaned in. "I do. You sound surprised. Am I alone in that sentiment?"

"No. You are not. I care enough to be scared of you. How's that for a breakthrough, Doc?" The look in Trish's eyes turned playfully naughty.

Josie tilted her head in surprise, trying her best to contain the jolt of interest Trish had injected into the conversation. "Scared, huh? I don't even know what to do with that information. Exactly how much wine have you had tonight?"

"Not enough to say anything I don't mean." Trish sat back in her chair, proud of herself for the candid admission.

"Yeah, but are you going to regret saying it tomorrow?"

"I guess I'll find out tomorrow, but for tonight, I just thought you should know."

"Well, for the record, I am *terrified* of you. Will you have dinner with me tomorrow night?"

"Is this a date?" Trish asked, surprised by her sudden excitement.

"That's your decision, my friend."

# Chapter Four

## JOSIE 1998

JOSIE SAT AT HER kitchen table the following day, weighing the pros and cons of the journey she was about to embark upon. She'd been down this road before, probably more times than she cared to admit. Women, love, loss, ecstasy, heartache—not necessarily in that order.  At eighteen, her first love kissed her in her 1953 Ford Crestliner on the way home from a drive-in movie. How cliché. Of course, except for the part about it being a woman, which wasn't at all cliché in 1961. That night, the fear, so profoundly rooted thanks to societal taboos, faded into the summer heat, and she yielded to her desires.

"Just let it happen," her lover had whispered into Josie's ear. Sitting at her table on this pre-dawn morning, she remembered 'the dance.' The dance was Josie's self-coined term for the start of a relationship when everything was new and magical, and all was right with the world. Love songs had more significance and every look had meaning, every word a poem from the new lover's lips. The dance was the intoxicating endorphin/dopamine cocktail that began the romance, but the beginning led to the middle, and the middle led to the end. The end was the debilitating hangover that inevitably came when the drugs all wore off. The music had ended, and the partners had left the dance floor. This was how the fairytale concluded throughout Josie's adult life. She thought of Trish and wondered if she had the stamina to go through it again. She looked down at Max as if he knew the answer. He barked at her—maybe it meant he wanted her to go for it. Or perhaps he just wanted a treat.

\* \* \* \*

Josie drove up in front of Trish's house, admiring the lovely flowers in the front yard. She slowly walked to the door and knocked, nervously shifting her weight from one leg to the other. Trish answered the door looking beautiful in a pair of beige dress pants and a cream-colored sweater with a brown scarf draped over the back of her neck. Her blond hair was pulled into a French braid, and she wore several bracelets on both wrists that made her hands look lovely. Seeing her outfit, Josie was even more convinced this was, in fact, a date. Trish probably would have been in jeans if she wasn't trying to impress her, right? Josie had this same conversation with herself a few hours earlier as she stood in her closet searching for something she thought Trish might appreciate. She had settled on black pants and black boots with a bold red button-down blouse. Trish subtly gave Josie a once-over, then smiled in approval. "You look lovely," Trish said.

"Thank you. As do you. That French braid is quite beautiful."

"Thanks. I was hoping you would like it."

"Mission accomplished. Shall we go?" Josie led Trish to the car and opened the passenger door for her. They shared a comfortable silence as Josie drove to her favorite little French restaurant a few miles from Trish's home.

Once inside the restaurant, the hostess seated them at their table in the corner, and the waiter handed them menus and the wine list, then filled the water glasses.

"Can I interest you ladies in something to drink before we go over the specials?"

Trish replied with an immediate and emphatic, *yes*, while Josie put her hand up and asked him to give them a minute first.

"So, listen, Trish. There was wine last night. Quite a lot of wine, as I recall, and there were things said that perhaps, in retrospect, you wish had not been said. Is wine the way you want to go tonight?"

"I remember everything I said last night. And for the record, I regret nothing. To prove it to you, I will abstain from the wine tonight. So let's see where the non-alcoholic conversation takes us this evening, shall we?" Trish said with a hint of self-satisfaction.

"Okay." Josie shook her head, impressed by her response. The last thing Josie wanted was for Trish to say something she'd regret just because the wine made the words flow more freely. Instead, she wanted a sober Trish sitting across the table tonight. Josie reached for her water glass, nodded for Trish to do the same, and offered a toast.

"Here's to an evening of good food, good friends, and good conversation." They clinked their glasses and Trish smiled before adding her own comments along with a wink and a nod.

"And to whatever else may come."

Josie nearly coughed up her water. "I can see you aren't wasting any time making sure I'm just a little bit on edge."

"Why, whatever do you mean, Josephine?" she replied with her best southern twang while giggling and fanning herself with the menu.

"Whatever else may come? You love making me squirm, don't you? Oh, and may I remind you only my mother was allowed to call me Josephine." Josie flashed a mischievous grin.

"Yes, you are a bit of an easy target, so I get carried away. My apologies, *Josie*," Trish said, leaning in as she said Josie's name.

"I'm glad I can make it so easy for you, but on the other hand," Josie playfully pointed at Trish, "*you* are the opposite of easy. You confuse me more than anyone I know."

"Oh, you mean because I told you I was straight multiple times, and now I'm shamelessly flirting with you?" To emphasize her point, she wiggled her eyebrows.

"Yep. That's it."

"Also because you told me you have a crush on me and I'm totally taking advantage of that bit of information." Trish laughed and put her palm on top of Josie's hand.

"Yep. That too. You have a mean streak in you, don't you, Trish?"

"I think I just might. This is kinda fun."

"I'm glad you are enjoying it," Josie said sarcastically.

"I am, but it's no fun if you're not, so let me try a different approach. I know it may not seem like it, but I'm really not trying to mess with your head." Trish changed her tone from playful to serious. "The truth is, after last night, I thought about what you said quite a bit. About whether I was really in love with Andrea and how you scare me a little. A lot, actually."

"And?" Josie asked, anxious to hear the magical words that would ignite her passion. She did her best to keep a poker face.

"I think I realized something. You're right. I probably am one of those previously married women from our generation, and I did many things back then because it was expected. If I had it to do over again, I might have done things differently."

"Although I do enjoy being right, this is not quite as satisfying as being right usually is."

"You think I'm going to be the same as all of those other women, don't you?"

"Well, that *is* what the evidence suggests, don't you think? But still, I'm not minimizing your feelings. I know it's difficult to come out at our age."

"It's probably difficult to come out at any age, but that doesn't change where we sit today. I mean that literally. I'm sitting across the table from a woman with these thoroughly hypnotic green eyes; a woman who intrigues me perhaps more than I care to admit. And try as I may, I cannot get you out of my head. I know what I said last night. You scare me, and I don't know what to do with you."

Josie squirmed in her chair and reached for her glass. She lifted it to her lips, realizing it was only water instead of wine. With a whisper of a sigh she placed it back on the table. Josie looked around the restaurant, pulled on her collar, then made her own fanning gesture with the menu.

"It's a little hot in here, don't you think? Whew! Damn, Trish. Whenever I think I'm going to control myself and you and I are just going to be friends, you throw me a curveball." Josie leaned in. "You don't know what to *do* with me?"

"I know. I'm sorry." There was no sarcasm in Trish's voice this time. "If you want, we can pretend the last twenty-four hours never happened. We can go back to being Friday-night drinking buddies. Do you want to do that?"

Josie thought about that for a moment, quickly concluding that there was no turning back. She had to see where this was headed. "Can I ask you something?"

"Of course," Trish said as she grabbed a cold mozzarella stick from the center of the table.

"When you thought about tonight, assuming you gave tonight some thought, how did you see it going? And perhaps more importantly, how did you see it ending?"

"Oh, believe me, there was thought—lots of it." Trish hesitated, deciding just how much she wanted to say. "So, I figured we'd talk, we'd laugh, we'd eat and drink, just like we've done every Friday night for the last couple of months. Then you'd drive me home, and..." Trish paused, took a deep breath, and said, "You'd kiss me goodnight." She sat back in her chair, pleased with herself for successfully verbalizing those last five words.

"I see." Josie nervously tapped her index finger on the table. "Are you still sticking with your 'I'm not gay' theory?"

"It was just a theory." They sat in silence for a moment, then both burst out laughing.

Josie picked up the water glass again, and this time, she took a good long drink. "Okay. I have a proposition for you. I say we dial back the sexual tension and just enjoy each other's company tonight. You can probably even have wine if you like as long as you're sure it won't make you want to attack me." Josie smiled and winked at Trish. "We will talk and laugh and eat and drink. Well, you will drink, then I will soberly drive you home. And I *will* kiss you goodnight. If you feel so inclined, you will kiss me back. Then, when you are alone, you will take some time to think about your feelings. Sleep on it. Maybe sleep on it for a couple of nights if you want. If you think this thing between us is something you want to pursue, then call me. If I don't hear from you, I will assume we will go back to drinking buddies, and I will see you at the bar next Friday night. No harm, no foul, no hard feelings. How does that sound?"

"I think that sounds like a very sensible and mature plan." Trish put her water glass on the table, raised her hand to flag the waiter, and said, "Excuse me. Can I see that wine list again, please?"

* * * *

Driving back to Trish's house, Josie could tell Trish was nervous because their usual flirty banter was noticeably absent. The radio was on, but so low they could barely hear it. It was just enough sound to make the otherwise silent ride slightly more comfortable. Josie thought about letting Trish off the hook with the kiss, but she'd been looking forward to it all evening. She could visualize the kiss. She *had* visualized it. They pulled up to Trish's house, and Josie parked the car and turned off the engine. No need to make it seem like she would be in a rush to drive away. She turned to face Trish, who stared downward.

"Do you wish to be released from the kissing pact we made earlier?" Josie asked reluctantly.

"What makes you ask me that?" Trish raised her head and met Josie's gaze but twiddled her fingers nervously.

"You're fidgeting. You seem anxious."

"I am. Two hours is a long time to think about a kiss while pretending you're not thinking about that kiss."

"You continue to surprise me; you know that, right?"

"Why?" Trish smiled devilishly.

"Because here I was thinking I was letting you off the hook from the heavy conversation we were having, and you were still thinking about it!"

"Weren't you?"

"Of course I was, but I'm the gay one, remember? I *want* to kiss you. I've wanted to kiss you since the day we met. You, on the other hand, are conflicted about your feelings. So I figured I'd give you an out by setting it aside for the rest of the evening."

"Just because we didn't talk about it doesn't mean it wasn't still there." Trish rested her hand on Josie's forearm.

"Just so we are both crystal clear, what specifically is the 'it' you are referring to? Just the kiss, or something more than that?"

"This." She pointed her finger at Josie, then back to herself. "Us. This attraction, this chemistry, this, well...for lack of a better word, heat."

"Heat. Yes." Josie sighed and reached up to touch Trish's face. She caressed her cheek. Josie paused for a moment, then leaned in and kissed her softly, opening her mouth just a little. No tongue—not yet. Maybe that would come another day. Perhaps not. But for now, just a tender, beautiful kiss. Trish kissed her right back, even trying to escalate it with a little more passion, but Josie wouldn't let her. She deliberately suppressed her desire and controlled the intensity. With a slight feeling of sadness, she stopped and pulled away. She took her hands off Trish's face, even though her urge to play connect the dots with those beautiful freckles nearly won the battle of wills going on in Josie's head.

Instead, she gathered her thoughts and said, "You remember our deal, right? Think. Sleep on it. Either I will talk to you on the phone, or I will see you Friday. You are in the driver's seat—metaphorically speaking—and I will be fine no matter what you decide. Scout's honor, okay?" She raised her right hand with the Boy Scout's two-finger salute.

"Okay. Good night, Josie." Trish flashed her dimple-laden smile.

"Good night, Trish. Sleep well." Trish stepped out of the car, walking quickly toward her house. She turned and waved before she entered through the door.

Josie drove home thinking about the kiss. *Damn. How the hell am I going to go back to being her drinking buddy after that kiss?*

* * * *

Josie walked into her house, gave Max the usual belly rub greeting, and took off her coat. On the way to the closet, she pressed the button on the answering machine.

"That was one helluva kiss. Call me."

# Chapter Five

## JOSIE 1998

THE PHONE RANG, AND Trish ran from the bathroom to her bedroom to answer it, flopping on her queen-sized bed in the process. She raised the antennae on the cordless phone handset and greeted Josie.

"Hey, sexy. How are you?" Trish asked, without even saying hello.

"I know you don't have that caller-id thing, so how did you know it was me?" Josie asked.

"You are the only one who calls me at six o'clock in the morning, Josie. Plus you always seem to catch me just barely out of the shower."

"That's because you are telepathically signaling to me you are naked."

"You wish," Trish said.

"Well, are you naked right now?"

"Um...yeah." Trish instinctively pulled the covers up over herself.

"See? It works every time. How are you today?"

"You'd think you'd be tired of talking to me after our two-hour phone conversation last night."

"No chance. You have a very sexy voice. We could go for another two hours this morning, and I still wouldn't be tired of it."

"Yeah, except you are going to make me late for work."

"The kids can wait, can't they?"

"Have you ever tried to get twenty-three seven-year-olds to wait for anything?"

"Okay, fine. I'll let you get to work. Are we still on for our first 'real' date tonight?"

"I wouldn't miss it. I've been looking forward to it all week. My students are going to have one very distracted teacher today."

"Just hand out a bunch of encyclopedias and have them read quietly to themselves. They will learn something, and you will get to daydream about me for the whole day."

"I think you've done the children of this generation a huge favor by choosing a non-teaching profession as your career."

"Well, you know me. I'm a giver," Josie said, laughing at her own joke. "I'll pick you up at six-thirty. Have a good day, Trish."

* * * *

The music in the dining room was lovely and just loud enough to make their conversation private. Josie diverted her eyes from Trish every so often so as not to draw unwelcome attention from the other patrons, but to no avail. Anyone with a lick of sense and an ounce of people-watching skills could see they were falling in love. *Cliches be damned*, Josie thought. *Those eyes are irresistible.* Josie knew she had to refrain from reaching across the table while they were in public. She only had one means of communication here—her words. They came slowly at first until emotion took over.

"You look beautiful tonight," Josie began.

"I think you might try removing those rose-colored glasses."

"Are you questioning my judgment?" Josie said with a wry smile.

"No, I just think you have a slightly biased opinion. You did admit to having a crush on me, remember?" Trish said with a coy smile.

"Indeed. Yes, that must be what this is. Just a crush." Josie did all she could to demonstrate her sarcasm. "Tell me something. Did your husband ever look at you the way I am looking at you?"

"No one has ever looked at me like you do. It's almost like you are looking through me. I'm both unnerved and completely turned on," Trish admitted.

"Well, the unnerved part is not exactly what I was going for, but turned on is good, right?"

"I think 'good' is perhaps too small a word for it."

"Okay, let me see if I can come up with a better word for it, at least from my perspective. How about enthralled? Captivated? Unable to form coherent thoughts?"

"That last one was more than one word. You're cheating."

"That just proves my incoherency. Is that a word, incoherency?" Josie tried not to laugh.

"Yes, I believe it is. Incoherency—noun. Nonsense that is simply incoherent and unintelligible." Trish folded her arms across her chest as she sat back in her chair.

"Always the teacher. Good thing I'm relatively bright. I have to be able to keep up with you."

"I think you can hold your own," Trish said.

"Okay, so back to 'turned on is good.'"

"Yes. Good. Turned on. Good."

"I think we may need to leave this restaurant sooner rather than later. If we don't, I will be forced to make a public display of affection, which is probably not wise. But before we do, I have a few things to say while I have you as a captive audience." Josie took in a deep breath and blew it out slowly.

"Uh-oh," Trish said ominously.

"No need to panic, but please consider my fragile ego before you laugh at what I have to say," Josie said, pretending she was being facetious.

Trish saw right through it, and responded in a more serious tone. "Unless you've chosen this moment to start telling jokes, I seriously doubt I will laugh."

"Okay then. Here goes." Josie took a generous sip of her wine, put the glass down, and took a deep breath. "Patricia Marie McCann, I am hopelessly, helplessly, and completely in love with you. My heart and my body literally ache for you. It's palpable. It's physiological. I do not know how to control it, and quite frankly, I don't want to. I want to take this feeling and sear it into my brain so I never forget it. I want to let it multiply, day after day, month after month. When I wake up, you occupy my thoughts immediately. I look at the clock and wonder where you are at that moment. Are you having your coffee? Getting dressed for work? Have I crossed your mind? Do you feel even a fraction of what I feel for you?

"I know I'm probably scaring you to death. You are only just discovering this 'thing,' which could very well be just a passing phase for you. If I were a better person, I'd give you the space to figure out who you are and who you want to be with, but I've already failed at that endeavor. I know this. At least I have enough self-awareness to recognize my failures."

Josie looked down at the table, unsure of where to go from there. She knew she may have overplayed her hand and said too much. Feelings of both relief and regret flooded her brain. She was glad she finally said it but terrified at what the reaction would be. Josie breathed deeply, looked up, and attempted to assess the damage.

Trish locked eyes with her for a moment, then looked around the restaurant, searching for the waiter. Their food hadn't even arrived yet, so Josie was confused by the gesture.

"Waiter? Can you please box up our meals and bring us the check? My apologies. We've had something come up, so we have to leave."

Josie started to panic. Maybe this was about to go wrong. Trish wanted to leave, which couldn't be a good thing.

"Josie, look at me, please. I want you to take me back to your place. I can't respond the way I want to respond here in public. I need to be alone with you. And yes, I can see you suddenly have a look of paralyzing fear in your eyes. There's no need for that. Just get me home, please, and I will show you that you don't need to be afraid."

* * * *

The ride to Josie's house was quiet, both women deep in their own thoughts. Once inside her house, Josie felt a chill in the air and turned up the thermostat. She took both of their jackets, and put them in the hall closet while Trish greeted Max with belly rubs and kisses.

"He likes me," Trish said with a smile on her face.

"He does. He has good taste."

"Does he need to go for a walk?" Trish asked.

"No. There's a doggy door in the kitchen, so he's fine. He'll settle into his bed any minute now. It's past his bedtime."

"I love your home, Josie. It's very welcoming." She pointed to a painting of a woman over the fireplace. "That is gorgeous. You have excellent taste in art."

"Thank you. Something about her expression drew me to that painting. She's beautiful, but she's sad, and obviously, we don't know why. It leaves it up to the imagination of the viewer to build a story around it," Josie explained.

"What story have you built?" Trish asked, tilting her head as she spoke.

"I think she's lost someone important to her, but not something as obvious as a lover. Maybe it's a child or a beloved parent." Josie looked at Trish as she studied the painting. *God, she's beautiful*, she thought.

Josie's nerves returned after the momentary distraction of the painting. She went into the kitchen and reached for a couple of glasses and a bottle of wine.

"Can I interest you in some liquid courage?" she called out.

"I don't need it. Do you?" Trish asked with a confident tone. Josie found her conviction both sexy and intimidating.

"I'm not sure. I might. Do I?" Her hands trembled. She hoped Trish didn't notice any fear that may be present in her eyes. This was either going to culminate into her fairytale or the recurring nightmare of her previous relationships.

"Come and sit down next to me, please." Trish patted her hand on the cushion of the plush beige couch, moving aside the pillows that Max had obviously arranged to his liking while they were out.

Josie set down the glasses and the wine on her marble countertop. It was probably for the best, anyway. Her hands shook so much she had no doubt she'd have dropped something. With unsteady legs, Josie slowly made her way from the kitchen to the couch. She wiped her sweaty palms on her pants and took a deep breath as she sat down.

"Tell me why you look so fragile right now," Trish said, reaching for Josie's hands.

"Because I think I've said too much too soon. I've scared you. These feelings are *so* new for you, and I've not allowed you the time to figure them out before I put you in this position."

"Well, there are a couple of things wrong with what you just said. Am I scared? Yes, I am. Terrified, quite frankly, but not because of what you said to me tonight. I told you. I've been scared since the minute I met you. I'm scared of my feelings for you, which are more intense than anything I've ever felt. I'm scared I don't know what I'm doing and will blow it. I'm scared to kiss you because what if I do it wrong?"

"You've already kissed me. You definitely didn't do it wrong." Josie giggled.

"You're interrupting me."

"Sorry. Continue."

"I'm scared that when I am out in the world with you—like just now, in that restaurant—everyone *will* see how I feel because I can't possibly be doing a good job of hiding it. It has to be written all over my face, right? You're right; I don't know how to process everything I feel, but there's no doubt about *what* I'm feeling. None. I've spent my entire life pretending to 'feel.' Pretending to be in love with my ex-husband, tricking myself into thinking what I felt was real when I know now it was all just a show. The world wants me to be what *they* think is 'normal,' and I tried—believe me, I tried—to be that woman."

Trish looked at Josie, who stared at the floor. She put her hand under Josie's chin and raised it so she could gaze into her eyes. "But then I met you, and now I know I can't play that game anymore. You've changed the rules. All I want to do right now is start being who I'm supposed to be. With you."

Josie stood up and reached out for Trish's hand. She pulled her to her feet. With both hands, Josie gently cupped Trish's cheeks. She inhaled Trish's intoxicating scent, feeling a heady rush of excitement. Josie leaned in and lightly brushed Trish's lips with her own. They kissed for what seemed a lifetime. Neither willing to break the trance. Trish released her tense shoulders and made a sound she didn't know was possible. Hearing it sent a bolt of electricity through Josie's body. She leaned in closer and kissed just a little bit harder, aching for more. Josie moved to kiss Trish's neck, wanting to savor every taste her body offered. Josie kissed and nipped her way toward Trish's ear.

"You have no idea how much I want to make love to you."

"Oh, I think I do. I've thought of almost nothing else since the minute I saw you tonight."

Josie resumed her gentle assault back toward Trish's neck, then down to the top of her cleavage. She reached for the top button of Trish's shirt, but Trish grabbed Josie's hand.

"No. Not yet. Not here. Take me up to your bedroom. I want the first time we make love to be in your bed."

They held hands while Josie led them up the staircase and into the darkened bedroom. Josie reached for one of the wall switches, illuminating two soft yellow sconces on either side of the king-sized bed. Trish looked around, admiring the warmth of the room, having nothing to do with the temperature. She kicked off her shoes and nodded for Josie to do the same. They came back together and kissed tenderly. Each connection of their lips became stronger, harder.

"I don't know what to do," Trish said, nervously taking a step backward.

"Yes, you do. There's no magic to it. Whatever feels right for you is all you need to worry about. I will only do what you want me to do. If you want me to stop, just tell me."

Josie's respect for her feelings touched Trish deeply, and she could feel her fear melting away. Trish timidly reached for her own top button and slowly made her way through each one, staring directly into Josie's eyes. Josie's breathing quickened into light pants as Trish pulled each sleeve off her arms. The bra followed in one quick hand motion to the front clasp. She reached for Josie's hand to place it on her breast. Trish closed her eyes and leaned her head back, allowing herself to feel what she had imagined so many times since they first met. Trish placed her hand atop Josie's, guiding her. Trish pushed their entwined hands down to her waist. Without the need for words, she encouraged Josie to undo her belt. Josie lost her breath for a brief moment before she continued kissing Trish's neck while she unhooked the buckle. She stopped, pulled her own shirt over her head, and quickly unsnapped her bra. She didn't want Trish to feel vulnerable while Josie stood before her, fully clothed. When Josie looked up after removing her clothes, Trish had tears in her eyes.

"I know I'm not all that attractive, but you don't have to cry about it." Josie smiled and wiggled her eyebrows, trying to add a little levity to put Trish at ease.

Trish laughed. "Your penchant for self-deprecation, while amusing on occasion, is poorly timed."

"Tell me why you're crying."

"I don't know. I can't explain it. I've imagined this moment a hundred times. Maybe more. And not once have there been tears in the picture. So I think I'm just a bit overwhelmed with a flood of emotions."

"Do you want to tell me what they are?" Josie asked as she brushed her thumb across Trish's cheek to wipe away the tears.

"Excitement, fear, anticipation, desire. But most of all, joy. I haven't felt this good in a very long time."

"Do you want me to stop?" Josie asked, genuinely concerned. She did not want to ruin this moment with an ill-timed joke or force Trish to do anything she was not ready for.

"Not a chance. If you do, I will never forgive you."

"Well, we can't let that happen, can we?"

Josie moved in closer, circled her arms around Trish, then guided her toward the bed. She pulled the belt out of its loops, unbuttoned and unzipped Trish's pants, and eased them down to the floor, taking her panties with them.

"You put on your best Victoria's Secrets, I see. Very sexy."

"Well, the Girl Scouts taught me to always be prepared."

Trish stepped out of her pants while Josie removed her own. Josie used her foot to push their clothing off to the side. It would not be very sexy if one of them became entangled in their clothes and fell to the floor. She returned her attention back to the beautiful woman standing before her. She snaked her arm around Trish's waist and placed her hand upon the small of her back. In turn, Josie wrapped her left arm around Trish's slender neck, cupping her hand to rest on the back of Trish's head. They kissed, long and slow, tongues exploring each other. Trish moved to sit on the bed, but Josie guided them to lie down. Josie was now on top of Trish. The intensity between them skyrocketed. Both breathing heavily, Josie momentarily stopped.

"I want to learn your body. Don't be afraid to show me and tell me what you like. Your wish is my desire – literally. Promise me you will tell me."

"I promise..." Trish whispered.

Josie moved half of her weight off to the side so her left hand was free to explore. She moved her fingers slowly but with purpose. As she caressed Trish's breasts, Josie lowered her head so she could kiss them. Trish did not disappoint. A rock hard nipple standing at attention told Josie she was on the right path. Her tongue circled the nipple, alternating between kissing, licking, and sucking. Trish groaned while running her fingers through Josie's soft brown hair. Josie moved her hand down to Trish's stomach, slowly progressing lower until her fingers felt the small patch of well-manicured hair. She paused, waiting to see if Trish would stop her. Instead, Trish lifted her hips ever so slightly, giving Josie the needed consent. She could feel the heat from Trish's body, almost begging her to touch her. Her fingers slid even further, finally landing on her clit slick with moisture. Trish nearly jumped from euphoria, but suppressed the urge, allowing Josie's fingers to explore and arouse every part of her.

Trish tilted her head up toward the headboard. Her eyes disappeared toward the back of her head, and her mouth hung partially open, emitting soft, guttural moans of pleasure. Never, in all Trish's years of sex with men, had she ever felt what she was experiencing at that moment. Within a short time, her body tingled, close to a powerful orgasm. Sensing this, Josie pulled off just a bit, not allowing her to have that moment just yet. These things were not to be rushed. Josie moved back on top so most of her weight was pressing down on Trish again. She slowly kissed the front of her body, starting at the neck and working her way down. When she reached Trish's hips, she took her fingers away from her clit and put them in her mouth, tasting her. Trish watched with anticipation. She had imagined Josie's tongue on her so many times as she fell asleep each night. *Finally.*

Josie darted her eyes upward, still ensuring Trish wanted her to proceed. Her tongue took its place where her fingers had been just a few seconds earlier, and she finally lost her ability to be slow, soft, and tender. The excitement overpowered her, and Josie became ravenous, darting her tongue between Trish's clit and into her vagina. Her hands put pressure on Trish's hips, holding her tight enough to keep her from pulling away but loose enough so that if she wanted to stop, she could do so. She did not. Trish called Josie's name, called God's name, and made inarticulate sounds of pure ecstasy.

Josie sensed Trish was going to come, so she eased the pressure from her tongue on Trish's clit. She waited until she could feel her lover's muscles contracting, ready to release. When the moment came,

Josie slowly pushed two fingers into Trish's vagina, moving them in rhythm with her hips. Trish screamed, releasing thirty-five years of frustration, pain, and hurt, allowing the first real moment of truthfulness to course through her veins. Josie held her close while she cried. "Trish. Look at me. Hold your breath, hang on to it, and look at me. My god, you are just...so beautiful. It doesn't get any better than this."

# Chapter Six

## TRISH 1998

TRISH WOKE TO THE aroma of coffee, toasted bread and bacon. She untangled herself from the twisted sheets and tiptoed to the bathroom. The image in the mirror revealed a little bit of everything. Hair in a tousled mess, eyes a bit bloodshot from lack of sleep, and a wide grin on her lips, demonstrating a satisfaction she didn't often see in her reflection. She threw on her underwear and one of Josie's tee shirts she'd found in the dresser and trotted down to the kitchen.

"I hope there is a cup of that coffee in my future," Trish said, greeting Josie with a kiss.

"And here I thought you would be an herbal tea kind of girl." Josie reached for a mug and poured another cup.

"Definitely not. Black and strong, please." Trish took the mug from Josie's hand, sat at the table next to her, and grabbed a piece of toast. The hunger pangs in her belly were a reminder that last night's dinner from the restaurant remained in the refrigerator. "How long have you been up?" Trish asked with a mouth full of food.

"Awake or out of bed? Cause I've been awake for hours, but I only got out of bed about an hour ago."

"You didn't sleep well? Why not? Is everything okay? I slept like a *rock*."

"Everything is fine. I slept a little, but you'll think I'm crazy if I tell you why I didn't sleep for too long."

"Try me."

"Do I have to? It shows my insecurities, which is a side of me I'd rather not reveal to you just yet. The longer I can postpone that, the better."

Trish tilted her head. "I think you saw a whole lot of my vulnerability last night, so it's only fair."

"That's true. Okay. I was afraid you might get up in the middle of the night and leave. Maybe you'd changed your mind and decided you hated being with me or you couldn't come to terms with all of this. It happens, believe me. I wouldn't blame you if you did, but I didn't want to miss saying goodbye if you had to go. So, I stayed up."

Trish took a swig of coffee before speaking. "Hmmm. Are you trying to burst my post-coital bubble?"

"I wasn't aware you were in a post-coital bubble. Please, do tell."

"I am. I hope you are too. It will be a bit of a blow to my somewhat fragile ego if you're not."

"Oh, I am. Trust me, I am."

"Okay, to address the first point, 'maybe you decided you hated being with me.' I have to ask—were you there when I had *the* most powerful orgasm I've ever experienced and cried tears of joy in your arms?" Trish asked. A look of concern spread across her previously happy expression.

"I was there. I wasn't aware it was the most powerful orgasm of your life, but from my perspective, it was quite a lovely sight to behold."

Trish put down her coffee and toast and leaned across the table. She reached for Josie's hands, brought them both up to her lips, and kissed them. "Do you think I was faking it?" Trish asked as she wiped the butter off Josie's hands.

"No, I don't. If you did, you are an outstanding actress."

"Acting is not my thing. I tried community theater once. Sucked at it. Everything you saw last night was one hundred percent me. All real."

"So, no regrets yet?" Josie asked.

Trish reached for her toast, taking a rather large bite. "I regret we didn't do it sooner," she said, again with a mouthful of toast.

"Very funny."

"What makes you think I was making a joke? You have to remember what I said last night. I have spent my entire life wasting time being what everyone else wanted me to be. I was the dutiful girly daughter for my parents and the dutiful wife for my husband. No one ever asked me what *I* wanted. Not even me, for a good number of years. Then you came along, and even then, I wasted time pretending I didn't feel anything for you but 'friendship' when you knew all along. I don't want to waste any more time, Josie. I'm tired of running from this. Last night was the first time in my life I allowed myself to *feel*. And my god, did I feel. Now that you've opened that floodgate, I'll be damned if I'm going to slam it shut."

Josie looked at Trish in awe. "Wow. I love this forceful side of you."

"Are you sure? Because there is plenty more where that came from."

"Lay it on me."

"Fine. Feed me breakfast and take me back to bed, please."

# Chapter Seven

## JOSIE 1998

JOSIE WALKED INTO HER bedroom, her arms full of a large bowl of popcorn and two cans of soda. She paused as she entered, enjoying the view of Trish naked on her stomach with her feet at the head of the bed. She had the remote in her hand and flipped through the channels on the television far quicker than her eyes could register the program on each station.

"Are you looking for something in particular, or is your finger stuck on the channel button?" Josie asked as she put the drinks down on the nightstand.

"There's nothing on anyway," she said as she turned off the television and flipped her body around to meet Josie at the head of the bed. She reached for her, and Josie reached back, only to discover that what Trish was really after was the bowl of popcorn. This had become a familiar routine for them in the two weeks since they first made love. Josie would make dinner for them, and they would clean the kitchen together. Then they'd retreat to the couch to watch television, with Max right next to them, his head on Trish's lap. Once Max decided he was ready to put himself to bed, they would make out on the couch, working themselves up like horny teenagers. Sometimes, they would move up to the bedroom, and other times, they would make love on the couch, unable to tear themselves away from each other to head upstairs. If it was still early enough after they were both sufficiently satiated, Josie would make popcorn, and they would lie naked in bed together, enjoying the after-sex euphoria.

"Tell me about your ex-girlfriends," Trish said as she fed popcorn to Josie.

Josie nearly choked on a popcorn kernel. "That's an odd question to ask right after we've had sex. What brought this on?"

Trish playfully patted Josie on the back in response to the choking gesture. "Nothing in particular. You've become my favorite subject to study, so I guess I'm just trying to learn."

Josie took a sip of her soda. "Hmmm. Must I? I'm afraid I don't always come out looking good in those stories, and I prefer to keep you in ignorant bliss for a little while longer."

"I think you are probably exaggerating. Besides, I've already figured you out. It doesn't take a rocket scientist."

"Are you saying I'm 'simple'?" Josie faked pulling a dagger out of her heart while smiling at Trish.

"Uncomplicated. How's that? I'm saying I'm usually a pretty good judge of character. I've met a couple of your friends. One can tell a lot about a person by meeting the important people in their lives. I've also noticed you still have several of your exes as friends. What's that all about?"

"It's a 'lesbian thing.'"

"Really? What does that mean—a 'lesbian' thing? Is that some secret code that straight people are not privy to?"

"Very funny, smart aleck. It means straight people tend to think you can't be friends with someone with whom you've had a prior relationship. Many lesbians, me included, think if someone was important enough to share an intimate relationship with, shouldn't they be important enough to figure out how to keep them in your life for friendship? After all, people you love and trust are hard to come by in this world."

"It's interesting logic; I'll give you that."

"There are, of course, a few women in my life who don't subscribe to this way of thinking. This explains the reason you haven't met them. Or maybe it's because they wish I'd rot in hell, and I thought it might undermine my purpose by introducing you to them."

"Those are the ones I want to hear about," Trish said emphatically. She fed another piece of popcorn to Josie while casually dropping a few on the floor for Max.

"Of course you do." She took a deep breath, partly because she was thinking about how much to say and partly because she had filed those memories away. "Well, let's see. We're talking thirty-five years' worth of history. You sure you want all that?"

"You can start with the abridged version. We don't need to cover it all in one night."

"You aren't letting me off the hook, are you?"

"Nope." Trish settled in for the explanation.

"Fine. Let's see. I've had a bad habit in my life of being the one who needs to be the fixer. I had an old girlfriend once say, 'rescuer to the rescue again, I see.' So I think I've managed to get into relationships with women who were a little bit broken, and I thought I could fix them. But of course, that's no basis for a long-term relationship. They either A) didn't want to be fixed, in which case they resented me, B) they didn't think they needed fixing, and they were insulted I thought they did, or C) they knew I was in it for the wrong reason and they took advantage of me. That's not to say that I was always the good guy doing the fixing, and they were the bad guys who were broken. I've certainly made more than my share of mistakes. I cheated on Amy, and we were in a ten-year relationship. To this day, it is probably the number one thing I've done that I regret the most in my life. She didn't deserve that. She was good and kind, and she loved me, and I trampled on her heart. Big mistake— huge regret. I was young, but that's a terrible excuse and a cop-out. Did you ever cheat on your husband?"

"No, but he cheated on me. And stupidly, I forgave him. Multiple times, which, in hindsight, I obviously regret."

"So now that you know I was a cheater, has your opinion of me changed?"

"I think it is unreasonable to expect that we have lived this long and never made any mistakes. And yeah, some of them are probably big, giant ones. I'd be naïve to go on thinking you are perfect forever, wouldn't I?"

"I didn't realize you thought I was perfect until now. Damn, I blew it. In any case—yeah, that was a big giant one. I left her for the person I cheated on her with. By some miracle, both of these women still love me. I don't deserve them, truth be told. In my defense, all I can say is I learned a *lot* from that time in my life. I've tried to do better. You know what Maya Angelou says—when you know better, you do better. I'm sure I'm butchering her exact quote, but you get the idea. One might think I should have known better to begin with, but maybe you can give me the benefit of the doubt on this one.

"I could probably make up several bullshit reasons and say I didn't have good role models for relationships and blah, blah, blah, but when all is said and done, I knew it was wrong, and I did it anyway, and for that, I'm not proud."

Trish tapped her index finger on her cheek as she considered her next question. "Since you opened the door, I want to hear more about the role models and blah, blah, blah, because I think a *lot* is going on there that you aren't saying. Am I right?"

Josie sighed. "Yes, I guess that's true, but can that be a conversation for another day, please?  We are lying in bed naked. Talking about my mother under these conditions makes me more than just a little bit uncomfortable. I require clothing to have that discussion."

"Chicken."

"Damn right."

# Chapter Eight

## TRISH 1999

TRISH HAD THE FIRST week of April off for Spring Break, so Josie took some of her well-earned vacation days and they sequestered themselves in Josie's house. They passed the time talking, eating, making love, and not a whole lot else. They saw no one and left the house only to walk the dog and get food. It was a blissful retreat from the rest of the world, and Max highly approved of the extra company. He followed Trish everywhere, slobbering her with doggie kisses and asking for belly rubs.

On the first day back at school after the break, Trish reluctantly walked into the teacher's lounge and poured a generous cup of aromatic coffee into her "World's Best Teacher" mug. She reached for the refrigerator door to deposit her lunch. When she turned around, Cassie, one of the other teachers and a close friend, was standing within inches of her face.

"Ahhh! Geez, Cass. You scared the hell out of me! What's up?"

"*You* are what's up. What's going on with you? I've hardly heard from you in weeks. And what's with that look on your face? Has there been *sex*?" Cassie opened her mouth to indicate her surprise, then quickly covered it with her hand. "There has! I can see it in that grin. You are holding out on me, McCann. Spill it."

Panicked, Trish turned bright red. That pale skin of hers gave her away every time. She had to think quickly. Cassie was a good friend, but putting her career on the line by confiding in her didn't seem wise. She wasn't ready for that just yet. So, employing the quick-thinking teacher routine, she stalled, diverted, and flat-out lied.

"You really shouldn't sneak up on people like that. You nearly gave me a heart attack! What makes you think I've been up to something?"

"It's written all over your face!"

"Your eyes are deceiving you. Besides, I spent the break with my family. We like to keep the discussion of sex off the table in my family." She gulped some coffee then refilled her cup, hoping the caffeine would help her think faster. "It was a relaxing yet boring break. I'm ready to get back to dealing with second-grade problems. I can usually solve those." Trish hoped Cassie didn't notice the stress-induced perspiration on her upper lip.

"I'm still not buying it, but obviously, you are not ready to share, so I won't pry it out of you—yet. Lunch today?"

"Sure. I'll even split my tuna fish sandwich with you if you want." Trish escaped the lounge with a parting wave and took a big deep breath as soon as she was out in the hall, away from Cassie's glare. She needed to do a better job of hiding her newfound bliss with her colleagues. She said a silent prayer that her second graders were still far too young to pick up on her change in demeanor.

* * * *

Back in the classroom, Trish stood in front of her kids. A feeling of sadness overcame her when she realized as soon as she'd left the house that morning, she'd gone into hiding. It would always be this way—free to be in love when they were alone, captives in their proverbial closets whenever they associated with the outside world. Now that she knew what that freedom tasted like, the idea of pretending it didn't exist brought that stark reality into focus. Most parents still frowned upon having their little children taught by one of those "lesbian types."

Her mind was elsewhere as she stood at the head of the class, spouting so-called facts about George Washington as the United States' first president. It was incredible how her brain could simultaneously keep track of two wildly different thought processes. And her mood, which started so wonderfully at the breakfast table with Josie feeding her grapes and making her laugh, suddenly came crashing down around her. She fumbled through the lesson, feigned a migraine, and bailed on lunch with Cassie. She went to her car during the break and called Josie on her cell phone.

"Hey, you. Is everything okay? You don't normally call during the school day."

"I know, but I'm having a bit of a panic attack."

"What happened?"

"Two things. Cassie cornered me, said she could tell I was having sex and wanted me to spill my guts."

"Oh boy. So much for your poker face, huh? Were you that transparent? And before you answer that, give me just a moment to congratulate myself on my ability to sexually satisfy you so completely it shows on your face hours and days later. I didn't realize I was *that* good." Josie laughed.

"Very funny. You are patronizing me."

"No, I'm trying to make you smile. Is it working?"

"Yes, dammit. Can I refocus your attention, please?"

"Yes, sorry. I was just thinking back to the look on your adorable face during the post-coital bliss you talked about, and I got *very* distracted. Continue, please. What did you tell her?"

"I lied! What else could I do?"

"You don't think you can trust her to keep your confidence?" Josie asked.

"I don't know. I've never done this before. The idea of risking my career made me panic," Trish answered with obvious angst in her voice.

"Okay, you don't have to decide today whether or not to tell her. You can think about it and maybe even feel her out and decide later. But, in the meantime, you did what you had to do in the moment, and you put her off, at least for now. Right?"

"Yes, I suppose you're right. But then, I got back in front of my class, still thinking about the conversation with Cassie, and I realized I'm in hiding. The safety of your home, your bedroom, it was gone. So when I'm out in the world, it's all a secret again."

Josie sighed, understanding exactly what Trish was feeling. "Welcome to my reality for the last thirty-five years, my love. I know you won't believe me, but things *are* better than they used to be. Now at least there are some people you can tell who will understand. Maybe Cassie will be one of those people. Or maybe even your mom, someday."

"What happened when you told your mom?" Trish asked, already knowing the answer.

"That story is counter-productive to this conversation," Josie said reluctantly.

"Right. I thought so. How do you deal with your whole life being a secret? It feels like I'm lying to everyone."

"Well, it's a sin of omission, and it's for self-preservation. In your case, as a teacher, you've got no choice in the matter. They will fire you. Maybe someday that will change, but let's face it. We live in a very homophobic society. Those parents don't want you polluting their snow-white children with what they all see as our sick behavior, but I have to believe that people will eventually start to realize we are just like them at some point. Yes, we have sexual desires and experiences they don't understand, but we feel the same as they do—we fall in love, get our hearts broken, pick up our pieces and carry on—just like they do. Knowing that this realization will happen someday, maybe even in my lifetime, is how I deal with it. The more society sees people like us living every day, productive lives, the more acceptance there will be. Maybe I'm naïve, but that's how I do it. This is all new for you. You are in the 'shout it from the rooftops' stage, which is admittedly the *best* stage, but is also the hardest to conceal."

"You don't want to shout this from the rooftops?"

Josie chuckled. "I do, but differently than you do."

"Explain, please."

"I want to shout that I've met this amazing woman who I'm madly in love with. You want to shout that you've finally discovered real orgasms."

Trish giggled while she considered that statement—and considered the orgasms. "While the orgasms are shout-worthy, that's oversimplifying and underplaying it just a bit, don't you think? It's not even in the top five of the things I want to shout about."

"Oh, really? I'll give you twenty bucks if you show me that list."

"I'd do it for ten, but you have to give me time to compose it first. Then I have to figure out the correct order. And then I might have to change it a couple of dozen times. You know me. Tasks like this bring out the neurotic teacher in me. I'll do it when school lets out this afternoon and share it with you when I see you tonight. Deal?"

"Deal." Josie said enthusiastically. "Let your OCD run wild. In the meantime, do you feel any better now? Are you ready to go back to the classroom and face the seven year olds?"

"Yes. You're pretty good at this *calming me down* thing," Trish said with considerably less angst in her voice than when the call began.

"Thanks, but I hope I'm good at working you up as well."

"Let's try that approach later this evening, shall we?"

"With pleasure."

# Chapter Nine

## TRISH 1999

JOSIE SET THE TABLE for dinner while Trish prepared the meal. The smell of garlic in the pasta sauce permeated the room. The ease with which they had settled into a domestic routine was paradoxically comforting and a bit scary for both of them. Josie opened a bottle of Merlot, poured two glasses, and handed one to Trish.

"Give it a minute to breathe. How was the rest of your day? Were you able to put aside the panic attack for the sake of the kids?"

"Yes, thanks to you. And after dismissal, I composed my list. I put it in order. Reordered it. Changed it. And reordered it again."

"Figures."

"You want to hear it or do you want to mock me?"

"Mocking you is fun, but I'll refrain until after you reveal the list."

"Do you want to hear it now, or is it better as a 'lying in bed and talking after sex' kind of thing?"

"Now, please. I'm impatient. We can revisit after sex."

"Okay." Trish pulled a piece of paper from the pocket of her Levi's. "I've titled it 'Things I want to shout from the rooftops.'"

"How original."

"You are mocking me again," Trish said with attitude, but the smile gave her away.

"Sorry. Continue, please."

"Number five."

"Oh. Reverse order. Even better. Building up to the main event."

"Ahem. Number five. Kissing a woman is quite possibly the sexiest thing ever. And as a corollary to that, men have no idea how to kiss."

"Can't argue with that."

"Number four. Being honest with others is rewarding, but it pales in comparison to being honest with yourself. Number three. It's incredible how much better you sleep in the arms of your lover. Number two. I am in love with Josie Molina." Trish glanced up at Josie for a reaction to hearing that phrase for the first time.

"If that's number two, I can't wait to hear number one." Josie leaned in for a kiss, enjoying the hint of Merlot on Trish's lips.

"The number one thing I want to shout from the rooftop is…"

"Is this pause for dramatic effect?"

"Yes. And because I'm nervous to say it," Trish admitted.

"You mean it's really not the orgasm thing?"

"It's really not." She stepped back and took a deep breath. Then, as she started to speak again, she dropped a knee to the floor. "Josie, will you marry me?"

Josie looked at her in shock. "Oh my god. That is *not* what I expected you to say. I'm not sure *what* I expected, but it wasn't that."

"You are avoiding the question. Do you need some time to think about it?" The look of disappointment on Trish's face was unmistakable.

"No, no, no..." Josie took her hand and guided her off her bended knee. She cupped her cheeks and kissed her as tenderly as she knew how. Tears filled her eyes, but she held them back, at least momentarily. She brushed the hair from both sides of Trish's face and tucked it behind her ears.

"Trish, I'm so in love with you." She kissed her softly before continuing. "But I can't marry you. Yet. And before you get upset, let me explain."

Trish pulled away and started to cry. "No, it was a silly idea. I'm sorry. I shouldn't have done that. No explanation is necessary."

"Yes, it is absolutely necessary. Listen to me, please." Josie grabbed her by the elbow and pulled her into her arms. "The first night we made love, I knew I would spend the rest of my life with you. There wasn't a doubt in my mind—there still isn't. I have stopped myself from asking you to marry me about five times already. And at least one of those was in bed, which is probably never a good idea. You know, endorphins, serotonin, etc. They likely hamper decision-making just a bit.

"But here is the thing. You are *just* coming out. I know you think you will feel this bliss forever, but at some point, real life is going to kick in. There are going to be days when not only do you *not* want to have sex with me, but you are probably going to want to punch me because I've irritated the crap out of you with my sarcasm or my annoying habits or any number of other reasons. It's inevitable, and there is no getting around it. But I can't even imagine the joy I will feel when you are on the *other side* of Mount Blissful, and you *still* want to marry me. I want you to ask me again when that happens. Assuming I haven't already asked you first, of course. So, no. I won't marry you—*yet*. But someday—hopefully someday soon—I will marry you."

She kissed the tears on Trish's face and looked her in the eye. Both of them were crying now.

Josie hesitated. "I'm having trouble reading these tears. Are they sad tears or happy tears?"

"Maybe a little bit of both. I know you're right. It's so quick. It's just...I've never felt anything like this, and maybe I wanted to do something bold to make sure it sticks. It's like you came to me through this little, tiny pinprick to my heart, and now it just feels like you are rushing right through me. I don't know where to put all of this emotion."

"I know. I feel the same way. So let's take our time and enjoy this. Just hold on for the ride and know I am committed to you and us in every way imaginable. You are the center of my world. We can take all of that emotion that we don't know what to do with and put it right back into our own little universe."

The pot on the stove started to boil over, and Trish jumped to lower the flame on the burner and stir the pasta. Finally, Josie decided to break the high emotion with a bit of levity.

"So, did you get me a ring? Because you know I'm not gonna marry you unless you shower me with jewels and nice things. No ring is a deal-breaker." She smiled from ear to ear.

"As a matter of fact, I did get you a ring, but now you don't get to see it since you turned me down."

"For the record, I didn't turn you down. I *delayed* you."

"Tomato, tomahto."

"Can I see it? Are you going to hold on to it or return it?"

Trish put down the pasta spoon, walked into the other room, and pulled it out of her coat pocket. Josie feigned outrage.

"What kind of proposal is this where the ring was stuffed away in your coat pocket when you asked me? Aren't you supposed to have that in hand when you go down on one knee?" Josie laughed and reached for the box, but not before Trish put it in her other hand and raised it high in the air so Josie couldn't get to it.

"If I had put it in the pocket of my slim-fitting jeans, I think you would have noticed something was up. Besides, I thought you would choose the "talking in bed after sex" option."

"Patience is not my forte. Haven't you figured that out by now? Can I see, please?"

"Fine." Trish opened the lid and handed the box over to Josie. "I remember you telling me you loved sapphires."

"I do." The tears in Josie's eyes returned. Now it was Trish's turn to kiss them away.

"Do you like it?"

She caught her breath. It was gold with an oval blue sapphire in a setting with two sparkling half-moon diamonds. "It is the second most beautiful thing I've ever seen."

"If you tell me I am the first, I will take it away just because your sheer corniness warrants swift and significant punishment." Trish closed the ring box and put it behind her back.

"Corny or not, it's true. So, what are you going to do with it?"

"I will tuck it away somewhere safe until an appropriate amount of time passes that society deems acceptable for a new relationship before engagement."

"I hate to break it to you, but society thinks it is never appropriate for us to get engaged."

"Well, aren't you a killjoy? Screw 'em. Like it or not, I will put this ring onto your finger at some point."

"I know you will. Do I get to see if it fits?" Trish hesitated, then pulled it out of the box and reached for Josie's left hand to slide the ring on her third finger. Perfect fit.

"I guess I have to take it off now." She scowled in a melodramatic manner.

"That's what you get for turning me down."

# Chapter Ten

## TRISH 1999

AFTER MAKING LOVE, JOSIE leaned on her elbow and pulled the sheet up to cover her naked breasts. She looked over at Trish.

"I know that look, Josie. You have something to say. Spill it," Trish said.

Josie traced her fingers down Trish's arm. "You think you know me so well already, don't you?"

"I do. Remember when I said you were uncomplicated?"

"I remember. I think you said 'simple' actually."

"No, *you* said simple. I said uncomplicated."

Josie reached over, pushed the hair out of Trish's eyes, and leaned in to kiss her. "I was just thinking," she said in between kisses, "if I had said yes to getting married now, would you come out to your mother before we have a ceremony?" Josie lifted her head again to look Trish in the eyes while waiting for her answer.

"Josie, we agreed not to discuss our mothers while naked, didn't we?"

"No, I said I didn't want to talk about *my* mother while I was naked. We made no such agreement about yours."

"Well, that's convenient, but to answer your question, I've been thinking about coming out to my mother anyway, having nothing to do with my failed proposal to you."

Josie sighed. "You aren't going to let this proposal thing go, are you?"

Trish playfully poked Josie's nose. "No, it's too easy to tease you with it."

Josie fell back onto her pillow and sighed in faux exasperation. "Seriously though, are you going to come out to your mother?"

Trish rolled over and nestled into the crook of Josie's arm. "Yes, I'm just waiting for the right time."

"That time never comes. Trust me, sweetheart. You just have to bite the bullet and speak the words out loud. It doesn't get any easier with time."

"Yours didn't go well, did it?"

"No, it did not, but that was a long, long time ago. Your mother is probably very different than mine."

"I wish I had met your mother before she died."

"I do too. I also wish I could say she would have loved you and accepted you as her daughter-in-law, but honestly, I have no idea if that would be true at this stage of our lives. She certainly struggled with it. She took it as her personal failure." The dull ache of an old wound was obvious in Josie's tone.

Trish sat up and looked at Josie, scrunching her eyebrows in confusion. "How so?"

"I guess because she let me be a total tomboy with my brothers, which never changed in my teenage and young adult years. And, since her relationships with my father and stepfather were failures thanks mostly to her issues, she thought that influenced me somehow. She never bought into the idea that we're born this way. Something or someone made me gay in her mind. So, it must have been her."

"That's kind of sad." Trish leaned in and gave Josie a tender kiss on her cheek.

"I know. We had a very complicated relationship. Then she died, so we never really got the chance to figure it all out."

"That's even sadder."

Josie lightened her tone, trying to encourage Trish. "Maybe your relationship with your mom is different. I'll bet she already knows and she's just waiting for you to say the words out loud."

"Oh, I doubt that. It's a nice thought, though." Trish nuzzled back into the crook of Josie's arm. "You sure you don't want to tell her for me?"

"Sorry, love. We each get to go through this special kind of hell all on our own."

"I was thinking about inviting her over here to tell her."

"Here? As in this house? Won't she find that odd since she doesn't even know me? Don't get me wrong, she's certainly welcome, but you might want to consider doing it somewhere more comfortable for her and where it is just the two of you. She will feel ganged up on if I'm sitting there with you."

"Why?"

"Come on, honey. If you were her, wouldn't you want to be in a place where you felt comfortable speaking freely if you had to have a potentially difficult conversation? I think it's only fair to her. Give her the best chance to react positively. Bringing her here will put her on guard. I know you want me to be with you, and I get that, but I think she will take it better with just the two of you."

Trish sat up again and faced Josie. "I guess you are right. I'll invite her to my place soon," she replied reluctantly.

"Soon, when?"

"Okay, pushy. Your patience in helping me through this process is heart-warming."

"Just doing my job. You said you wanted to tell her. So, yes. I'm pushing you to keep from procrastinating." She leaned over and gave Trish a peck on the cheek, then worked her way down to Trish's neck again.

"That sounds like something I would say to my students."

"Then you should take your own advice, *Mrs*. McCann." Josie sat up, picked up the notepad they kept by the side of the bed, and made a reminder note in giant letters.

*CALL MOM TOMORROW*!

"You'll thank me when this is all over," Josie said confidently.

"That remains to be seen," Trish replied. "You've never met my mother."

# Chapter Eleven

## TRISH 1999

TRISH STOOD AT THE stove, putting the finishing touches on her mom's favorite meal—a roasted lemon-pepper chicken, potatoes au gratin, and a green leaf salad with tomatoes Josie had grown in her backyard garden. She'd made sure the place was spotless and put on soothing music in the background. Earlier in the day, she'd spent over an hour in her closet, picking out an outfit she thought her mother might like. With all these preparations in place, Trish felt confident her mom would be at ease when she arrived. The aroma of the chicken in the oven was lovely, and she hoped her mother would appreciate the effort. Trish was not known for her cooking skills, so this was a rare occasion.

Marilyn McCann arrived fashionably early, as usual. Trish expected this. She would often tell her mother to come thirty minutes later than she wanted, knowing she would likely show up early anyway. To learn this trick took many years of answering her front door in a half-dressed state. Today, she was armed and ready.

"Mom, you look lovely as usual. Is that a new blouse?" She kissed her on the cheek, then took her coat and hung it on the wrought iron coat rack by the front door.

"Oh, it smells just wonderful in here, Patricia. Did you hire someone to cook for us?"

"Very funny. No, I did it all myself, thank you very much. I'm not a complete failure in the kitchen, you know."

"I didn't say you were, dear. I just recall a few burnt meals you served back when you were married. Richard was always very understanding about it, but I could tell he was putting on a good show." Her mother made her way to the swiveling recliner chair in the corner of the room. She made a squinting face as she looked around as if signaling to indicate her displeasure that it was too dark in the room for her liking. Before Trish even had the opportunity to rectify the lighting situation, Marilyn pulled the chain on the light next to her chair.

Trish shook her head, ignoring her mother's quirks, and continued the conversation. "I see you aren't wasting much time bringing up my ex-husband and my marriage." Trish tensed, took a deep breath, and tried to start over again. "What can I get you to drink?"

"I think maybe just some water for now."

*Damn.* Trish was hoping she would have asked for something a little more...well, alcoholic. Her mom was a happy drinker, and some wine might have made this news go down a little easier. She headed to the kitchen to open a bottle anyway to let it breathe for a bit before they sat down to eat. Trish noticed her hand visibly shaking while holding the glass of water on the way back out to the living room. She paused to steady herself—her mom would not have missed a bright, flashing neon sign of nervousness like that. She decided to waste some time on small talk to calm herself down before revealing her big news. She sat on the leather sofa next to the recliner, putting her glass of wine down on the "Teachers Have More Class" coaster on the coffee table in front of her.

"Mom, I ran into your old friend Karen McDougal in the grocery store the other day. She told me to say hi to you."

"Oh my! How is she? Geez, it's been ages. I'll bet she's got a boatload of grandchildren by now. Maybe even great-grandchildren."

Trish tensed. *Uh-oh. Grandchildren. Damn again.* Another landmine topic. So much for the small talk. The subject of grandchildren was an especially touchy one for them. Marilyn was so disappointed when Trish and Richard decided not to have children. Given their divorce, Trish took this moment to thank the stars above or whoever was looking out for them when they made that decision. Parenting was something she was always very iffy about. Single parenting was undoubtedly never on her radar.

"Patricia, do you regret your decision not to have children with Richard?" Marilyn gave her a look of genuine curiosity as she asked this question, not with the intent to trigger a mother-daughter argument.

Trish paused, giving the question due consideration. "No, Mom. I don't. I know it broke your heart, but I just didn't think I was cut out to be a parent. I'm happy with my little seven-year-old kids in my class, and I get to send them home at three p.m. every day."

Marilyn shook her head, accepting the answer even though she didn't like it, but it wasn't her decision, and she had reluctantly come to terms with that long ago. When Trish was growing up, it always seemed like she conformed to the norms but was never truly happy about it. But this was the one decision she didn't waver on. Richard agreed, as he also did not see himself as a dad. Even though Marilyn wished it was different, she was glad they had found each other. It would have been a shame to have one person in the marriage who wanted children if the other did not. So in this regard, Patricia and Richard were a good match, but unfortunately, they still couldn't make it work, which broke Marilyn's heart.

Trish went back into the kitchen to check on the chicken. When she reached the stove, the timer buzzed, and Trish pulled the chicken and the potatoes out of the oven. She gave herself a small pat on the back because the meal looked surprisingly good.

"Mom, dinner is ready," she called into the living room. "Come on in, and I'll pour you some wine." She brought the serving dishes to the table.

They ate and talked and laughed, much like they had time and time again over the years. It felt good for Trish to have this alone time with her mom. In the last few months, she'd spent nearly all of her free time at Josie's place, and she didn't realize until just now that she missed her mother's company. The feeling seemed mutual because Marilyn brought it up in the same context.

"I haven't seen much of you these days, Patricia. It's nice to just catch up with you. You've been somewhat scarce lately. Why is that? Is there a new man in your life?" Her mother looked at her curiously. "And as I say that, and I sit across the table from you, it occurs to me you look rather, well...content. Dare I even say happy? Am I right about that?"

Trish chuckled internally. *Content. Yeah. That is a good word for it. If she only knew.*

"Well, now that you bring it up, there is something I've been meaning to talk to you about. It might explain the content look upon my face."

"I knew it! There *is* a new man! I'm so happy for you. Who is he? Tell me all about him!" Her mother's face lit up like a Christmas tree.

"Mom, wait. No. It's not a new man." Trish paused, took a deep breath, and a rather large sip of wine. *Here goes.* "But there is indeed someone new in my life."

"You're confusing me, dear. It's not a new man, but there is someone new. Are you adopting a child or a dog or something?"

"No, Mom. I just said I'm not cut out to be a parent." Trish sighed in exasperation. "It's a woman, Mom. I've been seeing a woman, and truth be told, I'm in love with her." She paused long enough to take another deep breath. "I know this surprises you, but I'm hoping you can be happy for me because I am happier than I've ever been."

Marilyn's expression changed from joy to dread, and she didn't say anything for what seemed like an eternity. Then, she slowly took the cloth napkin from her lap, dabbed her mouth on either side and pushed her chair away from the table. Trish's heartbeat quickened, and she took another drink while waiting for the next move. Josie's theory that she probably already knew and was waiting for Trish to say it was becoming less and less likely with each excruciating second that passed.

"I see. Yes, that is a surprise. Perhaps I should go, Patricia."

"Mom, please. Don't go. We need to talk about this."

"Maybe you feel the need to talk about it, but I'm quite certain I am not interested in hearing it." She tossed her napkin onto the table and got up from her seat.

"You just got done saying how content I look. Don't you want to know why?"

"No, not if it means you are content because you are having sex with another *woman*!"

"I'm content because I'm in love, Mom. Maybe even for the first time in my life, if I'm honest. I'm content because I've met someone who makes me truly happy and brings balance, laughter, and intelligence into my life. Isn't that something worth talking about?"

"You've been married! How can you be in love with a woman?"

"Seriously? C'mon, Mom. You're smarter than that. You know one has nothing to do with the other."

"Well, I'm sorry, but if you were just expecting me to embrace this news, you were sadly mistaken. I've got to go. Call me when you've come to your senses. And Patricia, I'm so incredibly disappointed in you."

She grabbed her things, headed for the door, and walked out. Trisha followed right behind her and caught her before she went down the steps.

"Mom, wait!" she pleaded.

Marilyn turned back, clearly displeased. "What?"

Trish wanted to explode into tears, but instead, she just shook her head and said, "You never even asked me her name."

Marilyn sighed, turned, and walked away.

# Chapter Twelve

## TRISH 1999

TRISH DRAGGED HERSELF BACK into the house and stood over the dinner table for a moment, the half-eaten meals an indicator of the disaster that was the last fifteen minutes. She picked up the plates to busy her mind with the clean-up process, but as she grabbed her mother's dish, she quickly spun around and threw it against the wall, chicken and potatoes au gratin splattering everywhere. The wine glass followed, shards of glass shattered across the room. She grasped the pretty, floral tablecloth on her little dining table, and with both hands, she pulled the cloth out from under the items remaining on the table. Plates, silverware, salt and pepper shakers—all crashed onto the floor and against the wall of the narrow dining room. Her legs gave out as she bent over to pick up the broken glass, and she sank to her knees and screamed. A piece of glass pierced her skin, adding blood to the food and wine concoction on the floor. *This is going to require one hell of a stain remover,* she thought. She screamed in frustration and fury, mad at herself for thinking her mother could have embraced this news.

\* \* \* \*

Josie checked the caller ID and looked at the phone quizzically. It was much too early for the mother/daughter dinner to be finished.

"Hey, honey. How's it going? I didn't expect to hear from you so…"

Trish cut Josie off. "Josie, it was a disaster. Can you come over, please? I need you. I…I…I don't know what I'm doing. Everything is a mess—literally and otherwise. Please, babe? I need you." Her voice broke up with a mournful cry.

"I'm on my way. Five minutes. Just sit tight." Josie could hear the heartache in Trish's voice, and it devastated her. She grabbed her keys and bolted out of the house.

\* \* \* \*

Josie arrived at Trish's house, knocked lightly on the door and let herself in, not waiting for Trish to answer the door. She found Trish sitting on the dining room floor in a mess of food, broken dinnerware, and even some blood.

"Trish! Why do I see blood? Did this get *physical*? Where is your mom? What the hell happened here?"

"She's gone," Trish said through her tears. "And no, the blood is a self-inflicted accident, as is the rest of this mess. I had a bit of a meltdown after she left. I have glass in my leg, that's all." She whimpered as she spoke.

Josie tiptoed over the glass, cleared a spot on the floor to ensure she wouldn't add her blood to the mix, and sat down facing Trish. "A *bit* of a meltdown? Wow. Now I know never to get on your shit list."

Through her tears, Trish grasped for a bit of humor. "If that's the lesson that comes out of this, maybe it will all be worth it."

"Consider the lesson duly noted because apparently, my life is at stake if I piss you off. But seriously, what the hell went on here today?"

"She didn't take it well."

"Oh really? I couldn't tell."

"Your theory was completely wrong, by the way."

"I can see that. Tell me what she said." Josie grabbed her hands and held them tightly.

"She didn't say very much at all. She put down her fork, pushed her chair back, and said she needed to go. And if I expected her to be okay with it, I was crazy. Oh, and the worst part. She said how disappointed she is in me."

"Oh, that's a killer. Disappointed is almost worse than mad. Parents sure know how to use that word to cut to the quick, don't they?" Josie reached up to wipe the hair out of Trish's eyes. She handed her a stray napkin, scattered and dirtied by the fury of the earlier episode of destruction. Trish wiped her eyes and blew her nose in the least lady-like fashion, and Josie smiled to poke a little fun. Then Josie grabbed another napkin and blotted the blood from the cut on Trish's leg.

"We need to get this cleaned and bandaged. Is there still glass in there?" She leaned in close and poked at the incision.

"No, I don't think so. I picked at it while I was waiting for you to get here."

"Too bad you don't have a dog. It would sure make the cleanup of all this food a whole lot easier. If it weren't for the glass, I'd go get Max. He would have a field day in here! He loves chicken."

"I'll clean it. I'm considering it my punishment."

"Punishment for what, exactly?" Josie tilted her head in confusion as she asked the question, knowing what Trish was going to say.

"A little of everything, I guess. Disappointing her, not being who she wants me to be, and thinking she would accept this without question. Oh, and smashing everything to the floor. I probably deserve a bit of punishment for that too."

"Look, I know you think you are in some way responsible for what your mother is feeling right now, but you know as well as I do that we cannot live our lives for our parents. You've already done that for far longer than you should have. So at what point in your life does it become about you? When your mom is gone? You could be an old woman by then, and look at how much of your life you'd be wasting just because you are trying to please her and everyone else besides yourself."

Josie could feel herself getting worked up and angry at the pain Marilyn had caused. "If you feel the need to place some blame here, how about putting some of it on her? Look at what she's done to you tonight!" Josie gestured around the wreckage of the dining room. "You don't deserve this. All you did was tell her you met someone and that someone just happens to be a woman."

"I didn't *just* say I had met someone. I said I was in love with a wonderful woman who makes me so very happy. My mother even commented about how content I looked before we started talking about it. You'd think she could just be happy that I'm happy. Why is that too much to ask?"

"It's not, but you have to remember, T, she's from a very different generation. She was born in the twenties, for goodness sake! It was taboo to them then, and it still is. Hell, some people in our generation still feel like she does. The pace of change is painfully slow."

"But I'm her daughter, dammit!"

"We both know it's not that simple. For her generation, a gay child is a negative reflection of the parents. My mother felt the same way. I was her big failure, remember? She once told me if I continued my sinful lifestyle, I would never be happy and deserved whatever misery life bestowed upon me."

"That's a horrible thing to say."

"I know. It took me a *long* time to get over that one, but I did—eventually. Time will make things better for your mom. And for you. She has to get used to the idea that her child is very different from that picture every parent has in the back of their mind of the perfect child."

"I think I had already destroyed that picture when I told her I didn't want children and that Richard and I were getting divorced."

"Did she adjust to that idea?"

"Yes, eventually. Reluctantly."

"Okay, so there is hope here. It might take a little longer because the gay thing is difficult for her generation to wrap their heads around. Just promise me you will be patient with her and keep trying to help her understand, okay?"

"I don't think I have a choice in the matter. I have to be patient. She doesn't want to see me until I've 'come to my senses,' to use her exact words."

"Do *you* feel like you've lost your senses?"

"No. Just the opposite. This *is* me coming to my senses. It happened the day I sat next to you in your car and melted in my seat when you kissed me. My senses are what pulled me out of that car, sent me flying into my front door to pick up the phone and tell your answering machine what a hell of a kiss that was. *That's* when I came to my senses."

Josie smiled. She leaned over and kissed Trish just like she had done that night. Soft, tender, controlled.

"Here you are sitting on a floor that is a disaster of a mess surrounded by broken glass, food all over the place, including on your face, your shirt and pants, and I still think you are the most beautiful thing I've ever seen."

Trish bowed her head in embarrassment but smiled. "You are so corny."

"I know. And I make no apologies for that. If it's corny for me to tell you how beautiful you are, then so be it."

Trish kissed her again, then picked herself up off the floor. She grabbed Josie's hand and pulled her up and into her arms. "You can head home now. I'm better. I'll be okay. I just need to clean up this mess before the damage to my carpet is permanent."

"That ship has sailed, honey. We'll clean it up together. If I leave you to your own devices, you'll end up in the emergency room with glass in your feet, and I will have to carry you, and I'm way too old to do that."

# Chapter Thirteen

## TRISH 1999

THEY SPRAWLED ON THE couch on a Saturday evening with Max lazily resting his head on Trish's leg. In an attempt to alleviate her sadness, Trish plowed through a bag of potato chips with a beer in hand as she mindlessly scrolled through channel after channel. Josie finally grabbed for the remote, having had just about enough of the channel surfing.

"I'm taking that away from you. We've got to talk this through to get you out of this funk. This cold beer and remote control therapy isn't working for you. Or for me, for that matter. It's been two weeks since the blow-up with your mother. Have you thought about calling her?"

"No. She doesn't want to talk to me. We've already established that."

"No, we've established that she didn't want to talk to you two weeks ago. We have no idea what she's thinking now, do we? What if you sent her flowers or something? Extend the olive branch. Is she the type that would be moved by such a gesture?"

"I doubt it. She once got flowers from my dad when I was a kid, and she said he took the lazy way out instead of using his imagination to find a gift she might like."

"Your mom sounds so easygoing," Josie said sarcastically.

"Yep. That's my mother. Easy going."

"Who does she talk to when she's upset? Does she have a best friend?"

"No, but she sometimes calls her sister, my Aunt Judy, when she feels like talking."

"Okay, and what's Aunt Judy's situation? Is she as happy-go-lucky as your mom?"

"They are polar opposites."

"Well, that works in your favor in this case. How does she feel about you?"

"She says I'm her favorite niece." Trish grinned a big, toothy smile as she described her aunt's affection for her.

"How many nieces does she have?" Josie flashed the same grin, hoping to emphasize the joke and get at least a hint of a smile. It worked. "I think Aunt Judy is your go-between. You need some insight into where your mother's head is, and maybe Judy knows. Who knows? Maybe she can even play mediator. Call her."

# Chapter Fourteen

## TRISH AND JUDY 1999

TRISH WAS ALREADY SEATED at an outdoor table when Judy arrived. The brunch crowd was lively on a warm Sunday morning, and a duo of singers with their acoustic guitars played folk favorites in the corner of the patio. The smell of bacon permeated the air, and the wait staff carried out dish after dish of omelets and Eggs Benedict. Trish stood up to greet Judy and gave her a kiss and a hug, holding on to the embrace for a few extra seconds.

In typical Judy fashion, she jumped right in. "Oh, Trish. I was so happy to hear from you. Your mother has been driving me crazy, calling me every day." Judy's thick New York accent punctuated each word. "You've got her in quite an uproar, you know." She sat down, scooted her chair in, and motioned to the waiter. "Can I have a large mug of your strongest coffee, please?" Trish smiled, listening to her order *cawfee.*

"Yes, I gathered that from her abrupt exit from my house a couple of weeks ago. It seems I've disappointed her yet again. I do that rather well, don't I?"

"It's not difficult to do. I know from experience, but I gave up trying to live up to Lynn's ideals long ago." Judy waved her arms as if dismissing her sister's tiring behavior. Judy never shied away from saying what was on her mind, especially when it came to her younger sister Marilyn, whom Judy still referred to as Lynn, just as she had when they were little girls.

"Did she tell you what she is upset about, um...specifically?" Trish quizzed, testing the waters to see if Aunt Judy had heard the coming-out saga.

"Not at first. I could tell it was something big, but she wouldn't say what it was. She kept saying she was 'too ashamed,' and I should just leave it at that. Ha! It's as if she didn't know who she was talking to because obviously, there was no way I was going to leave it at that. So eventually, she gave me your news. She could barely get the words out."

"And...?" Trish could feel her hands shaking as she reached for her coffee cup. Judy reached across the table and grabbed her hand to steady it.

"I'll tell you what. Before we spend another minute talking about my oh-so-tolerant sister, why don't you share your news with me? Because I suspect sharing it was a big deal for you, and it probably broke your heart to have it received that way, am I right? Unlike your mother, I would like to hear about it."

Trish closed her eyes slowly and released the tension in her shoulders. "Oh, Aunt J," and she started to weep. Ever conscious of the people around her, she brought her napkin up to her face, just enough to muffle the sounds of her crying. Judy held tight to her hand, giving her the time she needed to compose herself.

"Tell me about the woman in your life, sweetheart. What is her name?"

"Her name is Josie."

"Josie. I like that. How did you meet her?"

"She came to talk to my class on career day. She works in IT, and she was so great with the kids. We went out for a drink afterward, and things progressed little by little from there. We talked for hours on end. I've never felt so, um...I don't know, just...at ease. It's like how you imagine it's supposed to be when you finally meet *that* person. Do you know what I mean?"

"Yes, I do. I had that with your Uncle Jimmy. I knew it almost immediately. I wouldn't call it love at first sight, but it was definitely something at first sight. A recognition that this person is different, you know?"

"Yes, that's exactly what I mean. I pretended I didn't have feelings for her for a while. I guess I was just scared. Terrified, to be honest, but then it occurred to me—I'm in my fifties. So what the hell am I waiting for? Why am I denying myself happiness? Because my mother will disapprove? That doesn't make any sense."

"If you only did the things your mother approved of, you'd miss out on quite a lot in life. I love her, but she certainly does know how to impose her issues on those around her. To say that she is a killjoy is an understatement."

"She does, and she is. I still don't know how to deal with it. She's not speaking to me at all now because of her shame and disappointment in me, and I have no idea what to do to make it better. It's killing me, Aunt J."

"Let me stop you right there. I don't like you using the word 'shame.' I don't think she is ashamed of you, even though she may have said she is. Shame is a powerful word. Your mother loves you dearly.  She just doesn't know how to adjust to this news. It's also brought up a lot of old baggage for her."

Trish gave her a puzzled look. "Baggage? What baggage?"

"Yes. I wasn't going to get into this with you, but I think you need to know. There is a story here that hasn't been discussed in this family for many years. As far as your mother is concerned, it's the Big Family Secret. I have significantly less angst about it than she does. Truth be told, I probably have even more *reason* to be upset about it than she has. It was my wedding day! But that just goes to show you how different we are."

"Well, now you have my interest. Are you going to share this with me? Because I have no idea what you're talking about."

"Your mother is going to kill me, but yes. I will share." She raised her hand to flag the server. "Waiter, can I have a double espresso, please?"

"Am I going to need a shot of whiskey in my coffee, Aunt J?"

"It's possible."

* * * *

*On the first Saturday in June of 1939, Judy O'Brien and Jimmy Callahan were married at The Milleridge Inn in Jericho, New York. Jimmy donned his tuxedo in the groom's quarters while Judy and her sister Lynn got ready in the bridal suite. Lynn looked beautiful in her maid of honor dress, but it paled in comparison to the stunning, lacy white wedding gown she helped her sister into that morning. They had worked together for weeks to sew it, wedding dresses being a luxury well beyond their Depression-era means.*

*The guests gathered in the vestibule, waiting for the ushers to direct them to the right or the left. The bride's mother, Anna O'Brien, was inexplicably going back and forth, in and out of the dressing room. Judy and Lynn were confused by what she was doing, but were much too preoccupied with other tasks to give their mother too much of their attention.*

*As the organist started to play their entrance music, Lynn took the best man's arm while Judy latched on to her father Patrick to make their way down the aisle. Patrick, who had been beaming with pride earlier in the day, showed a significant change in demeanor. Judy leaned in and whispered in his ear, asking what the matter was.*

*He stared stoically ahead and said, "Nothing. I'm fine, sweetheart. Ignore me, okay? This is your day. I'm so happy for you. Jimmy is a lucky man."*

*Obviously, he was not fine, but walking down the aisle at her wedding seemed an inappropriate time and place to have the discussion, so Judy attempted to put it out of her mind. Unfortunately, her parents had probably had yet another argument, an all-too-common occurrence these last couple of years. Judy took just a moment to reflect upon the unhappy state of her parent's marriage, even as she began her own, but she refused to let them dampen her day.*

*At the reception, the tension between her parents became even more apparent by their decision to ignore each other completely. They didn't dance together, talk to each other, or even sit together. Instead, Patrick planted himself in his seat at their assigned table while Anna was off with her best friend, Mary Monahan, talking at the bar, dancing, or going out for a smoke.*

*When the band finished their set, Judy and Jimmy left the floor, overheated from dancing the jitterbug to a Cab Calloway tune. Judy fanned herself, grabbed her drink off the table, and went to get Lynn.*

*"Lynn, come outside with me! I'm so hot, and I need some air."*

*Lynn put down her drink as Judy grabbed her other hand and led them out of the crowded reception area. They avoided the front entrance where the other guests talked and smoked, and headed for the back door. They rounded the corner, pushed the latch on the exit door, and stopped in their tracks. Lynn was about to gasp aloud when Judy put her hand over Lynn's mouth to squelch the sound. Up against the building about twenty feet to the right of the door, they saw their mother, Anna, passionately kissing Mary Monahan. Neither of the women broke their embrace to notice that Anna's daughters had entered the area and spotted them. They were so focused on each other they were utterly oblivious to the outside world at that moment in time. Anna dipped her head to kiss Mary's collarbone, her hands trailing through Mary's hair. She kissed along Mary's neck and up to her ear, whispering something soft and intimate while Mary raised her head skyward and closed her eyes. Judy took Lynn's hand and quietly retreated into the hallway, ensuring the heavy exit door did not make any noise as it closed. Judy led them into the ladies' room and checked* to see if anyone else was in the stalls. Once they determined they were alone, she let Lynn react to what they had seen.

Lynn was near hyperventilation. "I...I...What was she...? What did we just see? Was Mary attacking her?"

"No, Lynn. Definitely not. If anything, Mother was in control of that situation, although truthfully, it seemed entirely mutual."

"But...but how? She's married! They both are. I don't understand!"

"Lynn, I know this is a shock, but don't be naïve. Just because they are married doesn't mean they aren't 'that way.'" She raised her hands to signify air quotes. "I read an article about this a couple of weeks ago. It's apparently just as common for women to be homosexuals as men."

"What? Common? This is not common! This is disgusting. It's sick! How could Mother do that?"

"The article said it happens more often than you might think, but people are so scared of being found out they have to hide it. So that's why we all think it's uncommon."

"Do you think they've...you know...done more than kiss?" Lynn whispered and put her hand over her mouth in horror. Judy grabbed it, trying to calm her down.

"By the looks of it, I would say yes. It certainly didn't seem like it was the first time, that's for sure. But I think we know why Mother and Daddy have been acting so strangely today. Maybe Daddy found out. Oh, my goodness. The poor man!"

"What should we do? Do we say something to her? Or him?" Lynn asked, still trying to catch her breath. She leaned against the wall and bent to put her hands on her knees, bracing herself.

Judy stood tall and collected herself, hoping Lynn would do the same. "No. It's my wedding, and it's still so early in the day. I think I get to decide what happens next, and I refuse to let this spoil my day. So, I'm not going to confront either of them today. Honestly, I'd just like to forget about it for now."

"I don't think I can do that," Lynn said with a sadness in her eyes that Judy had never seen before.

"I know. That's not your style. How about letting it go just for today. Will you do that for me, please? We have a hundred people here who do not need to see and hear our family drama. Please, Lynn. We will deal with it another time."

# Chapter Fifteen

## TRISH 1999

TRISH STARED BACK AT her Aunt Judy in disbelief. "My grandmother was a *lesbian*?" she asked, maybe a decibel too loud. Some heads turned at the neighboring tables.

"Yes, she was. Does that help you understand why your mom is reacting this way?"

"Well, yes and no. You are her sister. The same thing happened to you, and you aren't reacting like she is. And what happened after the wedding? Did she ever get used to the idea for your mom?"

"No, not really. It became a subject we never discussed as a family, but I was comfortable enough to talk to my mom about it in private. I don't have the same issues your mother has. So my mother and I talked about it quite a lot."

"Oh, I need to hear about those conversations. Does my mother know this?"

"I'm not sure. Probably. But truthfully, it wasn't my story to tell. My mom knew she knew, but Lynn was so uncomfortable with it, she didn't bring it up except when it first happened. Since Lynn shut those initial conversations down, that was the end of that. So now it's the Big Family Secret. Of course, your coming-out process forces her to think about it all over again."

"Has she specifically said that to you?"

"Yes, she has. And for the record, she wishes she'd handled it better with you. I think she just doesn't know how. My generation just can't escape that old mindset that says it's unacceptable and must be hidden. Given my mother's obvious aversion to that way of thinking, I'm not sure how Lynn grew up with those old-fashioned ideals. My mother was way ahead of her time. She knew she was interrupting the status quo, but I think she just didn't care anymore. I suspect, my dear niece, that you are at that same point in your life."

"Yes, I'm just too old to pretend anymore. I'm in love with a woman. I have to be true to my feelings, and I don't care who thinks less of me for it. My biggest concern, honestly, is my job. Gay teachers are not looked upon very kindly, so as much as I'd like to be out, I still have to be careful, but as for anyone else not associated with school—including my mother—they can accept it or not," she said defiantly.

Judy reached across the table and grabbed Trish's hands. "I'm proud of you, Patricia."

"Thanks. You must be because you called me 'Patricia.'" She smiled at her aunt, happy she accepted her but wishing she could say the same about her mother.

# Chapter Sixteen

## TRISH 1999

TRISH TOOK THE LAST few bites of her eggplant parmigiana, then pushed her plate forward. She looked at Josie, who had momentarily paused her chewing, and waited for her reaction.

Josie nearly choked on her lemon-lime soda. "So, let me get this straight. Your mother has shunned you because you announced that you are in love with a woman, but meanwhile, her mother was a lesbian and had an affair with her best friend?"

"Yep," Trish confirmed, shaking her head. When Josie let out a shriek of laughter, Trish looked at her with intense annoyance. "I can't believe you think this is so hysterical," Trish said, clearly annoyed.

"I can't believe you don't. The irony is fantastic! Her mother has an affair with a woman, she never talks about it, pretends it didn't happen, and then her daughter tells her she's in love with a woman. It's as if the universe is repaying her for not dealing with it the first time. Kudos to badass Grandma Anna! Nineteen thirty-nine and she was kissing a woman in public? Wow! I want to be just like her when I grow up. What happened with her and your grandfather? Did they stay together? Did she and Mary keep seeing each other? Were they in love? This is better than a soap opera."

"I'm glad we can entertain you." Trish put her fork down. "Can you be serious for a minute, please?"

"Okay, I'm sorry. Go ahead." She reached across the table to put her hand on Trish's. "I do want to know what happened. Maybe there is some insight to be found in that story."

"My grandparents did not get a divorce. It was almost as taboo as homosexuality was in the thirties. They stayed married for the rest of their lives, although they did separate eventually. Till death do they part, blah, blah, blah. But Aunt Judy said she thinks my grandma and Mary continued to see each other for many years. Knowing what I know now, I feel sad for them. Imagine how difficult it must have been. They probably spent years lying to themselves about how they were feeling. That could have been me. If I hadn't met you, I could have spent the rest of *my* life in the same boat, lying to myself about what I wanted and needed out of life."

"I think you had reached a point in your life where you were just ready, and I happened to be in the exact right place at the right time, but I think you would have found your way on your own even without me. I suspect there is a lot of Grandma Anna in you, and I'll bet she'd be very proud of you." Josie put her hand on Trish's cheek.

"I hope so. I remember her. I always loved going over to her house. I would sometimes fake being sick to stay home from school, and my mom would take me there. We'd sit and watch her stories while she ironed my grandfather's shirts and handkerchiefs. She would show me how to bake Christmas cookies."

"Am I going to reap the benefits of those tutorials when the holiday season arrives? Who the hell irons handkerchiefs?"

"I said she would show me. That doesn't mean I could ever actually do it. You've sampled my cooking and baking. I may have inherited her *badass-edness* but I certainly didn't get her culinary skills. Or her ironing skills."

"Badass-edness? Really?" Josie laughed.

"Not a word?"

"I don't know. You're the teacher. You tell me."

"In that case, I say it's a word," Trish said defiantly.

"Fair enough."

"Do you think Grandma and Mary had sex?"

"Uh, yes, honey. They did. I'd bet my life savings on it. They would have had to be so discreet, but I'm sure they found a way. What a tough time it must have been. I get upset sometimes about what we have to deal with now, but we forget how far we have come. In the thirties, I'm sure it was a thousand times worse. The more I think about it, the more I admire her."

"But what about the fact she cheated on my grandfather?"

"Well, yeah. There is that, but it was completely unacceptable to be a lesbian in those days. She didn't have much choice. It's not a total justification, but it's something."

"I wonder what the sex was like with them," Trish pondered, with a hint of embarrassment in her voice.

"I'm sure it was a lot like sex between you and me. If they had been together for all those years, they had to have loved each other. You and I both know how that feels. I'm sure they showed each other how they felt whenever they got those infrequent opportunities. Speaking of opportunity..."

"Nice segue." Trish smirked.

Josie got up from the table, went over to Trish, and reached for her hand. "Thanks. I thought so." She pulled her into her arms and said, "Would you care to join me up in the bedroom, my love? All this talk of Grandma and Mary has made me a bit frisky." She kissed her and put her hands into Trish's back pockets.

Trish looked back at the table. "And leave the table with these dirty dishes on it?" She reached to grab for the dishes, only to be thwarted by Josie.

"I know it goes against every fiber of your being, but let's live dangerously and clean them up later." She laughed, kissed Trish's neck, and guided her toward the staircase. "Now that I know there's a rebel buried somewhere down in your DNA, I am going to take full advantage." Josie grabbed her hand and walked her up the stairs to the bedroom.

# Chapter Seventeen

## ANNA 1929

PATRICK O' BRIEN ANSWERED THE doorbell of the little house on the outskirts of New York City and greeted two burly delivery men with an extra-large wooden crate on a rolling dolly on their front porch. They hauled it into the living room of the tiny suburban home while eight-year-old Judy and six-year-old Lynn looked on wide-eyed.

"Daddy, Daddy!" Judy said excitedly. "What is it?" Lynn and Judy held hands, jumping up and down with impatience.

"You and your sister are just going to have to be patient until these nice men open the crate. Anna, are you coming in to look?" he asked his wife, who had remained in the kitchen to attend to the stew on the stove.

"I'll be right there. Don't wait for me." Anna answered.

As the delivery men removed the wood from the crate, the girls shrieked joyfully at the sight of the brand-new Zenith radio. They had been begging their father for a wireless for months, and they were beside themselves with excitement at the new piece of talking furniture.

"Oh, Daddy! You got us a wireless?" Judy asked. Patrick nodded and smiled. "My friend Maria has one. I can't believe you got one for us! Lynn, wait until you hear it. You'll be amazed!"

Anna appeared from the kitchen, surprised at this new piece of talking furniture that her husband neglected to mention to her. "Patrick, this is a surprise," she said, trying not to let on to her daughters that she was concerned about the extravagant expense.

Patrick gave her a look of reassurance. His job as a warehouse manager was going well. Business was booming in April of 1929, and he felt comfortable splurging on his family.

After dinner, Patrick and the girls planted themselves in front of the dials, searching for an exciting program to listen to as a family. Anna sat with them for a moment, but remembered she was supposed to buy flour for some baking she had promised to do the following day for the girl's school. She got up, put on her coat and boots, and headed out for the corner market.

Patrick looked confused and just a little bit upset. "Where are you going at this hour? Don't you want to listen to the new radio?"

"I do, but I forgot I need flour for tomorrow's bake sale. I promised I would bring cake and cookies. So I'll just run down to Marconi's Market and be back in a bit."

* * * *

While in the store, Anna remembered she needed more than just flour, so she wandered the aisles to find the other items on her mental list. Without looking in front of her, she bumped head-on into another patron. Her items scattered across the floor. "Oh, my goodness! I'm so very sorry! I wasn't paying a bit of attention."

The woman she collided with was equally apologetic. "No, please. It was my fault. I'm so clumsy, and I wasn't looking either. Goodness, I'm so sorry." They both bent to pick up the dropped objects, and the woman looked up at Anna, caught her eyes, and stared for a moment, just a bit unnervingly. Anna turned away, ready to move on, but the woman looked back at Anna and said, "Forgive me, but I have to say. You have lovely eyes." Anna, caught completely off-guard, attempted a graceful acceptance of the compliment.

"Really? Thank you! I don't think anyone has ever said that to me." They both stood, and Anna looked away nervously.

"I'm surprised your husband hasn't told you that. They're pretty hard to miss."

"Yes, well, my husband is not the type of man to say something like that. He wouldn't notice my eyes unless someone pointed them out, and he was *forced* to comment on them." She said it with a chuckle, even though acknowledging the fact gave her pause.

"Hmm...well, consider them noticed. They are quite beautiful. I don't think I've ever seen that shade of green. My name is Mary, by the way. Forgive me if I'm too forward."

"Hi, Mary. I'm Anna. And no, I don't think it's too forward. Even if it is, I forgive you because I like it! There are certainly worse things than having a stranger tell you that you have nice eyes. To be honest, you've made my day!"

Mary corrected her. "Don't sell them short. I said they are *beautiful*, not just nice."

Anna was visibly blushing now and lowered her head to hide her embarrassment. "Well, it was nice to talk to you, Mary. I'm surprised we haven't bumped into each other before—no pun intended."

"My husband and I just moved in about a week ago. A friendly face is always appreciated, so maybe we will see each other again sometime. Take care." Mary waved and walked away.

Anna paid for her flour, sugar, and baking powder, still thinking about the interesting encounter with Mary. She made her way back home with a spring in her step, and she picked up the pace so she could listen to the new radio with her family before the girls went off to bed.

Back at the house, Anna unloaded the bag from the market. She poked her head into the living room.

"Patrick, tell me what color my eyes are without looking at me."

"What?" he said, bewildered.

"Just curious. Do you know what color eyes I have?"

"Um...brown?"

"Never mind."

# Chapter Eighteen

## ANNA 1929

ANNA HEADED TO THE bake sale the next day, armed with cookies, an apple pie, and a chocolate cake. She walked to the school, arms overflowing with containers of baked goods. She was barely balancing them when a child on a bicycle cut her off, sending the tin of cookies well into the air. Before she could reach for it, a hand came out of the blue to grab it in mid-air. It was the woman from the market the previous night. The 'you have beautiful eyes' lady.

"Wow, we need a traffic cop out here for these kids on their bikes. They don't care who they run down on their way to get their sugar fix, do they? Are you okay, Anna?"

Anna spent an extra second collecting herself, trying to recall the new neighbor's name. The compliment, she remembered, but unfortunately, the name was not coming as quickly.

"Yes, I am, um…err…"

"It's Mary. From the market last night? The one who bumped right into you. Just as, I'm sorry to say, my son almost did just now. Michael! Watch where you are going. You're going to kill someone!" The boy looked over his shoulder, smiled devilishly at his mother, and kept riding. "Apparently, crashing into you runs in my family. So it might be best if you kept an eye out for us in the future. We're trouble."

"Right, right. Mary. Sorry. I'm so bad with names. That was a heck of a mid-air catch. Thank you!"

"No problem. I saw you down the street and had almost caught up to you when I saw my bratty—but equally cute, might I say—kid doing everything in his power to run you down. Just happened to be in the right place at the right time."

"Definitely. I'll be sure to give you all a wide berth going forward for my safety." She flashed a smile at Mary in an attempt to return the humor. It seemed to work because Mary grinned right back.

"Looks like you've made some wonderful stuff here, Anna."

"I love to bake. It works out well because my husband and girls love to eat, so everyone is happy."

"I can see why. It all looks so delicious. I can't wait to try some of it. Maybe I will buy up all your goods before anyone else has a chance to steal them from me."

"Well, if you are that interested, I'd be happy to bake something just for you. Consider it a 'welcome to the neighborhood' gift." Anna surprised herself with this invitation, and Mary seemed equally taken aback, although not unhappily.

"Ooh. I would love that." She smiled with a bit of a devilish grin. "Maybe you could teach me a thing or two. Honestly, I am a terrible baker, and my husband would be ever so grateful if you tutored me. He says he married the only woman in the world who doesn't know how to bake. I reply that I married the only man in the world who doesn't know when to keep his big mouth closed if he knows what's good for him. It usually works to shut him up, making the kids laugh in the process, so it's a win-win."

"How many kids do you have, Mary?"

"Twin boys, Michael and Kevin, who are seven, and a two-year-old girl, Linda. I suspect my kids will also be thrilled if I improve my baking skills, so the whole family will owe you one. Especially me."

"Teach the girl while she's young—that's what I always say! We'll do it at your place and make sure she's watching. Kids absorb so much at their age. When would you like to do this?"

"The sooner, the better! Besides, I'd love to have the pleasure of your company. It's tough moving into a new neighborhood. It can be a bit lonely."

"Well, I'm happy to do anything I can to make you feel at home. With my girls in school during the day, I can help you get settled. Will Thursday work for you?"

"I think that's a great idea. In the meantime, I obviously didn't bake for the sale today, so I volunteered to help with the setup. Let's get you inside and put out all this stuff so I can sample the merchandise. I need to make sure you are good at this before letting you teach me." Mary winked at her, clearly indicating her sarcasm. When Anna caught her eye, Mary stared for a moment and said, "It's those eyes of yours, Anna. Really. They are just...captivating."

Anna quickly bowed her head to the floor in embarrassment. "You are making me blush again! If you were a man, I'd think you were flirting with me." She looked back up, held her gaze with Mary for a second, and said, "Last night when I got home, I asked my husband to tell me what color eyes I had without looking at me. As expected, he got it wrong. I told you he'd never notice." *Of course, he never notices anything,* Anna thought to herself, somewhat disappointed.

"Well, forgive me for saying so, but your husband sounds like he needs glasses. If I was him and I had the opportunity to see those eyes every day, I'd pay more attention. What color did he think they were?"

"He said 'brown?', almost in the form of a question. As if he thought the laws of probability might work in his favor and keep him out of trouble."

"He wasn't even close. Silly man."

A voice in the back of Anna's head told her she should probably find this conversation odd, coming from a woman, yet for some reason, she didn't. It was quite lovely. She felt *seen* for the first time in ages.

At the bake sale, Anna and Mary giggled like schoolgirls and commented on the other women. Anna gave Mary the scoop on all her neighbors.

"That's Mrs. Baker over there," Anna said as she discreetly pointed to the other side of the room. "She's very sweet, but she's clueless to the fact that her children are hellions. And her husband is hardly ever around to notice."

"I'll be happy to send one of my little devils over to their house if you think it will help," Mary said, jokingly. "I'm sure they can give her kids a run for their money."

"Oh, please send the one that nearly ran me over earlier!" They laughed together as if they had known each other for years, and Anna felt a lightness that had been recently missing from her life. Things at home with Patrick had become rather mundane in the last few months. His idea of excitement was getting the new radio, which meant they would spend all their free time listening to it without talking to each other. It was lovely to have a new audience—someone who seemed genuinely interested in Anna, the person. Not Anna, the wife. Not Anna, the mother. Not persona non grata.

# Chapter Nineteen

## ANNA 1929

THE KITCHEN COUNTER WAS messy, and the baking lesson was in full swing. A rolling pin, measuring cups, and flour littered the entire surface area. Mary and Anna sat at the kitchen table, cookies and coffee mugs in hand, waiting for the next batch to come out of the oven. The aroma in the room was delightful. Mary's daughter Linda played quietly in her playpen, remnants of chocolate on her cheeks. The morning passed quickly and the conversation flowed easily.

"You know, Anna," Mary said, taking another gulp of her coffee, "I think maybe we should introduce our husbands and send them out for a beer one of these days. Get them out of our hair so we can talk about them behind their backs."

"Better yet, send your husband to my house, and I'll come over here. Since he got that new wireless, he barely wants to leave the house. It's like he loves that thing more than he loves me."

"Johnny has been talking about getting one, but we haven't been able to afford it, what with all the costs of the move. He'd love it. He read they have baseball games, and someone at the game describes everything that's happening. It's amazing, isn't it?"

"Send him over Saturday. Patrick is all excited about listening to the Yankee game. Bring your boys along too. They can all have their time without the women in their hair. I'll come over here, and we can bake again. Sound good?"

"Yes, except let's introduce them first. Johnny is a little shy and won't want to come over to the house of a guy he's never met before."

"I understand. I have an idea. We have all these baked goods. We'll come over after dinner tonight for coffee and cake. Once the guys get to talking about baseball, they will be best buddies."

That evening, Anna introduced Patrick and the girls to Johnny and Mary and their children over coffee and cake. As expected, the men got involved in baseball conversation, discussing their high hopes for the upcoming Yankees season.

"Sure, Ruth and Gehrig are great players, but what about Tony Lazzeri? You can't underestimate him," Patrick theorized. "Why don't you come over on Saturday and we'll listen to the game?"

"Oh, wow. Thanks, Patrick. I would really like that."

Anna smiled and turned to Mary. "See, Mary? I told you they would be fast friends once the baseball topic came up. Guys, how about you go into the living room and listen to the radio so you don't bore us with this baseball talk?"

"Happily," Patrick said, grabbing his coffee and his cake plate and motioning for Johnny and the boys to follow him.

* * * *

A few weeks later, the men decided to stay at Mary's house with all the children while Mary went to Anna's. They were planning an event for the PTA, and neither the men nor the kids were interested in any part of that conversation.

As usual, the coffee was plentiful and the conversation was animated. First, they laughed when they recounted how the president of their PTA had an embarrassing gas passing at their last meeting. Then they gossiped about their neighbor Martha, whom they suspected was having an affair with their plumber. Mary snickered and said, "I'm not letting him come over to clean my pipes, that's for sure!"

"Mary, can't you come up with a more original joke than that?" Anna scoffed.

"Okay, smartie pants. What would you say?"

"How about 'he better keep that snake of his away from me!'"

"How is that joke any more original than mine?" Mary asked, pretending to be upset that her joke was not good enough.

"It's the snake. Much better play on words."

"Hmph..." Mary got up and went to the kitchen for another cup of coffee.

"Oh, can you grab another cup for me as well, please, while you're in there?"

Mary filled the cups and walked across the room to hand one to Anna. She bent down to give it to her, but instead of retreating to her seat, she paused and put her hand over Anna's. Mary took Anna's hand off the cup and put it onto the coaster on the coffee table. The look in Anna's eyes was one of utter confusion. Mary leaned in, then bent down on her knees so her face was level with Anna in the chair. She gently kissed her cheek, not with passion but with purpose. Anna pulled her face back and Mary followed just as closely. She put her hand on Anna's face and caressed it. Startled, Anna pulled away again. This time, Mary leaned in and kissed Anna's lips softly. Anna didn't resist initially, but as if physically extracting herself from the moment, she stood and backed away.

"What are you doing, Mary?" she said angrily. She straightened her skirt nervously, then put her hand on her face where Mary had touched her just a moment ago.

Mary recoiled, her face turning bright red with humiliation. "I...I'm...um...I'm sorry. I thought I was getting a signal from you that you wanted to kiss me as much as I wanted to kiss you. I must have misunderstood. I'm...I'm very sorry, Anna."

"Yes, you did misunderstand! I'm not like *that*! I didn't know you were! Is this why you wanted to be my friend? Do you think I'm a lesbian?" She whispered the word of taboo. She could feel her face turning a deep red, a mixture of shame and embarrassment. Anna wanted to look at Mary but couldn't force herself to do so.

Mary moved closer and reached out her hand. "Anna, please. Just give me a minute to explain."

Anna pulled away. "No! I don't think I want to hear any explanation. I think you should leave, Mary. You've got me all wrong." Anna said the words but shamefully realized she wasn't quite sure she believed them. And that scared her as much as the kiss itself. Her heart was pounding through her chest.

Mary was visibly shaking. "Okay. I will go, but I need to ask you one question first, and I'm asking you to be honest with me. More importantly, be honest with yourself." Mary came closer to look directly into Anna's eyes. "Are you telling me to go because you think you *should* or because you want me to go? Because I can't help but notice your hand is still on your face where I touched you."

Anna quickly brought her hand down to her side in embarrassment. She turned her eyes to the floor and stepped away from Mary as her mind raced in search of the true answer to that question.

"Anna. Look at me. There's no one else here. It's just you and me. There are no husbands, kids, or gossipy neighbors. No one to judge us. If I am wrong, I will apologize and leave, but am I really wrong? These last few weeks...it feels like something is happening between us. I can't explain it, but it's a feeling I can't shake. I feel so comfortable, so...at home with you. Do you feel it too?"

Anna returned to the kitchen table and sat down as tears filled her eyes. She put her hands over her face to hide them from Mary, knowing it was a futile effort. Mary grabbed a tissue from the box on the counter and handed it to Anna. She pulled a chair closer and sat beside her as Anna wept openly.

"Mary, I can't do this. It's not right. I need you to leave, please." Yet, as the words came out of her mouth, she knew this time for sure she didn't mean them. It was as if a curtain had been slowly raised to reveal her true feelings for Mary, but she thought about her husband, her kids, and her family. *How is this even happening? No. This. Cannot. Happen.*

"Okay. I will go. I'm sorry I've upset you. Goodbye, Anna."

Mary grabbed her purse and slowly made her way to the door. Anna fought back the urge to stop her. When the door closed behind her, Anna's crying reached a fevered pitch, so much so Mary could hear it as she stood outside, her back against the door to hold her up as she attempted to catch her breath.

# Chapter Twenty

## ANNA 1929

ANNA TOSSED AND TURNED all night. Patrick gently snored beside her, oblivious. She wiped the perspiration from her face and sat up, unable to get comfortable in any position. Unable to breathe. The dream she'd awoke from felt like a betrayal to her husband. Peaceful in the ignorance of his slumber next to her. She quietly crept out of bed and retreated to the kitchen to make a pot of coffee. As it perked, she relived it. Kissing. Touching. Whispering. How could her brain process both ecstasy and terror simultaneously? Which emotion won the battle, or for that matter, the war? Her hands trembled as she poured a cup and took a sip, willing the caffeine to snap her out of this daze. She sat at the table by the kitchen window and looked at the horizon—five a.m. The sun cast a faint glow to announce its impending rise. The birds were already chirping on the towering oak tree in the yard. Anna itemized the ramifications in her head—children, divorce, shame, public ridicule. Jail? This was illegal, right? How could she even think about this, with all she had to lose? It was unspeakable. And yet, that dream was...spellbinding? Was that the right word? Maybe riveting? Enticing? Yes, all those things, but most of all—erotic. Her humiliation was profound. Anna tried desperately to block out the images replaying in her head, but instead, all she could think was—if Mary were to touch me like that, would it feel that good?

Patrick quietly made his way into the kitchen and called her name. She did not respond; her eyes instead focused out the window and her mind a million miles away from this room.

"Anna? Honey, are you okay?"

"Oh, I'm sorry, dear. I guess I was just daydreaming."

"Is it still daydreaming if the sun hasn't come up yet?" He smiled at her through his sleepy pillow-smushed face. "Why are you awake so early?"

"I couldn't sleep and didn't want to wake you with my tossing and turning, but I guess I did. I'm sorry, hon. I must have had too much coffee with Mary last night."

"You didn't wake me, but the smell of that coffee did, so I thought I'd see if you were okay. You seemed distracted last night before you went to bed. Am I in trouble?"

"Why do you assume that?"

"Because it's usually me, right? I didn't see the kids doing anything wrong yesterday, so I figured it had to be me."

"Everything is just fine. There's nothing wrong." *Lie.* "I promise." *Another lie.* "Why don't you go back to bed. You don't have to get up for another hour." *True, but trivial.* "I just need to have a bit more coffee and all will be well." *Lie number three.* He kissed her on the cheek and ambled his way back into the bedroom.

At eight a.m., as the kids were scrambling around the house getting ready for school, putting on their shoes, and grabbing their books, there was a knock on the door. Anna handed each kid their lunch sack and opened the door. She turned and stopped dead in her tracks. Mary and her kids stood on the other side of the door. The look of surprise on Anna's face was unmistakable. Mary pretended not to see it and greeted them cheerfully.

"Good morning, all! It's a lovely day outside, and I thought I would put Linda in the stroller, and maybe we could all walk to school together. What do you think?"

Anna hesitated. "Um...yes, sure. Um...why not. Let me get my sweater. Girls, are you ready to go?" Both girls responded happily in the affirmative, glad to have the company on the walk to school.

Anna's girls and Mary's boys ran ahead of the adults, finding the pace with the stroller to be much too slow for their liking. Little Linda was lulled to sleep with the morning sun on her face and the soft rumbling and motion of the wheels. Mary and Anna exchanged pleasantries, pretending everything was normal. Finally, when Mary was sure Linda was indeed sound asleep, she broached the topic Anna was dreading.

"Are you upset that I came over today, Anna? I'm sorry, but I just couldn't stay away. I was afraid if I let any time go by, you might never speak to me again." She looked straight ahead as she spoke, but her tone made it clear that if she could do so without making a scene, she would much rather be talking face to face.

"I was surprised to see you, that's for sure, but to be honest, I'm at a loss for words. I don't know what to say to you."

"Can we talk when we get back to your house? I want to explain myself if you'll let me."

"We can talk, but I'm not sure there is much to say. Nothing has changed since yesterday." *Lie number four.* Anna was racking them up this morning. Everything had changed since yesterday. Scenes from the dream flashed again in her mind.

* * * *

When they returned to Anna's house, Mary left Linda sleeping in the stroller and sat on the couch in the living room.

"Can I trouble you for a glass of water, please? I feel like my mouth has gone dry before I've even said a word." Anna grabbed a glass from the cabinet and went to the sink. While her face was hidden from Mary, she took a moment to take a deep breath. She wondered how she would reply once Mary started to speak.

"Listen, Anna. I know you probably hate me or are disgusted by me right now, but there are a few things I need to say to you. If you still hate me afterward, then so be it, but at least I will know I said my piece."

"Mary, I don't..."

"Anna, please. Let me get this out, okay? After I've finished, you can say whatever you want, and I will listen." She stopped and took a long gulp of the water, composing her thoughts. "I know I overstepped my bounds yesterday. I should have never tried to kiss you, and I am sorry. I wish I could explain why I did what I did in a way that wouldn't make you want to run screaming for the door. All I can say is I have been thinking about you ever since we met at the market—all the time. No matter what I'm doing, there you are. I don't know why! I've never felt this way before. Yesterday, you said you didn't know I was 'that way.' Neither did I. I swear. This has never happened to me before, but when I look at you, I see this brand-new thing I desperately want to explore. It started with those damned eyes of yours and hasn't let up since. Why do you have to look at me that way? Why can't I just make these feelings stop? Last night, I served dinner to the family and dropped a plate full of food on the floor. It's like I wasn't even present in the room with them. I was somewhere else—somewhere with you in my imagination. I don't want to feel this way! I'm scared, I'm embarrassed, and I don't know what to do. Please forgive me. I'm trying to figure it all out, but I never meant to hurt or scare you, and I'm so very sorry. It will not happen again, I promise."

Anna sat quietly for a moment, debating which one of the hundreds of responses on the tip of her tongue she intended to express.

Finally, she stood up and went into the kitchen to get herself a glass of water.

"You aren't the only one who needs a drink before speaking. I kind of wish this was vodka." She smiled and lifted her glass to Mary as if to toast.

"I'm sure we could get some vodka if that would help," Mary said.

"No, I think I'll pass. Perhaps a clear head is the most prudent course of action here."

Mary looked away toward the window; anything to avoid what she expected would be an unfavorable response to everything she had said.

Anna stepped back out of the kitchen toward the living room, taking a detour past the stroller to ensure Linda was still sleeping. She sat down next to Mary.

"Did you say everything you wanted to say, or is there more?"

"I think I've said enough. I'm just waiting for you to show me to the door."

"I can see why you might be expecting that, given it's what I wanted yesterday, but right now, I'm not so sure. Are you honestly saying you have never done this before?"

"I swear. I wouldn't lie to you."

"You've never kissed another woman?"

"God, no!"

"Did you ever want to? Remember, you just promised you wouldn't lie to me."

"When I was nineteen, a girl lived in the apartment above me who I thought was very pretty. I had what I can only describe as a crush on her, but that's all. I never did anything about it and I never told her."

"And you said it would never happen again between us, right?"

"Right. It won't. I promise," Mary said, with as much conviction as she could muster.

"But...what if...um, that is, what would you...what could we..."

"What, Anna?"

Anna sighed and took a deep breath. She looked Mary in the eyes, hesitated, and said, "But what if I *wanted* it to happen again?"

"What?" Mary asked with complete shock.

"I know you heard me. Please don't make me repeat it."

"But...but why? Yesterday, you were horrified. What changed?"

"Well, I'm not sure, exactly. Like you, I could barely think of anything else when you left yesterday. I went through all the motions of taking care of the kids, feeding everyone, getting them off to bed, and listening to the radio with my husband, but I'm not sure I can tell you a single thing that any of them said to me all evening. Only my body was in the room with them. I can't account for the rest of me. I went to bed long before Patrick did so I wouldn't have to speak to him. Also so I wouldn't have to...well, you know. I went to sleep, steeped in moral indignation about your indiscretion. I woke up at four-thirty a.m. in a sweat. I'd had a dream. About you. And me. And we...um...we were doing things. Things I would never imagine doing. Things that, in the light of day, made me ashamed of myself, but in that dream...oh my. I...we...I...*wanted* it. More than I've ever wanted it. I wanted you. I felt shaken, rocked to my core, but in the best way possible.

"I had to get out of that bed. It was like I had been unfaithful to my husband. I sat up in the kitchen by myself, trying to chase away the images of that dream, but I couldn't. I just kept replaying it over and over. Then I lied to my husband and told him nothing was wrong, but that's not true, is it? Something is wrong with me, right? And something is wrong with you too, but even knowing that, I still want it. Because if it's possible to feel in real life what I felt in that dream, there's no way I could stop it. It's like a train coming straight at you, and you know you should move out of the way, but your feet are frozen on the tracks. That's how I feel right now—frozen on the tracks. Frozen in my head, waiting to find out if it's possible to get that feeling back again. Does any of this make sense?"

"It does. I had a dream about you the first night we met. Scared the hell out of me."

"Did we, you know...in your dream?"

"No. We kissed, that's all, but it was enough. And here I am, sitting next to you and unable to move from the train's path. I feel it will run me over so completely I won't ever recover."

They let their gazes meet as if magnetically drawn, and Anna lost her fear in Mary's deep blue eyes. She swallowed what little moisture there was in her mouth. They both leaned in simultaneously, tilting their heads in opposite directions as if they knew exactly what position each was supposed to take. They kissed so softly, so slightly. They would have barely felt it if not for the hypersensitivity of their nerve endings. The kiss lasted only a few seconds, and both pulled away. They each caught their breath. Anna reached for Mary's hand. She was shaking so much she could barely get a grip. They grabbed each other to hold their hands steady and kissed again. The chaste kiss slowly increased in intensity. Mary put her hands on Anna's face and pulled her in closer. Their mouths were open now, and they let their tongues barely touch, taking yet another step toward the oncoming train.

Anna broke their bond and suddenly stood up and made a sound somewhere between a cry and a moan. Mary looked a bit stunned at the break in the kiss. She took a deep breath and a sip of water while waiting to see what Anna would do.

"Anna, what is it?"

"If we keep going, we won't be able to stop."

"Yes, I know, but I don't want to stop. Do you?"

"No. But I'm so scared."

"I am too. Petrified. Maybe if we can talk through our fears, we can figure out what to do about it."

"Okay," Anna said. She slowly paced the room, thinking of words that might do the situation justice. "I'm terrified that what I just felt for you, here and now on this couch in my living room, is unlike anything I've ever felt in my entire life. If we take the already overused train analogy just one step further...once it hits us, we'll be paralyzed and never be able to go back to our normal lives. What are you scared of?"

"Well, at the moment, I'm scared I'm having a heart attack because my heart is pounding so hard in my chest." Mary walked over to Anna, took her hand, and placed it over her heart so Anna could feel it thumping. "I am having trouble catching my breath. If I collapse, it will be no mystery as to the cause. My goodness, Anna. Wow."

Mary leaned in and kissed Anna again. Anna returned it but then stepped away.

"I thought we were supposed to be talking about what's scaring us. So I'm going to go out on a limb here and say that if you continue kissing me, it will probably not decrease the fear factor."

"I know, I know, but I can't help it. Okay, just let me regroup. Whew...it's just...okay. Have you ever ridden a roller coaster when the county fair comes to town?"

"Yes."

"Okay, so I have a love-hate relationship with roller coasters. The thrill of it makes me continue to ride it again and again. Every time the car reaches the top of the slope and creeps over the edge, I close my eyes because I'm terrified of falling, but the feeling of falling is *so* exhilarating. That's what I'm feeling right now. I'm on the highest roller coaster ever built, and I'm falling. It is frighteningly exhilarating. I just want to ride it over and over and over again."

"What are we going to do?" Anna said, with a sense of urgency in her voice.

"Well, I think we both know what we *should* do. The question is, have we passed the point of no return? Because what we want to do and what we should do are on opposite ends of the spectrum."

"Maybe we need to take some time to think about this. My heart and mind are on parallel courses, and it feels like never the two shall meet. The ramifications of the heart's course are enormous. We could both lose everything we have. Are we willing to risk that?" Anna had tears in her eyes as she asked the question.

"A stronger person than I would likely say 'No, it's not worth it' and leave this house right now, but what if it *is* worth it?"

"It may be. It probably would be, but I can't risk losing my family. Can you? Just imagine if anyone found out. We would be branded with scarlet letters. Our husbands would take our children from us, and they would have to move because of the embarrassment. I just don't know if I can do this to them. Patrick may not be the most romantic or interesting man, but he's still a *good* man, and he doesn't deserve this."

"I know. My Johnny is the same." She walked over and put her arms around Anna. "Oh, Anna, what the hell am I going to do with you?"

"I think we have both just concluded you will do nothing with me. So I think it's our only option."

"Of all of the things we've said today, that may be the saddest one of all." Mary sighed, kissed Anna on the cheek, then picked up her purse, gently grabbed the stroller's handles so as not to wake Linda, and left the house.

Anna stood stock still, except for the hand she put on her face where Mary had just kissed her. Then she cried.

* * * *

The dreams continued nearly every morning that week. Anna woke up breathing heavily, bathed in sweat. Patrick would ask what was wrong, and she would tell yet another lie about a recurring nightmare she'd started having. Daytime offered no respite. She spent the day faking normalcy, trying to stay interested and engaged with her husband and children. The kids were straightforward, but Patrick? That was much harder. He was typically oblivious to her moods, but he took notice. They demanded attention, and neglecting them was simply not possible.

"Anna, what's been going on with you? You have had a 'headache' every night this week. I don't understand what's wrong. Why don't you want to be with me?" he asked.

"I'm sorry, honey. I just haven't been myself lately. I really do have a headache. I'm not sure what's wrong with me. Maybe I need to make an appointment with the doctor. It's not you, really." The constant lying to Patrick weighed on her conscience, but not enough to stop. If she dared to be honest with herself, the truth was she very much wanted to have sex. Just not with Patrick. Even though she hadn't acted on it, she still felt as if she had betrayed her husband. She had. She had kissed someone else. She had sexual dreams about someone else almost every night. She technically wasn't cheating, but there was no honor in not cheating by a technicality.

Just to keep things as uncomfortable as possible, Anna and Mary still walked the children to school each day. They still went to Mary's house for coffee once a week, and they still came to Anna's house on the weekend to listen to the wireless. They knew staying away would make things easier, but it was an unbreakable attraction, like magnets unable to pull themselves apart. Self-induced torture. Pleasure and pain in equal doses.

# Chapter Twenty-One

## ANNA 1929

"PATRICK, ARE YOU AND Johnny going to listen to the game on Saturday?"

"Yes, I think so. Why?"

"I thought maybe Mary and I would take the kids over to the fair that night. Would you mind?"

"Of course not. You know the fair is not my thing. If you are offering to let me skip it, I will not refuse. I'm sure Johnny feels the same. Baseball on the wireless is a far better use of a Saturday."

"I assumed you would say that. You are nothing if not predictable, Patrick O'Brien. I could probably finish your sentences for you if I wanted to do so."

"Yes, you could. Does that make me boring to you?"

"I wouldn't use that word. Let's say 'reliable.' Does that sound better?"

"Only slightly. It sounds like just another word for boring to me. Maybe you should think about how we can make things more exciting for you around here."

Anna nearly choked on the coffee she was drinking. Yes, there were ways to make it exciting, all right. If Patrick only knew. When he kissed her, she pictured Mary in his place. When he made love to her—on the rare occasions she let it happen—she faked all the right moves and sounds, but her heart and soul were not with him. The guilt afterward was gut-wrenching. As Patrick fell asleep, she rolled over and wept. Inevitably, on those nights after sex with him, she dreamt about making love to Mary. Vivid, erotic, and extensive dreams. Pleasure and pain in equal doses. The morning came, and Patrick was none the wiser. For the first time in their marriage, his tendency to ignore his wife's demeanor worked to her advantage, but even that hardly felt like a victory. If her husband couldn't see what was right in front of his face—that his wife was in love with someone else—what did that say about their marriage?

Knowing the answer to that question but weighing the alternatives, Anna had no other option but to suffer in silence and feign happiness. The one person she could not do that with, of course, was Mary. When they walked home from school each morning, Linda slept in the stroller, and they whispered to each other as they walked down the street. Looking straight ahead, intentionally avoiding eye contact, they talked of their heartache.

"Anna, I can't sleep. I'm so tired. I can't stop my mind from racing as I lie in bed at night. Thank goodness Johnny is such a heavy sleeper. I don't know if he suspects that something is wrong with me. If he does, he's doing a good job of hiding it. He wanted to make love last night, and I just couldn't do it!"

Anna swallowed hard, understanding the feelings all too well.

"I couldn't put Patrick off again. He wouldn't have understood. So, we..."

"Oh...I see," Mary said in a tone to indicate her jealousy.

"I didn't want to, Mary."

"I have no right to be jealous, Anna. It's completely irrational. There is nothing about this that is rational. And yet, I am. The thought of him kissing you, touching you, it's just..." She trailed off, unable to complete the thought.

"Can we drop Linda off at your mom's house today and go back to my place to talk, please? If I don't get some of this off my chest, I will have a nervous breakdown."

"You aren't worried about us being alone?" Mary asked.

"Of course, I'm worried! Terrified. But we have to talk about this or it will tear us all apart."

"Okay, okay. Let's go."

* * * *

Once inside the door at Anna's house, they took off their sweaters and hung them on the coat rack. Anna nervously went to the kitchen to start a pot of coffee while Mary sat at the table, twisting her wedding band round and round. Anna set the coffee cups, spoons, and napkins out on the table while Mary watched her every move around the room. Finally, they let their guard down when it felt as if they could at least momentarily escape from the charade that had become their lives. Mary took a deep breath as Anna came to sit next to her at the table.

"Where do we start?" Mary asked.

"Maybe we start by being honest, for the first time in a long time. I can't speak for you, but I spend most of my days faking presence, faking joy. It's exhausting. I just want to be real for a minute. I want to say what I mean and feel what I feel."

"I've wanted to do that from day one, Anna."

"I know. It's probably my fault you haven't been able to do that."

"It's not anyone's fault. It's the way of the world. *We* don't even understand what is happening to us. I don't think it's fair to expect anyone else to understand it."

Anna gave that some thought and said, "I understand what's happening to me. I may not know *why* it's happened or what to do about it, but I understand what's happening. All too well, truth be told."

"Tell me."

"As complicated as it is, it's equally simple, Mary. I'm in love with you. In every sense of the word and with all that it implies." She exhaled after saying it as if a weight was lifted off her chest.

Mary's face flushed. For perhaps the first time in her life, she was speechless.

"Have I said something you didn't already know?"

"No. But knowing it and hearing it are two very different things."

"Would you rather I hadn't said it?"

"I wish I had said it first."

"Why?"

"Because I feel like I'm the one who started this. I'm the one who felt it first. I dragged you into this mess. I've known for weeks that I am in love with you, but I haven't dared to say it. If I hadn't tried to kiss you that night, you wouldn't be any the wiser, and everything would be normal." She lowered her head as she spoke.

"Mary, I don't think this is a competition to see who can say the words first. I had no idea you were so competitive." She put her hand under Mary's chin to raise it so their eyes could meet, and then she smiled to let Mary know she was kidding.

Mary smiled. "I'm glad you can poke fun at me at a time like this."

"If we don't laugh about it, we'll cry. As you know, I've cried about this quite a lot already. So I prefer the laughter."

"I'm having a little trouble finding the humor."

"Okay. If you can't find the humor, do you think you can find the love? Can you see it in the way that I'm looking at you right now?"

"Yes, I see it. Anna, I love you so much. I'm sorry I've put you in this position."

"I'm a big girl, Mary. If I didn't want to be here, I wouldn't be. Even if this ends in complete heartache and destruction, the simple act of falling in love so completely has to be worth something, doesn't it? Do you feel like this with your husband? Because I sure as hell don't. This…"

She pointed her finger back and forth between the two of them. "This happens maybe once in a lifetime if you're lucky. I would bet that most people we know have never felt this. There has to be a reason why you and I are here. Yeah, it's caused more complications than we know what to do with, but I'm not going to set aside the magnitude of what I feel right now. It's too good. Too real. Too rare!"

"To answer your question, no, I never felt like this with my husband. I love him, but not like this. This is overwhelming," Mary said.

Anna stood for a moment and walked to the window. Staring out into the yard, she sighed. "The flowers in the garden are so pretty this time of year."

"Is this your way of changing the subject because you are uncomfortable?" Mary asked as she got up and joined her at the window.

Anna turned to her. "Maybe it's my way of changing the subject because I don't know where we go from here."

"I think I do."

"Please—tell me, because I'm at a loss. I don't think I've ever been so completely sure of one thing while in the midst of abject confusion about everything else."

Mary looked into Anna's eyes. The green eyes that started this whole thing stared back at her with just a hint of tears that Anna was trying to hold back. Mary put her thumb underneath Anna's eye to wipe it away. Then she leaned in and kissed Anna tenderly.

"That was supposed to stop your tears, not make them worse."

"Kissing me like that will make me want to cry every time, Mary."

"Why?"

"Because I can feel everything you are putting into that kiss. Every emotion. Like you said—overwhelming."

They kissed again, this time with more urgency. They folded themselves into each other's arms, and the kissing became harder, stronger, faster. Finally, Anna broke away from the kiss and pulled Mary closer, holding her tightly in a bear hug. She breathed her in and smelled her hair, her skin, the scent of clean from her shampoo. She whispered into Mary's ear. "Do you hear that? It sounds like a train is coming. Hold on for dear life because it's headed right for us."

Mary giggled a bit, then replied, "I've always loved the sound of trains, don't you? I'm ready. You?"

"My feet are planted firmly on the tracks."

They resumed their kissing, getting more heated as they learned the feel of each other's lips, mouths, faces. Anna turned away and glanced at the clock. "What time is your mother expecting us to pick up Linda?"

"After school. It's only ten forty-five. We have plenty of time." Mary was breathing heavily now. They both were.

Anna took Mary's hand and led her down the hall and into the spare bedroom. They looked at each other nervously.

"Neither one of us has ever done this before. So how will we know what to do?" Anna asked.

"I think we just do what feels right and let it happen naturally. Let's go slow. I don't want to rush this."

They sat on the bed, fully clothed, and just kissed for the longest time. No wandering hands, no pushing to go faster, as often happened with their husbands. Just tenderness. Their eyes were closed, feeling the moment rather than seeing it. Then they both opened them simultaneously and lost each other in a trance. They could hear each other's breathing, steady but increasing.

Anna spoke first. "I love you, Mary. I love you more than I have the words to say."

Mary gulped and seemed unable to respond.

Anna kissed her with much greater urgency as if to make sure Mary knew she was ready. Mary leaned them both down so they were lying on the bed. While still kissing, she moved her hand onto Anna's breast, over her blouse. Anna made a sound of approval, and Mary fondled her with more intention. She reached her hand inside Anna's blouse, fumbling to get inside the bra. When she touched Anna's nipple, she felt it harden between her fingers. Mary let out a moan of pure pleasure. Anna stopped kissing, looked Mary right in the eyes, and began undoing the buttons of her own blouse. Mary took the hint and responded by pulling her sweater over her head. Both were in their bra now, and Anna said, "Will you do the honor, please?" She turned her body around so Mary could get to the clasp on her bra. Mary unhooked each hook, slowly and purposefully. When the last one came undone, Anna pulled it off and rolled back around to face her. Mary repeated the process, rolling on her side for Anna to undo hers. She moved back, and they were face to face, breast to breast.

Anna brought her hand forward and put it on Mary's breast. She was gentle and deliberate, having never touched any other breast but her own in all of her twenty-nine years. She circled the nipple, softly squeezing it between her thumb and forefinger. Mary tilted her head back and sighed in gratification. When Anna heard that sound, she leaned in and put her mouth on the nipple. She rolled her tongue over and around it, making it harder with each stroke. "Oh my god," Mary said. With each new sound from Mary, Anna increased the intensity of her touch. With both hands, she fondled the breasts while her mouth continued to kiss and suck on them. Mary wriggled beneath her, pushing into her as if she couldn't get close enough. Anna brought her face back to meet Mary's, kissing her passionately. Mary rolled them onto their sides and reached behind Anna for the zipper on her skirt. She unzipped and pulled the skirt down in one fluid motion. Then she pulled herself onto her knees and looked at Anna while grasping her panties at each hip as if waiting for permission. Anna took her own hands and put them over Mary's, and they pushed her panties down together. Mary took off her skirt and panties before lying down again next to Anna.

After all the angst, tears, confusion, and longing, they were finally lying next to each other, skin on skin.

Mary looked into those emerald green eyes, caressed her face, and said, "I never dreamed it would be like this. I knew I wanted you, but this feeling is beyond anything I ever thought possible."

Anna smiled. She put her hand behind Mary's head and kissed her. Mary moved her hand down Anna's body, feeling every curve along the way. Her breasts, her stomach, her ribs, her navel. She took her time learning the terrain. She lightly scratched the tip of her fingernails over Mary's stomach, making goosebumps appear. "Are you trying to tease me, Mary Monahan?" she asked with a devilish smile.

"Yes, as a matter of fact, I am. Is it working?"

"It is. I had no idea you were so good at it."

"Neither did I. I guess you bring it out in me."

Mary ran her hand down Anna's leg to her knee, then reversed course and came back up on the inside of her thigh. She gently pushed Anna's other leg to spread them just a few inches wider. Then, with her middle and index finger, she touched Anna right *there*. Anna breathed in deeply and moaned. Mary answered by sliding her fingers up and down, up and down. Anna had a fleeting thought that she had never been this excited in all the times she'd ever had sex with Patrick, but she quickly chased her husband out of her head. She forbade him from infiltrating this room and this moment. Anna's attention refocused as Mary picked up the pace of her strokes.

When Mary's fingers entered her, Anna arched her back and cried out. Mary nervously pulled back.

"Did I hurt you?"

"No. No. No! Please, Mary. I want you. Now."

Mary pushed her fingers back inside Anna, doing as she demanded. She pressed harder, her fingers exploring deeper and deeper inside Anna's vagina. With each thrust, Anna grunted and called to her deity repeatedly. Mary moved her head back up to Anna's and kissed her desperately, frantically.

Mary could feel and hear that Anna was reaching her point of no return. She stopped kissing Anna and said, "Look at me, Anna. I want to see your eyes when you go there."

Anna tried to focus, to keep her eyes from closing while she climaxed. She stared at Mary, gasping for breath and calling out her name. "Please, Mary. Please..."

"Oh, Anna. Oh my god. You are so beautiful. Oh god."

When Anna finished, her back arched again, her eyes closed, and her head tilted backward. Mary collapsed down onto Anna's chest, struggling to catch her breath. They lay together in the aftermath, replacing the air in their lungs and listening to each other as they recovered.

When Anna finally spoke again, she said, "I don't even know what to say after that."

"Are you okay, Anna?"

"I have never been better. I just can't form the words to tell you what I'm feeling. I...I just didn't *know* that it could be that good. What about you? Are you okay? Did you..."

"I am perfect. And yes, I did. It was worth the wait. None of my fantasies did it justice."

"Nor mine. All those nights, I dreamt about this. Not. Even. Close. You seemed to know just what to do. If I didn't know better, I'd ask you where you learned how to do that."

"I didn't. I just went on instinct. It feels like the most natural thing to make love to you. Your body made it easy to know what to do. You are so fucking sexy!"

"Mary! I've never heard you use that word. Hmm...I kinda liked it!"

"Regular words aren't working. I needed something *more*. That word works."

"In more ways than one," Anna said, fully intending the pun.

"Well, we've crossed the line over into the 'new us,' don't you think? So maybe the new me uses that word."

Mary rolled over onto her back, suddenly realizing she was sweating and still hadn't fully caught her breath. "Now I see why men collapse and fall asleep afterward. It takes a little while to recover when you do it the right way. I always thought they were faking it because they didn't want to snuggle or talk."

"Well, I do want to snuggle and talk, but not yet. I'm not done with you." Anna rolled over on top of Mary, grasping their hands together over their heads.

"Wait, Anna. Remember how I said I don't want to rush this?" Mary said.

"Yes. I don't either. There is too much good stuff here to explore."

"I want to just lie here with you for now. Is that okay? Let's leave a bit of mystery for next time. We only have a short amount of time before we have to go back to the real world. Can we just be *still* with each other for a while?"

"Hmmm...being still. I'm not sure I remember what that is. We don't get to do that very much, do we? It sounds lovely, but let me ask you this. After that, how on earth will we return to the real world? How are we going to fake this? How am I going to look at you across the room? I'm starting to panic about it."

"You are not allowed to panic for at least another hour. You are all mine until then. When that time comes, we will figure it out, but we're not allowed to worry about it now. We're being still, remember?"

Anna nuzzled into the crook of Mary's arm. She inhaled deeply, taking in her scent and reveling in it. She closed her eyes and released any remaining tension. They set an alarm clock to make sure they didn't accidentally fall asleep, which was wise because an hour later, the alarm woke them, thoroughly entwined in each other's arms. They kissed for a few moments, then playfully helped each other get dressed and fix their hair and makeup. Then they straightened the guest room, removed all proof they had been there, and prepared to get their kids. Neither wanted to face it, but the real world was right outside the door.

# Chapter Twenty-Two

## JOSIE 1999

JOSIE STOOD AT THE door of Trish's house, ready to pick her up for their date. She cradled a dozen red roses and a bottle of champagne in her arms. Trish answered the door with a look of surprise, thinking she would just run out to the car when Josie arrived and tooted the car horn.

"Wow. Isn't this lovely. You've come bearing gifts. To what do I owe the honor?" She let Josie in and closed the door, greeting her with a kiss. She took the flowers from her, dipping her nose toward the buds to inhale the luscious aroma.

"Well, I thought I would treat this occasion with an appropriate amount of fanfare, given that it is a special day."

"It is? Uh-oh. I should probably know this. Am I going to be in trouble for this? What day is it?" Trish brought her hand up to her mouth, covering it in a gesture of embarrassment.

"No, my dear. I know not everyone keeps track of these things the way I do, but since you asked…Six months ago, my boss asked a crowded room of people for a volunteer to go to a career day thingy to speak to a class of little ones. Not one person volunteered, including me, but in her infinite wisdom, she selected me for the task, not realizing she would, in effect, change my life forever. As soon as you walked into that principal's office, I knew I was doomed. Nothing has been the same since. Happy six-month anniversary, baby."

"Aww! I had no idea. I'm sorry, honey. I really should have known that. Flowers, champagne, and those sweet words—you are too much! I couldn't believe my luck that day. I thought they would send me some nerdy guy my kids would torture, so it was a fortuitous event for so many reasons. Thank you, babe."

"You are very welcome. Put the flowers in water and the champagne in the fridge. We will drink it when we get home."

"Well, maybe we need to stay home for a bit so I can thank you appropriately. Wanna sneak into the bedroom for a while?" She raised her eyebrows, flashed her 'come hither' grin, and turned her head toward the hallway, leading Josie to her desired location.

"Nope. I'm turning you down. Let's go. We have a reservation in a half-hour. The restaurant will give away our table if we are late. We're going to Raphael's down on the waterfront. I know it's one of your favorites."

"Damn. Do you mean I really can't tempt you? It could be a quickie!"

"No quickies. Let's go, missy. Chop, chop."

Trish pouted playfully, then made her way to the kitchen to handle her chores. Once the flowers were settled in the vase, they left for their dinner date.

Josie made sure they had a table on the patio overlooking the bay at the restaurant. She had arranged for even more flowers on their table—lilies this time—and the card with Trish's name was already resting against the wine glass in front of her. The hostess moved to pull the chair out for Trish, but Josie quickly walked around to the other side of the table to complete the task herself.

"I'm getting the royal treatment tonight, aren't I? I'm so honored."

"You are, and you deserve it. Tonight, it's about you, my love."

"How about we make it about 'us' instead?"

"I prefer to keep my focus on you right now," Josie said as she looked into Trish's eyes. "If you choose to turn the tables, I guess I can't stop you."

"I think I will do that. I kind of like the view. But seriously. This is so sweet, honey. I'm really touched."

"Open your card."

"Now? Already?"

"Yes, please. I had to go out of my way to get it to the table before you did, so I'd like to get the appropriate amount of credit for and attention from it." Josie laughed.

"We'll see about that." As Trish opened the card, a piece of paper fell onto the table.

"Read the card first. Then you can see what that is."

"Aren't we pushy today!"

"Yep. Read."

Trish read the front and the inside of the card, taking her time to read it more than once. She was full-on crying by the second read-through. "I don't know what to say. This card is so beautiful."

"It just reflects the woman who is reading it right now. Open the paper."

Trish unfolded the paper to find a reservation for a bed and breakfast in Vermont.

"This is the place I showed you from that article in the Sunday paper last week, isn't it?"

"Yes, it is."

"Oh, my goodness! You are the sweetest woman I've ever met. I don't deserve you."

"That's true," she said sarcastically, "but I kinda like you, so I'm willing to take that into account." They both laughed, and Trish took the napkin she had been using to dry her eyes and threw it across the table at Josie.

"I don't know how to thank you." Trish reached across the table and took Josie's hands into hers, lifting them to her lips and kissing them.

"You're welcome, and you deserve it. I'm sure you can find a way to thank me intimately when we are alone later this evening. In the meantime, I hope this is the first of many vacations we take together." As she finished her sentence, she noticed Trish's eyes darted across the room, and her expression changed drastically. Josie turned her head to see what had caused her to go white in the face.

"Who is that, Trish?"

"It's my mother."

"Oh. Well, um...err...okay. Um, what do you want to do? What do you want me to do?" They were still holding hands across the table.

"Nothing. She is coming over here." Josie made a move to take her hand from Trish's. The death grip she felt signaled Trish wanted the hands to stay precisely where they were.

Trish looked up to meet her mother's glare. "Hello, Mom. How are you? This is Josie. Josie, this is my mom, Marilyn."

"Hello, Mrs. McCann. It's very nice to meet you."

"Hello, Patricia. Josie. It's nice to meet you as well," she said coldly.

"What are you doing here, Mom?"

"I'm meeting a friend for dinner. I didn't know you would be here, or I wouldn't have intruded on your evening."

Josie chimed in, "It's no intrusion. I'm happy to finally get the chance to meet you."

"It looks like you are celebrating something special. What's the occasion?"

"Oh, it's nothing, Mrs. McCann. We just..."

"It's the six-month anniversary of the day we met when Josie came to my school for career day. She gave me these lovely flowers and a gift."

"How nice," she said, clearly meaning the exact opposite of her words. "Well, I won't take up any more of your time. Enjoy your evening." She turned quickly and walked back to the table and her friend.

"Wow," Josie said. "She's...um. I, uh...I am *genuinely* at a loss for words."

"She's a real breath of fresh air, right? She brings sunshine wherever she goes!" Trish took a deep breath, trying to regain her composure. "I'm really sorry, hon. We were having such a nice evening, and now it's ruined."

"Does it have to be ruined?"

"Well, no, I guess not. But..."

"No, listen. Hear me out. I know she has tanked your mood. And having heard the exchange between you two, I can certainly see why, but think about this. Can she see you from where she is sitting?"

"Yes, she's looking right at us."

"Okay, good. So how about this. I say something witty and sweet to make you smile and laugh again, just like you were before she arrived and threw cold water over you. In return, you do your best to pretend she isn't here. Then we get the benefit of our well-planned and quite lovely romantic evening, *and* she gets to see how happy you are. Unless I'm mistaken, you *were* pretty happy about five minutes ago, so it's not like you would have to fake it."

"Hmm...Not a bad plan. Let me hear the witty and sweet things first, and then I will decide."

Josie laughed. "Remember the first night we went out for a drink and I said I knew you were gonna be a handful?"

"Yep."

"I was right, wasn't I?"

"Yep. Forewarned is forearmed."

Josie reached across the table again for Trish's hand. "I think I responded by saying I like a challenge, which meant you would keep me on my toes. I was certainly right about that. I can't think of any better way to have spent these last six months than with you. You are a handful and a challenge, and I couldn't be happier. So when I go to work on Monday, I should hug my boss to thank her for this."

"Hmm...is she attractive?"

"Yes. Very."

"Oh. I was hoping maybe she was old and decrepit. Maybe just shake her hand to thank her instead, okay?"

"Ooh. Are you getting jealous? Not to worry, she's straight and married."

"Yes, I remember your rule to stay away from straight women. How's that working out for you?"

"Good point. I guess you do have reason to worry." Josie sat back in her chair, flashing a sarcastically smug look on her face.

"Maybe just send her a thank you card. I'll even sign it, so she knows you are off-limits."

"Oh, so I guess I'm officially off the market now, huh?"

"That depends. Do you *want* to have sex with me ever again?"

"Yes, please. Hopefully, in about two hours or so." Josie pointed to her watch and shook her head vigorously as she answered.

"Then yes. You are off the market."

"So, what's happening at the grumpy table across the room?"

"She's pretending she's not looking over here, but she's not doing a very good job of it."

"Good. Then she's watching you smile. My work here is done."

"Yeah, except she's still not speaking to me."

"I know, but if she's like most parents—and I hope she is—all she wants is for her kid to be happy. So I guarantee we've made an impression with her tonight. Mark my words."

The waiter came over to open the bottle of champagne Josie had ordered, the popping of the cork capturing attention around the room. As he poured their glasses, Josie locked eyes with Trish and smiled. When the waiter left the table, she toasted their good fortune.

"Six months ago, I thought I was satisfied with just my work, my dog, and my house. When we get into our fifties, and the right person still hasn't come along, we accept that maybe it's just not meant to be. And that's what I had done. I could have lived out my life that way, being content. I probably would have convinced myself I was genuinely happy, but I would have been wrong. I didn't know happiness until you walked into that room. And as much as I tried to keep away from you, being one of those straight women who cause havoc, you wormed your way inside. I don't just mean into my heart. I mean inside every part of me. You are in my head and deep inside all my senses. When I go to work, I can still smell your cologne on my skin. I can taste your kiss on my lips. The other day, my boss walked by my desk and tried to get my attention. She had to call me three times to get me out of my trance. I was just staring at my computer, thinking about making love to you just a few hours earlier. She said, 'Oh, you've got it bad, don't you?' I said, 'Yeah, I sure do.'"

Josie took a breath, brought her glass to Trish's, and clinked them together.

"Here's to you, Patricia Marie. Thank you for making me aware of what I've been missing. Thank you for being honest with yourself and with me. For crashing into my life like a meteor. For making me laugh every single day. For loving me and for letting me love you right back. Happy anniversary, sweetheart."

They drank their champagne, and Josie wished she could lean over and kiss her, but that would have drawn too much unwanted attention. So she settled for a tight grip on her hand and an 'I wish I could kiss you' smile. Trish put her glass down and reached for her napkin to dab her eyes.

"There's something I've never told you about that day you came into my classroom."

"Oh, really? I'm all ears."

"Okay. You're going to think I'm crazy, but here goes. You were in mid-presentation, talking to the kids like you were one of them but still commanding the room with the fun facts you were handing out to them like candy. At one point, you caught my eye—I guess that's when you were looking for my reaction like you said afterward—and I had a vision flash through my brain. It was kinda blurry and fast, but I know exactly what it was because I saw it again later that night as I was falling asleep. You were looking at me, just like you are right now. You smiled, and I smiled back. You just said, 'Hello, love.' That was it. It was over. I blinked myself out of that daze and back into the moment with you and the kids. In the back of my mind, I was thinking, 'what the *hell* was that?' I had no idea, but I knew I wanted to find out. That's what made me ask you out for a drink that night."

"Well, there's only one explanation, isn't there? Clearly, I had died and gone to heaven when I met you, and I was visiting you from the great beyond." She started laughing.

"Oh, geez. Your corniness knows no bounds, does it?"

"Nope."

"Whatever it was, it got my attention, and here we are today. While I wish the sour puss on the other side of this room would have taken the news a little better, there is otherwise nothing I would change about the last six months. It's as if I suddenly got a do over and figured out who I'm supposed to be. And who I'm supposed to be with. I love you, Josie. Thank you for breaking your 'no straight women' rule for me."

"My pleasure. Rules need to be broken sometimes. Breaking it for you has been one of the wisest decisions I've ever made."

Dinner ended, and a massive slice of decadent chocolate cake rounded out the meal. As they drank their coffee and indulged in their sugary treat, Trish rechecked her peripheral vision to find that they were still being watched. Marilyn inadequately concealed her curiosity in monitoring the activities of the couple. After Josie paid the check and they prepared to leave, Trish passed by her mother's table and politely interrupted, knowing that Marilyn would not cause a scene at the table with her guest.

"Mom, it was nice to see you this evening. I'd love to talk soon if you are willing."

"Sure, dear. I will call you."

"When? Let's plan it, okay? I want to make sure I'm available for you."

"I don't know yet, Patricia. I'll have to get back to you," she said, with increasing snippiness.

"Right. Got it. Well, good night, then."

"Good night."

Trish caught up with Josie again in the vestibule and said, "Why do I even bother?" Then she stormed out.

Josie rushed out of the restaurant to catch up to her. She grabbed her arm and said, "Let's take a little walk before we get in the car, okay? I think the night air might do you some good." Trish's pace slowed, and they walked with their elbows locked together. They meandered toward the back of the building, where the dock from the marina joined with the restaurant's patio. Then, arm in arm, they strolled past the boats clanking against the dock, gently rocking from the warm late-summer breeze.

"I know she's hurt you," Josie said. "I can see how upset you are. You have every right to be, but she's just going to have to come to her acceptance in her own time. Nothing you can say is going to rush that for her."

"I know, I know. It was stupid of me to go over to her table again. I should have known. I guess I was just hoping that, as you said, she saw I was happy. Like...really happy. And dammit...it's just that I can see my relationship with her deteriorating right before my eyes, and there's nothing I can do about it! I set myself up for disappointment by going over there, didn't I?"

"Maybe, but I can see why you had to try. She's your mother. There's probably no more complex relationship than between mother and daughter. It's like one puts a lifetime of expectations on the other. A heavy burden to put on a child, especially since the daughter has no idea those expectations are there while she's growing up. My mother once told me she was disappointed she put 'all of her eggs in one basket' with me. I have a feeling your mother may be experiencing something similar. She had a vision. She just needs time for that vision to change."

"But what if it doesn't?"

"That is a possibility, I suppose, but in my heart, I do believe she's going to come around."

"I'm sorry our anniversary got ruined," Trish said.

"It wasn't ruined. Interrupted, maybe. Ninety-nine percent wonderful with just a *hint* of uncomfortable. We still got to celebrate, and I still got to make you smile and laugh. Now I'm walking with you in the moonlight with the sound of water lapping against the dock. That's a good night in my book. Yeah, there's all that other stuff that I know is killing you, but I'm in it for the good and the bad with you."

"I got pretty lucky that day six months ago."

"You sure did." Josie gave her a wry smile as she spoke.

Trish laughed. "So did you."

"You're damn right, I did. C'mon. Let's go home and celebrate in private."

As they made their way back to the car, their arms still entwined at the elbows, they heard the sound of several men walking behind them in the parking lot. They were inebriated and making cat-call noises to another woman getting into her car across the lot. Rattled by their attention, she hurried into her vehicle, started the car, and sped away. As she pulled out, the calls continued.

"Hey, baby! Let me hop in the passenger seat and take you to my place. I'll show you a good time, guaranteed!"

"Aw, c'mon, honey. Don't leave. You're missing out on the best offer you'll get all night!"

Josie and Trish kept walking, avoiding any contact with the obnoxious group. They had obviously upset the woman in the car, judging by the rate of speed at which she drove out of the lot.

"What a bunch of assholes," Trish said at a slightly elevated volume.

"Babe, please don't antagonize them. They will target us next. You've probably never been subjected to homophobic harassment before. I have. Trust me, you do not want to engage with them."

"What are they going to do? They're a bunch of drunk cowards showing off their Neanderthalic mating skills."

"Just, please. Let's go." Josie ushered them along a little faster. One of the men must have heard something Trish said because the group's attention suddenly shifted to Trish and Josie.

"Well, looky what we have here. A couple of lesbos out on a romantic date. How sweet. Hey, ladies! Oh wait, can I call you ladies? Cause you're more like guys, aren't you?"

Trish slowed down, clearly eager to respond, but Josie pulled harder on her arm to get her to move faster. Their car was still about a hundred yards away.

"C'mon," Josie said. "Do *not* speak. This could get very bad very quickly."

"Hey, dykes! Don't you want some of this here?" He grabbed his crotch. The others in the group laughed and joined in. "I'll bet you've never had a guy like me before. I'll make you straight in no time. C'mon, bitches!"

One of the others chimed in, shouting, "Hey, how about we all have a go at them?" The group started jogging toward Josie and Trish, and Trish realized Josie wasn't exaggerating. This was about to get serious. They broke into a full-on run, hand in hand. They were about ten yards from the car when one of the men caught up to them. He pushed Josie to the ground and got right in Trish's face. So close she felt his hot, beer-laden breath on her skin. When she resisted, he smacked her in the face so hard she screamed. Josie got up and wedged herself between the two of them, and she kneed him in the crotch with all of her strength. He fell to the ground, groaning in agony with his hands over his balls. Josie opened the car door and pushed Trish inside, then ran around to get in on her side and locked the doors. She sped out of the lot as quickly as possible, swerving to avoid running over the rest of the group who had finally caught up to their ailing ringleader.

Josie drove about a mile away from the parking lot, then pulled over to the side of the road. She was sweating, breathing heavily, and her hands were shaking. She looked over at Trish and found her palm on her face, covering a sizeable red handprint. They were both crying. Trish leaned over and lowered her head onto Josie's shoulder.

"Are you okay? Let me see your face, honey!" Josie pulled Trish's hands off her cheeks and assessed the damage. "I think we need to go to the hospital."

"No, please. It's okay. It was just a slap."

"What if he broke your cheekbone?"

"No, he didn't. It would hurt a lot more if that were the case. I'm okay. Mostly I'm just scared and embarrassed and mad at myself. I should have listened to you. They obviously heard me call them assholes. I'm so sorry, babe. Are you okay? You took a pretty hard fall on the concrete."

"I'm fine. This is not your fault! They did this, not us. Those fucking assholes harassed us! This is a hate crime, and we can't take the blame for their disgusting behavior." After they both calmed down and their breathing returned to semi-normal, she kissed Trish's forehead, put the car in drive, and pulled away. A few minutes later, Josie turned the car into another lot down the road in front of the Nassau County police precinct.

"Please, Josie. Do we have to do this? I don't want to go in there to report this. It's humiliating."

"Yes, we have to. Like I said—a hate crime. If people like us don't report them, no one knows the truth about the shit we have to go through. Plus, I want them to take pictures of the mark on your face. I'll call the restaurant to make sure they know about it."

After a two-hour wait in the police station to make a statement and take pictures, they finally made their way back to Trish's house. Josie flopped on the couch while Trish went into the kitchen. She returned with two shot glasses and a bottle of whiskey. She sat next to Josie, poured their shots, and handed one to Josie. They clinked their glasses instinctively and gulped them down, followed by a quick refill and another gulp. Finally, they leaned back on the couch, and Trish put her head in the crook of Josie's arm.

"Are you okay, baby?" Josie asked.

"Not yet, but I will be. I was so naïve. I had no idea this kind of thing still happens."

"Yep. And it probably always will." She caressed Trish's arm as she spoke. "We just have to be careful."

"I see that now," Trish said sheepishly.

"Look on the bright side. The debacle with your mother was *not* the worst part of our evening. In fact, in perspective, it wasn't so bad at all."

"Very funny. What do you think the police will do?"

"There's probably not much they can do. We couldn't give them a strong description, and the restaurant manager said there weren't any large tables of guys there tonight. I think they were just walking around the docks, getting drunk, and causing trouble. The chances of them being picked up are slim. Even if they are picked up, the odds of them being punished are almost zero."

"That was one of the scariest moments of my life. When I saw him knock you over, I was so frightened. You could have cracked your head open on the cement."

"When he got to you, I thought he was going to rape you. I was petrified. Thank goodness an overdose of adrenaline got me to my feet to get in between you and him. I'd never forgive myself if I was unable to protect you."

"Josie, it's not your responsibility to protect me. This was the work of a very disturbed group of guys who thought they had the right to terrorize us."

"True, and while it might not be my responsibility, protecting you is something I will always do, sweetheart. Haven't you figured that out by now? Like it or not, I'm yours."

Trish picked her head up from Josie's shoulder and faced her, looking into her eyes. "I'm yours too. Unfortunately, I didn't get to protect you, but I hope you know I would have if the situation had transpired a little differently. He just slapped me so quickly!" The tears began to roll down Trish's cheeks again, and Josie reached over to dry them.

"I know, honey. I think what we've learned from this is that we both have a lot to be thankful for, but we also have a lot to lose. It hasn't taken long for me to realize I don't want to be without you. So, we're in this together, whether it's cranky mothers or violent homophobes. Happy anniversary, my love."

"Most people just have a romantic dinner for their anniversary," Trish added, giving Josie a slightly sarcastic grin.

"Yeah, well, the universe obviously thought we needed some excitement. Maybe it was testing us. Do you think we passed?"

"I know we did. I love you more right now than I did before we left the house this evening. I didn't think that was possible, so thank you, Universe. Perhaps you didn't need to scare the shit out of us to make that happen, but so be it." Trish stood and grabbed Josie's hand. "Take me to bed, please. I need some calm, and I'm sure that falling asleep in your arms is the best place to find it."

# Chapter Twenty-Three

## ANNA 1929

ANNA LAY NEXT TO Patrick, feeling the weight of her betrayal like a boulder on her chest. He lightly snored, unaware of her torment, but in her head, the feeling of being trapped with no viable alternatives felt like a vacuum sucking all the air out of the room. Memories of the afternoon with Mary inflicted both pleasure and pain. She stared at the ceiling, waiting for an answer to come from somewhere out of the ether. When she closed her eyes, she saw the vision of Mary's body next to her in the tiny bed in the spare room. Her skin, glistening in the aftermath, invited her to touch. She could feel and smell Mary's breath upon her as they lay so close together. She heard the soft-spoken words whispered to each other as the afternoon sun beamed through the window and fell upon their faces. She felt their feet softly rubbing together while they drifted off to sleep. If only she could sleep now and avoid the torture of the nighttime. Her feelings for Patrick had suddenly diminished to that of just a friend. The father of her children, but not her lover. Not anymore. She had only one lover now. There was only room in her heart for Mary in that role. It was only a matter of time before she would have to either tell Patrick she was no longer interested in having sex with him or, worse, fake it with him just to avoid the conflict. There would be no explanation that would satisfy him if she told him she didn't want it. It would only make things worse. Before all this started, they had discussed having another child. Talk about making things more complicated! How would she explain the change of heart for that plan?

* * * *

Mary spoke first as they walked the children to school in the morning. "You're about a million miles away from me right now, Anna."

"I know. I feel a little lost. I can't see a way forward. I've never been so confused. My heart and my head are at war with each other."

"Who is winning?"

"No one. It's lose-lose, all the way around." Anna's voice started to crack a bit, holding back tears. "I can't sleep. Either I'm worried about what I'm going to do with Patrick, or I'm remembering what it was like to be with you. The thoughts of you are not without worry either, sexual arousal notwithstanding."

"I know I'm going to make the situation a hundred times worse by telling you this, but..."

"Uh-oh. What?"

"I had sex with Johnny last night. Not because I wanted to. Believe me. I just didn't see any other way to keep him from realizing something has changed. I...I didn't know if I should tell you or not. Are you upset with me?"

"No, of course not. How could I be? I've had the same thought myself. Telling him I don't want to will only invite more questions I won't know how to answer, but my god, Mary. How will I let him touch me now that you have touched me?"

"I think you have to, and you have to act as normal as possible. If you liked it before, you need to make sure he sees that you like it now. Did you, um...err...did you, um, like it with him?"

"It was...fine. Nice. Not bad. But nothing...I mean *nothing* like what it was with you. I don't dislike it with him."

"But 'fine' is kind of a lackluster word, don't you think?"

"Well, knowing what I know now, lackluster kind of covers it. The funny thing is you convince yourself you are satisfied until you find out what true satisfaction feels like. I never really thought anything was wrong with my relationship with Patrick, but now, all I can think of is you. And us. Will you stop back at my place on the way home? I just need to be alone with you for a minute, Mary. I know we can't be together very often because it's too risky, but just hold me for a minute and tell me it will be okay. Lie to me if you have to."

It started to drizzle on their way home. Mary pulled the top over the stroller to keep Linda from getting wet. She slept through these walks every day, and the rain had no impact whatsoever. They only had one umbrella between them, so Anna put her hand on Mary's back and held it over them while Mary pushed the stroller. When they got to Anna's house, Mary closed and locked the front door behind them and wheeled Linda over next to the couch to continue her nap. She met Anna across the room and folded her body into Anna's arms. She could hear Anna weeping into her shoulder and just let her cry.

# Chapter Twenty-Four

## ANNA 1930

ANNA SKIPPED THE WALK to school. The morning sickness had gotten the best of her, and Mary offered to take care of the kids. Unfortunately, the nausea with this pregnancy was considerably worse than with her other kids, and some days she could barely get out of bed until lunchtime. Eleven weeks along, and it got worse every day.

The doorbell rang, and she finished chewing the salty cracker she'd been nibbling on in hopes it would ease the sickness. She opened the door to find Mary alone and without Linda.

"Where's Linda?"

"Well, hello to you too."

"Sorry. Just not used to seeing you without her."

"I dropped her at my mother's house. I wanted to see you and didn't want to risk her waking up. How are you feeling?"

"Like death. This baby is doing a real number on me. I hope it's not an indication of what a troublemaker they intend to be. If it is, I'm in real trouble."

"Or maybe it's getting its difficult period over with now, and it will be an angel when it's born."

"It would have to be a real angel to make up for this. It's probably a boy. They are always troublemakers."

"The pregnancy with my boys was a challenge as well. I guess you're right. It's the boys." She hesitated for a moment, then continued. "This is going to sound crazy, but I wish you and I were having this baby together." Mary lowered her eyes in embarrassment as she spoke. "We could live together as a family. I know it sounds ridiculous, but it's nice to dream."

"That could never happen."

"I know. People will never get over the idea that we are abnormal perverts."

"Do you think we are abnormal perverts, Mary?"

She walked over to Anna and put her arms around her neck as she answered. "No. If we were, I can't imagine it would feel like this. Like this is the way it's supposed to be for us. Why would God make us this way?"

"I'm not sure I believe in God anymore. As you said, He made us this way and then gave us a life of torture where we can never be truly happy as we are. What kind of god would do that?"

Mary looked surprised at the admission about God. Then she leaned in and kissed Anna tenderly. "It's not all torture. When we are alone, especially when we make love, it's anything but torture. We could see it as God giving us a gift that only we get to share just between ourselves."

"That's an optimistic viewpoint. I wish I could be more like you in my thinking. However, I have difficulty understanding why this is happening to us. Why would we meet and fall in love, only to maintain this huge secret for the rest of our lives so we could have sporadic moments of bliss only when we are certain others won't see us?" Anna choked up as she finished her thought.

Mary put her hands on Anna's cheeks. "Anna, please don't let anger consume you. It's not good for you, the baby, the rest of your family, and it's not good for us. We have only two choices here. We can decide it's too painful and we end it and never see each other again. Or we live with our situation, treasuring those sporadic moments of bliss when they come. For me, the thought of ending it and never seeing you again is just too painful to consider."

"I can't end it with you. I'm too deeply in love with you."

Mary smiled and kissed her again. "Then we have only one choice. We have to choose love." She put her arms around Anna and held her, attempting to block out everything except the two of them. "Are you still feeling sick, or would you like to take a walk? It's a beautiful day, and the air might help."

"Okay. Let's try. I think my stomach has calmed a bit. Just give me a minute to put on some makeup. I'll be right back." Anna went into her bedroom to freshen up.

Mary walked around the room, looking at the family pictures on the walls and shelves. She picked up the ones with Anna to stare into those eyes she loved so much. Photos of Lynn and Judy when they were babies. Anna and Patrick at their wedding. Anna, with her parents and her brother and sister, out on the stoop of their brownstone in Brooklyn in 1915. She was as beautiful then as she was now. As she moved from one photo to the next, she heard Anna calling from the next room. The urgency in her voice was unmistakable.

"Mary, please. Come here. Hurry!"

"What's the matter? Are you all right?"

"No, I'm bleeding. Something is wrong with the baby. I don't know what to do!"

"Okay." Mary ran into the bedroom and helped Anna over to the bed. "Lie down. It will be okay. I'll get the doctor over here right away, and I'll call your husband at work. Just relax. Breathe. You're going to be okay."

Mary ran to the telephone and got the doctor's receptionist on the line. She explained the situation and cried, "Please! Send him as soon as possible. We have an emergency here!"

She hung up then called Patrick's work. Unfortunately, they had to page him into the front office to answer the phone, which took several minutes. Mary paced as far as the phone cord would allow, twisting it around her hands subconsciously.

"Hello, this is Patrick. Who is this?"

"Patrick, it's Mary. You need to come home right away, please. Anna is bleeding and is worried about the baby. I've called the doctor, and he is on his way. Hurry, please. She needs you." Saying those words stung a bit, realizing Patrick would be the one who got to be by her side while Mary had to take a back seat and pretend to be just a friend.

"Oh my god. No, no, no...Please, God, don't let her lose the baby. I'll be home as quickly as possible. Please tell her I love her, and I'll be right there!"

Mary returned to the bedroom, sat on the bed, and held her hand. "Anna, I've made all the calls. The doctor will be here soon, and so will your husband. So just lie still and relax. Patrick wanted me to tell you he loves you." She paused and took a breath. "He does, you know. He really does love you. I could hear it in his voice."

"I know he does. He's a good man. It kills me to betray him like this. What if this is my punishment?"

Mary leaned in, coming face to face with her. She could feel the panicked breathing and hear the cracking in her voice. She reached for a tissue from the box on the nightstand and dabbed at Anna's perspiring forehead. "Stop. Don't even think that. You are *not* being punished. You are a good wife and an excellent mother. You will get through this, whatever it is. I will be here for you in whatever way I can. I promise." Mary kissed her lips, then kissed away the tears rolling down her cheeks.

A knock at the front door interrupted the moment of tenderness between them. Mary ran for it and let the doctor into the house.

She ushered him into the bedroom, and he turned to her and said, "Thanks. I'll take it from here," and he closed the bedroom door behind him. The distress at the inability to be by Anna's side suddenly crippled Mary, and she leaned against the wall and slid down to the floor, sobbing. Anna was scared and alone, and there was nothing Mary could do about it. Protecting Anna from whatever was happening in that room was not an option. She was just...helpless.

Patrick came rushing into the house and went straight to the bedroom. He saw Mary on the floor but barely registered her existence as he burst into the bedroom. He was welcome in that room. Mary was not. That's the way it was and the way it would always be. Sadness overtook her.

* * * *

Mary went to school to retrieve both her kids and Anna's and then stayed at Anna's house to watch them. The doctor did not explain what was happening when they left for the hospital, just that she would be in good hands. Every aspect of the reality of their relationship came crashing down on her, and the irony of their conversation just a few hours earlier hit Mary like a cruel joke. 'We could look at it as God giving us a gift that we get to share just between ourselves,' she had said to Anna. That gift seemed intangible at this moment, as the kids chattered to themselves while Mary struggled to hold back the tears.

Patrick came home at eleven-thirty that night, clearly exhausted and distraught. The children were asleep, the girls in their bedroom, and Mary's boys on the floor in the spare room. Patrick looked in on them, making sure the doors were closed so he could talk privately, then sat at the kitchen table.

"She lost it. The baby is gone." He lowered his head, put his hands over his face, and started to cry.

"Oh, Patrick! I don't know what to say. I'm devastated for you."

He sniffled, composed himself as best as he could, and said, "The doctor said that sometimes these things just happen. There's no explanation. But I don't understand! Everything was fine. She was perfectly healthy!"

"I know, I know. It makes no sense. It's one of those things we will never know why it happens. How was she when you left her?"

"Heartbroken. Inconsolable. I didn't know what to say. I didn't know what to do. I felt so helpless."

"I know. I felt the same while waiting for you and the doctor to arrive this morning. I just wanted to help her, but I couldn't. It broke my heart." Little did Patrick realize just how true that was.

"Can you please go see her tomorrow? She was asking for you. She knows how much she scared you today and wants to thank you for calmly handling it. Maybe you will be able to console her. I'm just no good with words. Sometimes I think she would rather talk to you than me anyway."

Mary did not react to that statement, at least not how she wanted to react. "It's just because we relate to each other as women and mothers. It's not because of you, Patrick. I hope you know that. She loves you." Well, at least that much *was* true, even if it was not in the way she and Anna loved each other. Skating on the edge of truth wasn't exactly lying, was it? "I'll go see her while the kids are in school tomorrow. I'll ask my mother to watch Linda. In the meantime, you must be starving. I made a casserole for the kids tonight. I just need to warm it for you. Have a seat, and I'll take care of it."

"Thanks, Mary, but I can't eat a thing. I need to just go to bed. You don't have to wake the kids. Why don't you sleep in the spare room tonight?"

"Thank you. I think I will. It's been an exhausting day all the way around, and the thought of trying to get the kids up and then back to sleep at my house is a little daunting."

Mary lay in the spare bed, remembering the last time they were in this room together. That day's joy and ecstasy were replaced by sadness, thinking of Anna alone with her grief in her hospital bed. Her sons lay sleeping on the floor, breathing rhythmically and providing some much-needed sound to calm the endless stream of thoughts running through her brain like a freight train. *I will see her tomorrow,* she told herself. *I will be better when I see her,* knowing that better was a relative term. A baby had died today. Nothing was going to make that better.

# Chapter Twenty-Five

## MARILYN 1999

CONSUMED WITH DESPAIR, ANNA was curled up in the fetal position facing the window when Mary arrived at the start of visiting hours. The room was sterile and cold, with an empty second bed and a deafening silence. As Mary approached the window side of the bed, Anna barely acknowledged her, except by closing her eyes to stop her tears. Mary reached for her hand, squeezed gently, and sat down at her side on the bed.

"Hi," Mary said.

Anna made a faint attempt at a *hi* back to her, but no sound came from her lips.

"I know there is nothing I can say to make your heartache disappear. Just know I love you and will do anything I can to ease your pain."

"Remember I said yesterday I was being punished?" Anna whispered. Mary nodded. "I was right. I keep thinking back to our conversation a couple of months ago. I told you Patrick wanted another child, and I said I didn't. I'd betrayed him with you even before that. I've been a terrible wife and I deserve this, but the saddest part is that baby was the innocent victim in all of this. It never got a chance to know how much I would have loved it, regardless of what I said!"

"Anna, please. This is not a punishment. It's a horrible thing that has happened, but it's not God's vendetta against you. These things happen every day. Just last week, Sharon Murray had a miscarriage. And two months before that, Lucy in the house next door to me had one. Please. Stop blaming yourself. You were taking good care of yourself and the baby. It wasn't meant to be, I guess."

"The doctor said he doesn't know if I'll be able to have any more children. Patrick is going to be devastated. He wanted a son so badly."

"Oh, Anna." Mary leaned in and wrapped her arms around her as they wept together.

Mary composed herself and took a tissue off the tray to blow her nose. Then she grabbed another tissue and blotted Anna's eyes with it. "I wish I could kiss you. Not in a passionate way, just a kiss of love. I feel so incredibly helpless."

"You being here is helping some. I couldn't even form words when Patrick was here last night. How was he? Did you see him?"

"Yes, I was still at your house with all the kids. He was, well...he was trying to put on a brave face, but it was obviously crushing him. So I stayed at your house and slept in the spare room last night. It was late, and I didn't want to wake the kids. I hope you don't mind."

"The spare room..." Anna said as her voice trailed off.

"Yes, but let's not think about that right now, okay. It's neither the time nor the place. When did the doctor say you could go home?"

"Probably tomorrow. They want to make sure I didn't lose too much blood. Are my kids okay?"

"Yes, your kids are fine. I fixed their lunches and made sure they got off to school this morning. Patrick told them you weren't feeling well and had to stay where the doctor could keep an eye on you. He did a good job talking to them. I don't think they were too worried, especially since you hadn't even told them you were pregnant yet. I'll collect them all this afternoon and stay with them until he gets home. I'll get dinner prepared too. So don't concern yourself, okay? I've got it handled."

"I don't know what I would do without you. And even though I didn't say it before, I wish you could kiss me, too. I could use it right about now. I just feel so...lost."

"When a little more time has passed, I hope you will let me find you."

# Chapter Twenty-Six

## TRISH 1999

MARILYN SAT AT JUDY'S table and drank her white wine spritzer while Judy stirred the chili on the stove. She pulled a spoon from the drawer and tasted her handiwork, adding a dash of salt and pepper.

"Not bad, if I do say so myself."

"You've never hesitated to say so yourself, have you, Judy?"

"If I don't, who will? Besides, it really is good. You can judge for yourself."

"Did I tell you who I ran into the other night?"

Judy chuckled. "You didn't, but your daughter did."

"Oh, Patricia called you, huh? I guess I should have anticipated that. She prefers talking to you."

"That's because I'm a lot nicer to her than you are, Lynn."

"Gee, thanks. So glad I have a sister to boost my ego for me."

"Well, am I lying? You are not known for being particularly easy on your daughter."

"I'm just not afraid to tell her what's on my mind, that's all."

"Yes, but the problem is what's on your mind is rarely complimentary toward her. So does it surprise you she doesn't choose to confide in you? Look what happened when she told you about her girlfriend. That was a huge deal for her, and you were, quite frankly, pretty awful to her."

"She didn't think I was going to approve, did she? That's absurd."

"Did you even listen to what she had to say? She told me you just left."

"No, I didn't want to hear it." Marilyn finished off her wine as she spoke.

"I'm amazed at you, Lynn." Judy grabbed the wine bottle and refilled her sister's glass. "Especially since being gay is not new to this family. As much as you hate to admit it, you *did* love our mother, and she *was* gay. You must have accepted it, at least on some level, before she died. She was a good mother to us. You can't deny that fact. And she loved Dad, maybe not the same way she loved Mary, but she did love him, and they did their best for us. Are you still holding this against her after all these decades?"

"I don't think I accepted it so much as I tolerated it. I was never comfortable with it the way you were."

"Well, that was obvious, but I can't understand how you can still be so narrow-minded about this subject. This is your daughter! She's happy. How can you be opposed to her having love in her life? At what point does her happiness finally become your primary concern? When you are on your deathbed?"

"It's not that I don't want her to have love in her life. Of course, I do."

"There's absolutely no evidence to support that claim," Judy said emphatically.

"Let me finish. Of course, I do. But why can't she find that same love with a man?"

"Maybe this is just who she is. Maybe something in her DNA makes her more comfortable with a woman. Maybe she *tried* living that life you wanted her to live for all those years, and she just can't anymore. It's exhausting to spend that much energy faking it for you and everyone else who tells her it's wrong. Only she knows what feels right in her bones. Having known your daughter for every minute of her fifty-odd years, I can tell you I have never seen her as at ease and content and genuinely happy as she is right now. The only thing wrong in her life at the moment is you."

Marilyn lowered her eyes. "Ouch. That hurts. Is that why you invited me over here tonight? To scold me about this?"

"I'm sorry, but it's true. Maybe it's about time someone told you that you are just plain wrong about this."

"It's my opinion. Opinions aren't wrong. They are what they are, and I'm entitled to them."

"Okay, Lynn. Let's go with that line of thinking. What exactly *is* your opinion about gays and lesbians? Take Trish out of the equation. Just tell me what you think of gay people."

Marilyn stood up from the table and walked over to the window, carrying her glass of wine. She sighed and stared out into the backyard. Judy went back to stirring the chili, giving Marilyn time to answer.

"Before we learned about Mom and Mary, I had naively never even given it a moment's consideration. Of course, we all knew people like that existed, but back then, they were deviants and freaks, and nobody even knew a gay person. But I remember that first night—the night of your wedding—when we saw them kissing. At that moment, I was horrified. Truly. I could barely breathe."

"I remember. I was the one who made you breathe." Judy turned the burner on the stove down to a simmer and sat down.

"I know you did, but afterward, I remember trying to sleep that night, and all I could think about was what Mom looked like while kissing Mary. She looked...entranced. Mesmerized. I've seen her kiss Dad a thousand times but never once did it look like that. I think it terrified me a bit. Maybe not so much that it was a woman kissing another woman, but that a woman could react *that* way to kissing another woman. We could have smashed a window in that room right next to them, and I don't think they would have known we were there. Do you remember that?"

"I do. I talked to Mom about it many times. I wish you had too."

Marilyn sat back down and continued. "I always wondered what it could be that made her so different that she could respond that way to a woman. Was something wrong, you know, like...biologically? Was she some kind of a pervert? And now, today, does that make my daughter a pervert as well?"

Judy reached across the table and took Marilyn's hand. "If you had asked Mom, she would have told you. Have you ever considered the possibility that some people are indeed just born that way? Marilyn, this is your daughter we are talking about. She's kind. She's smart. She teaches little kids how to grow up to be good people. She's always been so good to you, and you've been incredibly hard on her for so long. So why does what she does in the privacy of her bedroom make her any less of a person than what you know her to be in your heart?"

"Tell me what Mom would have said if I had asked her."

"Okay, what question do you want to ask?" Judy replied.

"What was it about Mary that made her so spellbound she didn't even care that she was kissing another woman at a wedding full of people? What was she feeling? How was what she felt for Mary different than what she felt for Dad?"

"She'd say she was truly and deeply in love with Mary. That they had spent years either denying or hiding what they felt. It was a life lived in secret. Sometimes, the overwhelming desire to be together spilled out into their day-to-day lives like a volcano, to the point where they couldn't control the eruption. That's what happened at the wedding. I know she loved Daddy, but in a very different way. She loved him as the father of her children, as the man who was strong and steady and took care of us, but she didn't have that passion for him as she did for Mary."

Judy gave Marilyn a minute to digest all that information. Then she continued. "Lastly, you asked how her feelings for Mary differed from what she felt for Dad. She told me Mary made her feel whole. She said maybe she could have ignored it or kept away from Mary if not for the way she felt about herself when she was with Mary. She liked herself better after she fell in love with Mary. Maybe because she was true to her heart, I don't know. Or maybe having that kind of love gave her confidence that she never had before. Whatever it was, you could see it in her eyes when she talked about it. She would smile in a way that we never saw with Daddy. I know it sounds *so* cliché, but it was almost a glow. I wish you had found the courage to talk to her after the wedding. That wasn't the first time Dad caught them, you know," Judy confessed.

"Really? I knew he knew about it before that night, but I didn't know he caught them."

"Yes. There had been several other times over the years. Eventually, he just accepted it because, well...because he was a good man, and he knew Mary made her happy. Mary calmed her and kept her steady. In the long run, he just wanted what made Mom happy, even if it meant he was missing out on that same sort of passion."

"What about Mary's husband? Did he know?"

"Yes, he knew. He didn't take it quite as well as Daddy, and they eventually divorced."

"Wow. I didn't know that."

"That's because you pretended it didn't exist, but you held it against her all those years. Do you want to do the same with Trish? It's such a waste of time and energy. Please, Lynn. I'm begging you. Make it right with her. She wants you to meet Josie. For what it's worth, I think she is someone worth meeting. She's good for Trish."

"I have met Josie. At the restaurant."

"That hardly counts. You were rude as hell to both of them."

"Rude is a bit of an exaggeration, I think. Is that what Patricia said? I didn't say anything bad to them."

Judy got up and stirred the food again, but spun back around quickly and said, "No, but you didn't say anything good, either. And when Trish asked you to set up a time to talk, you put her off."

"Have you met her and spent time with them?"

"Yes, I have. I've enjoyed watching their interactions. It's adorable. They dote on each other. Trish does not strike me as the doting type. She is *your* daughter, after all."

"Ouch again, Judy. You are killing my ego tonight. Have I done anything right where my daughter is concerned?"

"Go and have dinner with them. You will see first-hand all that you've done right with her, which is a *lot*. But *don't* go unless you plan to open your mind to accept her and allow her to be happy. Otherwise, it will just be another disaster."

# Chapter Twenty-Seven

## TRISH 1999

TRISH MOVED ABOUT HER living room and dining room, pushing the vacuum cleaner from corner to corner. As she did so, she remembered the last time her mother visited and the mess that ensued—literal and figurative. The stain on the carpet was covered with a planter now, and she moved it to clean underneath as she reflected upon that evening. When the phone rang a week ago, and her mother said she wanted to come over to 'properly' meet Josie, Trish nearly fainted. When she told Josie about it, Josie had almost the same reaction. The thought of sitting at the table *as a couple*, with her mother staring them down, was at best daunting. At worst, it was a train wreck waiting to happen.

Trish thought back to the night before when she lay in the crook of Josie's arm in bed. Trish was fidgeting like a fish who had just jumped out of the water and onto land. Josie rubbed her hand on Trish's arm, trying, but failing, to get her to lie still.

Josie finally spoke when she realized sleep was not coming any time soon for either of them.

"Babe, are you going to be like this all through dinner tomorrow? If so, we might have to give you a couple of doses of valium beforehand. This is not going to go well if you can't relax."

Trish got up and sat cross-legged, facing Josie. "Relax! Relax? How am I going to do that? Why is she suddenly eager to come over and have dinner with us? What kind of a scene is she planning? What is her motive? It makes no sense. Why?"

"Well, when she called, what exactly did she say?"

"She said she thought it was time you two met properly and could she come over for dinner one night. I was too flabbergasted to ask questions. I think I barely even answered with a yes, but I guess I must have because it's happening whether I like it or not."

"Don't forget this is what you wanted, after all. When we saw her in the restaurant, you said you wanted to get together with her. Do you think she's had some sort of an epiphany about it? Or maybe it's just guilt. Or just imagine this! What if she *genuinely* wants to see you and get to know me? I know it's a novel concept, but hey—you never know."

"My mother does not do guilt. Of course, she dishes plenty of it out, but I don't think she ever feels it."

"You make her sound much worse than she is, I think. I'll bet you five dollars I can win her over. Parents love me. On the other hand, their daughters tend to tire of me easily, but the parents are a piece of cake."

"For the record, this daughter doesn't think she will tire of you, but if you insist on punishing yourself, I will take that bet, and you'd better make sure you can pay up. You have no idea what you are in for." They shook hands to seal the wager.

"We shall see, but maybe now you can calm down about it a little if you know I will make every effort to win that five from you. I will charm her ass off. I promise."

"I can't wait to witness this. It will be entertaining if nothing else."

Trish curled back into the crook of Josie's arm. Josie contemplated her plans for the following evening, brainstorming ideas to make the night a success. She was about to share her ideas with Trish when she heard her breathing change and realized she had already fallen asleep. She pulled her in closer, kissed her forehead, and whispered goodnight.

# Chapter Twenty-Eight

## JOSIE AND TRISH 1999

JOSIE STOOD IN HER closet, trying to choose just the right outfit that wasn't too 'gay.' She usually didn't change her wardrobe for anyone, her feet planted firmly in the 'I am what I am' camp, but this was an exception. A semi-feminine outfit could only help the situation, so she decided to break her own rule. She chose a pair of flared blue slacks, a colorful belt, and a three-quarter sleeve blouse with a print that matched the pants perfectly. She even put on a bit of make-up, just for good measure.

When she arrived at Trish's house, she found her in her closet, with clothes scattered everywhere, and Trish standing in her robe, clearly distraught.

Josie looked around and gave her a smile with a hint of a smirk. "Um...babe? Are you having a bit of a meltdown here?"

"Yes, smart ass. Clearly, I am."

"Okay, I can see my sarcasm is not appreciated at this time, so I'll refrain from further commentary. Is there anything I can help you with? Do you want my opinion, or would you rather I just leave you alone?"

"Well, I'm not making any progress on my own, so your opinion might prove valuable. By the way, you look hot."

"Why, thank you. I think I'm going to blush. Although 'hot' is not exactly what I was going for. It was more of a 'don't look too gay' ensemble. Did I succeed?" She twirled a little and pretended to model her outfit.

"Oh yes. You are the epitome of the lipstick lesbian."

"I can't tell if you are messing with me or not."

Trish moved in closer, put her arms around Josie's neck, and whispered in her ear. "I'm not messing with you. Well...maybe the lipstick part, but honestly, you look wonderful. Thank you for making the extra effort for my mother's sake."

"I told you. Parents love me. I know how to push all the right buttons."

"Marilyn McCann is a hell of a button pusher in her own right. This should be fun, but before we get that far, I need to find something to wear. Being naked isn't going to cut it tonight."

"Too bad. I would have enjoyed that." Josie leaned in for a kiss.

* * * *

Marilyn arrived early, per usual. She was nothing if not predictable. When Trish answered the door, Marilyn greeted her with a kiss on the cheek and told her how nice she looked. Trish smiled and returned the kiss but felt confident this must be a trap of some sort. Trish moved aside to reintroduce Josie, but Marilyn stepped forward before the words even came out, and she held out her hand for Josie.

"Josie, it's so nice to meet you again. Please let me apologize for my rude behavior when we first met at the restaurant. I would say I was caught off guard, but that would sound like I was making an excuse. So let me just say I'm sorry, and I hope you will forgive me."

"Oh, Mrs. McCann. Please, think nothing of it. It's forgotten. I'm delighted to be here with you tonight. I was so pleased when Trish told me you were coming, and I'm honored that you invited me to join you both."

Trish looked at her mother, then back at Josie with a 'what on earth is happening' look on her face. Who was this imposter, and what had she done with her mother?

"Mom, can I get you a glass of wine? Dinner will be ready in about forty-five minutes, if that's okay. I hope you're hungry. I've made a lot."

"Wine would be wonderful. Can I help with dinner?"

"No, no. I've got it under control. Maybe you and Josie would like to sit in the living room and get to know each other better?"

Trish poured the wine and handed the glass to her mother as they sat on the sofa.

"So, Josie. Trish tells me you two met while speaking at a career day event at her school. What is it that you do?" Marilyn leaned in, seeming to be genuinely interested in the answer.

"I work in Information technology, and I got a chance to talk to the kids about what the future holds in that area. It was a lot of fun, and her kids were so well behaved. They got very interested when I gave them some hints about what they would do with computers in just a few short years. I really enjoyed it. Trish and I talked afterward, and we went out for a quick bite. The rest, as they say, is history, but I don't want to bore you with my work stuff. So please, tell me something about you."

Josie sat back and listened intently while congratulating herself for crossing off rule number one on the 'How to Make Your Girlfriend's

Mother Like You' list. Divert attention away from yourself and over to her. Then show interest and ask questions. Check!

Marilyn and Josie chatted easily while Trish listened from the kitchen in disbelief. Josie had her talking about the family, and she seemed to delight in doing so. Trish was almost afraid to call them over to the table for fear of interrupting.

As the food came out of the oven, Josie jumped up to help get it into the dining room. Rule number two—be helpful. Make sure she knows you pull your fair share of the weight in the relationship. Check! They all sat down, with Marilyn choosing the seat across from Josie and Trish. *Perfect,* Josie thought to herself. Eye contact. Rule number three would be a snap. Trish lifted the bottle to refill the wine glasses, but Josie put a hand over hers. "I'm good with just the one glass tonight, thanks." She winked at Trish when Marilyn wasn't looking to let her know turning down the second glass of wine was all part of her master plan. Rule number four – don't drink too much. Stay in control and do not, by all means, do *not* get drunk!

Marilyn talked effortlessly throughout the meal, and Josie looked her in the eyes and remained engrossed in the conversation. Trish and her mother volleyed back and forth with their conversation, much like they used to do when Trish was younger. Marilyn told Josie some of Trish's more embarrassing moments growing up, instigating significant discomfiture and blushing from Trish.

"When Patricia was about ten, we took her to Yosemite National Park. We were on a nice, leisurely family hike when Patricia decided she had to pee and could not possibly wait even a moment longer. So her father and I turned our backs as she ran into the brush. About two minutes later, we heard a blood-curdling scream, followed by the vision of Patricia attempting to run with her pants around her ankles. She claimed a snake was underneath her rear end while peeing and was concerned she had been bitten and needed anti-venom *immediately*. Her father returned to the incident scene, only to find an anthill looking curiously moistened. Apparently, she had chosen a very poor location to urinate, and there were several tiny, rather angry ants crawling on her behind. Not to mention the thousands of ants who suddenly found their home flooded."

Josie had to stop herself from spitting the water she was drinking all over the table. Once she regained her swallowing ability, she looked over at Trish, who seemed rather unamused, and laughed hysterically. Marilyn was equally tickled.

"I'm glad I could be a source of entertainment for the two of you." She feigned irritation, although it was evident the humor in the story was getting the better of her as she tried to hide her smile.

"Josie, haven't you done something embarrassing that you'd like to share with us?" Trish asked.

"Who, me? I'll never tell. I'm trying to impress your mom here, Trish. No way I'm wading into those waters. You are on your own here, my friend!"

They all laughed. "Gee, thank you so much for your support, traitor!" She continued to laugh while she started to clear the table of the dishes. "Mom, will you have some coffee with dessert? I made an apple pie. I know it's your favorite."

"Sure. I'd love some. But come sit down while it's brewing. If it's okay with you, I'd like to turn to a slightly more serious subject."

"Uh-oh," Trish murmured from the kitchen.

"No reason for an uh-oh. I promise."

Trish set the coffeepot and cleared the rest of the dishes. She sat down somewhat nervously, not knowing what to expect. "Okay, Mom. What's up?"

"I want to talk about the two of you. About your relationship."

"You do? Really?" Trish answered, her voice cracking in the process.

"Yes. Well, to be clear, not just about you, but sort of. Your Aunt Judy tells me she has explained the situation with my mother to you. Is it safe to assume you've shared this information with Josie?"

"Yes, I did. I hope that doesn't upset you."

"No, it doesn't. You are in a relationship. I would expect that. So, the thing is, I had dinner at Judy's a week or so ago. She told me a lot about my mother and her relationship that I never knew. If I'm honest, and I'm sure this won't surprise you, I didn't handle my mother's 'situation' very well." She made sure to emphasize the air quotes on situation. "And before you make any comments about how obvious that statement may be, let me try to explain."

Marilyn stood up from the table and took a deep breath, making Trish somewhat nervous. Josie took her hand and reached over to Trish's lap. She put her hand on her knee with a comforting touch, letting her know that wherever this conversation went, they would be okay.

Marilyn moved slowly about the room as she prepared her thoughts. "Let me preface all this by saying that when I found out about my mother, it was nineteen thirty-nine. The subject of, well...um, homosexuality was *never* discussed by anyone. It was nothing like it is today. I was naïve and judgmental. And, of course, I was scared that my parents were going to get a divorce. I was also scared that people would find out and she would be humiliated. Well, if I'm honest, I was scared that we would be humiliated—all of us. Me. So I pretended it didn't happen and never spoke of it again. Not to my father, and certainly not to my mother, but just because I never spoke of it doesn't mean I never thought about it."

"What do you mean 'thought about it'?" Trish made an air quotes gesture.

"No, it's not what you are thinking. I don't mean that I thought about it for myself. I just mean I thought about how she was with Mary, her...um, her girlfriend."

"What do you mean, Mom?"

She continued to pace slowly around the room, wine glass in hand. "I saw something in her with Mary that I never saw with my dad. It was a personality shift in her presence. She was always rather meek and soft-spoken when I was young, but once Mary came into the picture, she was suddenly just...more *alive* is the best way to describe it, I guess. It never registered until I saw them kissing at the wedding...you know about that whole story, right?"

"Yes. Aunt Judy told me."

"Right. So, after I saw them at the wedding and I knew what was happening with them, it suddenly dawned on me that Mary brought out something in my mother that no one else seemed able to do. Not us, and not my dad. Judy also told me the wedding wasn't the first time my dad had found them. They had been seeing each other for years before that, and he knew. The more I thought about it, the more I realized their marriage had taken a turn somewhere along the way. They were a seemingly happy couple until I was in my teens. And then something changed. It had to have been when he found out. How and why he stayed with her after that is a bit of a mystery to me, but there was a definite shift—happy marriage to unhappy marriage and then a permanent separation. From that point forward, the only time I saw my mom happy was with Mary. I didn't understand it and never asked any questions because it was too uncomfortable for me. Judy said that if I had just asked my mom about it, she would have gladly explained her feelings, which might have helped me understand. So, I asked Judy to tell me what Mom would have said if I had asked her those questions."

"What questions, Mom?"

"If I'd asked what it was about Mary that was different than what she felt for my dad. What made her so mesmerized by her? Because believe me, if you had seen that kiss, you'd have seen mesmerized right in front of your eyes."

"Did Aunt Judy know the answer?"

"Yes, she did. She told me my mom was just hopelessly in love with her. That she felt better about herself whenever she was with her. She thought she was a better person when Mary was around. And you know what? I think she was. It's like I said, she was more alive, more excited, more loving.

"So, after my conversation with Judy, I did quite a bit of soul searching. I had directly associated the collapse of my parent's happy marriage with my mother's relationship with a woman. When you told me about you, it all came flooding back to me."

She sat back in her chair facing Trish. "But I started wondering if that's how you feel too. Do you think you are a different and better person now? Do you feel more complete, to use a phrase that Judy said about your grandmother?"

"Mrs. McCann, do you mind if I interrupt for a moment?" Josie said tentatively.

"Sure, go ahead."

"I want to say two things here, if that's okay. First, I want you to ask Trish that same question without me in the room because I want you to feel comfortable that she's not just giving you an answer that she thinks I want to hear."

Patricia tried to interrupt. "Hang on, Trish. Just let me finish. I think it's important for your mom to get your unfiltered responses to her questions. But secondly, I wanted to say, Mrs. McCann, that I know exactly what your sister meant when she told you how your mom would have answered, because that is exactly how I feel. I had several straight relationships when I was much younger, and I always knew something was missing. Like, is this it? There's gotta be more to this life than just going through the motions. Something just didn't fit right. And for me, I think I have even a little more perspective to add because I've also been in several long-term relationships with other women. While I didn't necessarily get the 'is this it?' feeling with them, I didn't realize how much I was settling in my relationships with those women until I met your daughter. So, it's almost like it's a two-part equation. First, I had to be with the right gender, and then, I had to be with the right person.

Any other combination just wasn't going to work, evidenced by the fact that I was still single at fifty-five when I met Trish. Does that make any sense?"

Marilyn looked over at Josie and then again at Trish and nodded. "Yes, it makes perfect sense."

Josie continued. "And it sounds like your mother may have found both in her relationship with Mary." Marilyn shook her head in agreement.

Trish chimed in. "Um, excuse me. Does anyone want to know what *I* think?"

"Yes, of course we do, dear," Marilyn responded.

"I don't need to answer the question with Josie out of the room. The answer will be the same, and if you don't believe me, Mom, you can call me tomorrow and ask me again. My take on it is probably closer to my grandmother's experience since this is my first relationship with a woman. I want to explain how this whole thing came about. Not how we met because you already know that, but what happened *when* we met. When I walked into my principal's office to meet Josie that day, something physical happened to me. Don't worry, Mom. I have no intention of making you faint by talking about something sexual. That's not what I mean at all. It was a sensation that came over me, like a fog lifting. I didn't even know the fog was there. Something in my brain just clicked as if to say, 'Oh, *now* I get it.' Before Josie, the idea of soulmates always seemed like a Hallmark phrase that was about as real as a unicorn. I don't feel that way anymore. I honestly believe I am exactly where I am supposed to be right now with exactly the right person, the person that is my soulmate. And by the way, I was *so* sure of that when I met Josie that at the end of the day, I was the one who asked her out, not the other way around."

Trish took a breath and a swig of her water from the coffee table.

"Mom, does that answer your question?"

"It does. I'm sorry I reacted so poorly when you told me. It was fifty years of baggage that I was carrying around. It's time I let that go because I do want you to be happy." She reached across to grab Trish's hand again. Then she turned toward Josie.

"So, Josie, let me ask you. What's next for the two of you?"

"Mom, are you seriously asking Josie what her *intentions* are with her fifty-four-year-old girlfriend?"

"Yes. I am. We don't stop worrying about what's in store for our kids just because they grow up, Patricia."

Josie smiled at Trish and turned to Marilyn to answer. "It's okay, Trish. It's a fair question, and I'm happy to answer it. Trish and I have discussed the future, Mrs. McCann. It's early on—we know that—so we aren't making any rushed decisions. Obviously, we can't get married, at least not in the traditional sense, but we have said that if and when the time is right, we would like to commit to each other. Neither of us is selling our house and packing up the U-Haul. We're taking it a day at a time, giving each other room to breathe so we both are sure this is what we want."

Marilyn looked Josie in the eyes and smiled. "Trish, what happened to that cup of coffee you promised me?"

"Trying to get me out of the room, Mom?"

"Maybe." Marilyn winked at Josie.

Trish made a grunting sound and left to go into the kitchen.

"Josie, I want to thank you for being honest with me and for not holding my previous behavior against me. I spent the whole first part of this evening watching my daughter, looking for clues. Judy told me that you were good for Patricia, and to be honest, I think she may have even undersold it. She has a light in her eyes that I'm not sure I've ever seen. Patricia is a lot like me in some ways, which is not always good. You see, I'm well aware of my faults. Hers are similar. We're not always easy to get through to. It took my sister Judy a lot of effort to convince me that I've been unreasonable about this. Even when I knew she was right, I still stuck to my guns. But when she told me that you were, in her words, worth meeting, I finally gave in. My sister is much wiser and much less stubborn than I am. Watching Patricia tonight, I can see that she was right. Thank you for making her happy."

"Mrs. McCann, I..."

"Please. No more Mrs. McCann. It's Marilyn. Okay?"

"Oh...okay. Marilyn, your daughter is a gift I didn't expect to get at this point in my life. You don't have to thank me for loving her. That's the easy part. On the contrary, I would like to thank you for giving us a chance to have a relationship with you. Trish has been distraught these past few months. She's missed you."

"Can I come back into the room yet?" Trish yelled from the kitchen.

"Yes," Josie and Marilyn said in harmony.

* * * *

Later that night, as Trish came into the bedroom after brushing her teeth, she leaned over, kissed Josie, and handed her a five-dollar bill.

# Chapter Twenty-Nine

## PATRICK 1937

PATRICK STOOD AT THE loading dock in the warehouse, supervising the loading of a truck for local deliveries. It was loud on the dock, and the foreman had to call his name three times before he heard him say there was a phone call for him in the office. Patrick rushed to answer it, knowing no one ever interrupted him at work to give him good news.

"This is Patrick. Who's this?" he asked.

"Hi, Mr. O'Brien. This is Mrs. Gardner, the nurse at your daughter Lynn's school. I'm afraid she's not feeling very well, and I think she should go home. Are you able to come pick her up? She's running a fever, and I don't think it's wise for her to walk home by herself."

"Can you call my wife at our home, please? I'm working."

"I know, sir, and I'm terribly sorry, but we've tried your home a few times, and there is no answer."

Patrick sighed, realizing he didn't have much of a choice. Anna must be at the market or something. "All right, Mrs. Gardner. Just let me talk to my boss about getting off for a little while. I'll be there as soon as I can. Thank you."

"Thank you, Mr. O'Brien. See you soon."

Patrick hung up the phone and saw that his foreman was on the other side of the office, leaning against the wall with a cup of coffee in his hand. He nodded his head, signaling he had heard the conversation. "Go on, O'Brien. Just be back as soon as you can. Hope your kid feels better."

"Thanks, boss. Be back in a jiffy."

He decided to stop by the house first before heading to the school. It was on the way, and he hoped maybe Anna had since come home and she could pick up Lynn. He hurriedly opened the front door and called out Anna's name, hearing no response. Then, as he reached the back of the house in the hallway in front of the spare room, he saw them. The door was partially closed, and they hadn't heard him come in. He quietly stepped out of the doorway so they wouldn't see him if they looked up. As he peered around the door jam, he saw them lying next to each other on the bed, kissing. They were only partially dressed, their legs entwined in each other and the sheets. Their hair in complete disarray. They spoke softly as they kissed, whispering as lovers do in the aftermath. He averted his gaze and backed up against the wall, trying to find his breath. His legs felt weak beneath him, ready to give out. He was afraid they were going to see or hear him at any moment, and he was unprepared for that encounter. He just wanted to get out of the house as quickly as possible. Yet, as if drawn to the site of a tragic accident, he could not stop himself from watching them. His wife of seventeen years was lying in bed with a woman, speaking in a tone that she had rarely, if ever, used with him. He couldn't make out the words, specifically, but he could see their intent, hear their inflection.

A few interminable moments passed, and he quietly made his way down the hall and out of the house, doubling over at the waist with his hands on his knees, gasping for air out on his front stoop.

Patrick considered his options. Option one. If he went to school and brought Lynn home, Anna and Mary would likely still be there. That wouldn't work.

Option two. he could call the school and tell them he couldn't get away, and Lynn would have to stay there until her mother could come and get her, but that wasn't fair to Lynn. She wasn't the type of student to fake being sick, so she must have felt quite unwell to ask to go home. That didn't seem right.

Option three. He could go to a payphone and call the house. Maybe Anna would answer now, forcing them to end their mid-day tryst. If she didn't answer, he could keep calling so she would know it was urgent. Yes, that was the only feasible option.

He took his handkerchief out of his pocket, wiped the sweat off his brow, and took a deep breath. He calmly walked down the block to the payphone on the corner to call his house.

It rang almost ten times before Anna finally answered the phone, sounding winded.

"Anna? It's me. I've been trying to reach you."

"I'm sorry, dear. I was at the market and just ran to the phone when I came in. What's wrong?"

"Lynn is not feeling well. They asked me to pick her up since they couldn't reach you, but I can't get away."

"Lynn? What's wrong with her? Is she okay?"

"Yes, it's not bad. She has a fever, though, and is feeling rather poorly. Would you take care of it, please?"

"Of course. I'll just need a minute to uh...to get...to put away the groceries. I'll get there as soon as possible. I'm sorry they had to bother you, honey."

"Sure."

"Are you okay, Patrick? You sound upset."

"I'm fine. I'll see you later. Thanks." He hung up. He intended to head back to the warehouse, but instead wandered aimlessly, unable to focus on anything except the images playing in his head. Finally, he found himself in the park and sat on a bench under the trees. His breathing was still rapid, as though his lungs had simply deflated, and he could not inhale enough oxygen to refill them.

His wife was having an affair. And not just any affair—an affair with a *woman*. With her best friend. Did Johnny know? No, that wasn't possible. He wasn't the type of man to tolerate that if he knew. Did anyone else know? The girls? Mary's kids? The neighbors? No, the women in this neighborhood were far too nosey and gossipy. He would have known if anyone outside the house knew. How long had this been going on? Was this the first time? It didn't appear to be. They were certainly very comfortable with each other. Comfortable. That was an understatement, more like intimate. He kept picturing them facing one another, kissing and touching and whispering. They smiled as they spoke and touched each other's faces tenderly with love. This didn't seem like just a sexual rendezvous. There was more to it. Of this, he was certain. They've been best friends for the better part of a decade. Had this been happening all along? Should he confront her? He must, right? He couldn't just pretend it didn't happen. What would he say to her? 'Anna, I saw you having sex with Mary.' No, there was no way he would be able to get those words out. Besides, he didn't *technically* see them having sex, but he was pretty sure it had already happened when he arrived. 'Anna, are you having an affair with Mary?' That might work, but what if she denied it? He would still have to tell her what he saw. 'Anna, are you a lesbian?' Nope, those words weren't going to work either. 'Anna, do you want a divorce?' 'Anna, do you still love me?'

# Chapter Thirty

## PATRICK 1937

LYNN ATE THE SOUP Anna made for her and took her dose of aspirin. Her fever was down to just one hundred degrees, and she seemed to be feeling better.

"Get some rest, Lynn. You'll stay home from school again tomorrow. I hope your sister doesn't catch it from you. Judy, are you still feeling okay?"

"Yes, Mom. She's probably faking it anyway."

"You can't fake a fever, Judy. Now leave your sister alone. She needs her rest. Finish your homework then go to sleep, please. Good night, girls."

She closed their bedroom door and made her way out to the living room, where Patrick sat in front of the radio. It was on, but he didn't appear to be listening. Instead, he just stared off into space.

"Patrick, is everything okay? You are acting very strange tonight. I said I was sorry you got interrupted at work. Is that why you are upset?"

"Are the girls in their room with their door closed?"

"Yes. Why?"

"Good. I need to ask you something, and I'm not quite sure how to say it."

Anna tensed, afraid of what he might say. "What is it, dear? You can ask me anything, you know that." She steadied herself, trying to keep her voice light and calm.

"Are you...um. Did you and...uh..." He cleared his throat and took a sip of his beer. "This is so difficult. Are you having an affair with Mary?"

"Am I what? Patrick, what are you talking about?" she said, turning away from him, trying to hide her deceit. She was overcome with an acute sense of panic.

"Please *think* about it before you lie to me," he said emphatically. "Are you having an affair with Mary?"

Anna broke out in a sweat, and her hands began to tremble. Her heart pounded rapidly in her chest. The moment had finally come. Realistically, she must have known it was only a matter of time. The only thought that came to mind was...*Now what? Do I keep lying, or come clean?* Her breathing became erratic, and she struggled to speak.

"Patrick, I..."

"Anna! Just tell me the truth," he said with anger in his tone.

Anna stood up and turned away from him, toward the window. She folded her arms around herself as if a chill had suddenly filled the air. "How did you find out?"

"I saw you today. I came home after the school called. I thought maybe you had just gone to the market, and if you had returned, you would be able to go get Lynn, and I could go back to work."

Anna put her hand over her mouth and gasped. "Then I guess you already know the answer to the question, right?"

"I need to hear you say it. And I need you to explain it to me. I think I deserve at least that much, don't you?"

"Yes, you probably do." She went to the kitchen for a glass of water, her mouth suddenly dry. When she returned, he stood up, turned the radio off, and stared at the floor, waiting.

"Yes, it's true."

"My god, Anna! How could you do this to us?" He moved closer, angrily facing off with her.

"I know. I never meant to hurt you. I can't imagine what you must be thinking of me right now. I'm not sure if any explanation I give you will make it any better."

"Try me." He raised his voice again as he spoke.

"Okay." Her breathing was heavy and erratic. "What do you want to know?"

"I want you to tell me what the hell is going on, Anna. Are you...are...are you a lesbian?" His voice got louder with each word, and Anna gestured for him to quiet down. If the girls were to hear this conversation, it would be devastating for all of them.

She answered in more of a whimper than in a full voice. "Yes, I...I suppose I am. I can't explain it to you because I can't make sense of it myself, but yes, I guess I am."

"How long has this been going on?" he asked, almost afraid to hear the answer.

"A long time, I'm afraid."

"How long?"

"About eight years."

"What?" He raised his arms in the air in exasperation, as if not knowing what else to do with them. "Eight years! You've been having an affair with *a woman* for eight fucking years?" He had lost his ability to keep his voice down. Anna could see his face and neck getting redder, the veins popping out in fury.

"Patrick, please! I'm begging you to lower your voice. The girls will hear you." Anna sobbed through each word.

He approached her and got right in her face, pointing to her as he angrily spoke. "Don't 'Patrick, please' me. Do they know about this? Does anyone else know about this?"

"No, no. No one knows. We've been very discreet." Anna reached for his hands, but he pulled them away. She could tell by his gestures that he really wanted to smack her hands away, but he was too much of a gentleman to allow himself to hit his wife, even under these circumstances.

"If that were true, we wouldn't be having this conversation. Are you...do you, um...are you in love with her?" he asked incredulously.

Anna lowered her eyes, unable to look at him. He took a deep breath, waiting for the answer he desperately didn't want to hear. "Please, Anna. Just answer the question."

"Yes. I am. I'm sorry, Patrick. You have no idea how sorry I am," she said through her sobs.

He sat back down in his chair with his head in his hands. She walked to him and knelt before him, putting her hands on his knees. He pulled away from her.

"Please. Please try to understand," she pleaded.

"How can I understand? You haven't told me why yet. Or how? Or when? So far, the only thing to understand is that you've thrown our marriage away. Seventeen years down the drain, just like that."

"No, Patrick. No, please. Listen. I will try, okay? Just give me a chance to find the right words."

She got up off her knees and sat back down on the couch, attempting to compose herself. Her hands moved back and forth between her face and onto her lap, searching for words. She sobbed for a few moments, then wiped her eyes.

She steadied her breathing and spoke. "I don't know if I will be able to make you understand this, but I'm going to try. The only way I can do that is with complete honesty, even if what I say might be hurtful. Do you want me to do that?"

"Yes. I need to know."

"Okay. It started a few months after Mary moved in. We realized, each in our own way, that we were feeling something for each other that was, well...different—more than just a friendship. We tried; I promise you that we tried *so hard* to fight it. Neither one of us wanted to betray our husbands, but what we felt for each other was just too strong to ignore. It was like a tornado that just swept us both up. Nothing we could have grabbed onto would have kept that tornado from lifting us off the ground. Not you. Not the kids. Not the shame or the guilt we both felt. Nothing. It was an affair of the heart even more than a physical affair."

"But you *have* had a physical relationship, right?"

She paused, knowing that telling him the truth would gut him. "Yes, we have. I've lain awake nights wondering what is wrong with me to make me feel this way for her. There must be something wrong with me."

"What way?"

"I don't understand what you mean."

"You said you wonder what is wrong with you to make you feel this way for her. What way?"

"Satisfied. I don't use that word in a sexual context. Complete. It's all-encompassing. Just...where I'm supposed to be."

"Oh my god, Anna. I don't even know what to say. Where do I fit into all of those feelings?"

"I know you aren't going to believe me, but none of this means that I don't love you. I do. I truly do. This is just me being...I don't know...born with something wrong with me, biologically, I guess. I don't know why I feel this way, and I didn't *want* to feel this way for so long because I knew the damage I would be doing to you."

"How does Mary feel about all of this?"

"The same. We are two broken pieces of machinery who somehow managed to find each other. Equal partners in a mystery we will never understand."

"Does Johnny know?"

"No, definitely not. Are you going to tell him?"

"I don't know what I'm going to do, to be honest. Do you want to divorce me?" The agony in his voice was heartbreaking.

"No!"

"But I assume you don't want to stop seeing her."

"I'm not sure I can, but I expect that it's something you will probably ask of me. If I was in your shoes, I'm sure that's what I would want. Or maybe you just want me to get the hell out of here and leave you alone. Is it?"

"Where would you go? And what would we tell the girls?"

"I don't know, but I'll do just about anything right now if it will ease the pain I've caused you."

He pointed down the hallway. "Our spare room...that's where you, um...were together, right?"

"Yes."

"When I saw you today...I couldn't hear what you were saying, but I could tell just from the tone of the whisper that I didn't stand a chance. I could see that you were in love with her. It was so...just, um...*intimate*. Obvious. Like it was written all over your faces. How could I have missed it for so long?"

"I'm so sorry, Patrick." She sobbed as she spoke.

"I just can't even believe this is happening, Anna. I'm just...at a complete loss. I thought we were happy. It's like our whole marriage is a lie."

"No, it's not. I swear."

He put his head in his hands and rubbed his palms into his tear filled eyes. He paused for a long time as if waiting for an answer to come to him while simultaneously knowing it wouldn't.

After several minutes, he looked up and said, "If you think you are attracted to women—and I guess we've already established that you are—then nothing I can say or do is going to change that. Am I right?"

"Yes, you're right."

"I can't believe I'm about to say this, but...I think it's not the same as you cheating on me with another guy, right? Maybe it should be, but it isn't. Don't get me wrong, you *did* cheat on me, and this is one helluva betrayal, no matter how you look at it, but...I can't compete with Mary. It's apples and oranges, isn't it?"

"In a way, yes. It is."

"If it's a guy you're fooling around with, at least I could fight for you. I could show you that I'm the better man. I could find him and sock him in the face for messing with another man's wife, but this...what can I do? I've got two choices—stay or go. That's it."

"What do you want me to do? Do you want me to sleep on the couch tonight while you figure it out?"

"No. I don't want to make the girls suspicious. Just go to bed, Anna. I'll come in after you've fallen asleep. I need a good stiff drink, and I need to be alone for a while."

Anna retreated to their bedroom and readied herself for bed. She lay there crying for at least an hour, maybe more. She was still awake when he finally came in, but pretended not to be. He sat on his side of the bed, facing away from her, and whispered, "Are you awake?"

Anna hesitated but answered. "Yes."

He took off his shirt and pants, crawled in bed beside her in his boxers and undershirt, and lay down facing her, but he did not touch her. "Can I ask you something? And will you promise to answer me honestly?"

"Yes."

"Were you unsatisfied with me all these years?"

"No...no...not at all." The light from the three-quarter moon beamed through the window and onto his face. She reached over and put her hand on his cheek. He flinched away at first, but then let her caress him. The familiar stubble on his face calmed her.

"Did you hate being with me, you know...here, in bed?"

"No, honey. I didn't. I swear."

"Because I never forced you, right? I mean, I don't think I ever got the impression you didn't want to. Maybe I thought you were tired sometimes, but I figured that was because we had young kids running around."

"You never forced me. I did it because I wanted to be with you. I liked it. I promise you."

"But it's different with her, right?"

She stared into his eyes, afraid to answer and inflict more pain.

"You can say it. I already know." He put his hand over hers on his face.

"Yes, it's different."

"Are you able to tell me how? Without being too graphic, please. I don't think I can handle that."

"It's a deeper connection with her, mentally, emotionally. Like she knows me better than I know myself."

"Physically, too?" he asked tentatively. She nodded yes, and he rolled over onto his back with his hands on his chest.

"Will you see her tomorrow and tell her I know?"

"Lynn will be home sick tomorrow, so I can't. I won't discuss it while Lynn is here, even if Mary does stop by. So it will keep for another day." She paused, hesitated, then whispered, "Please don't hate me, Patrick."

"Good night, Anna." He rolled away from her.

# Chapter Thirty-One

## ANNA 1937

PATRICK WAS ALREADY UP and out of bed when Anna woke the following day. She rolled over to find a note on his pillow that said,

*Needed to get out early.*

*I'll be home late tonight.*

*Tell Lynn I hope she is feeling better.*

She sighed and laid back down. The day was starting the same way the previous one had ended—in tears. The girls would be up soon, and she knew she had to go out into the kitchen, but the thought of facing them filled her with dread. She heard rain on the roof, adding insult to injury for her troubled mind. Her head was pounding, so she went to the bathroom medicine cabinet for some aspirin.

The coffee was brewing when Judy came out of her bedroom. Anna had checked on Lynn earlier and found her fever was down, but she still wasn't back to normal. Lynn would stay in bed all day, so Anna would not be leaving the house. Mary would surely call later, and Anna would have to pretend everything was normal. They sat at the table on so many occasions and discussed this day's inevitable arrival, knowing they couldn't keep this secret forever. Mary said she wanted to leave her husband, but Anna talked her out of it. Where would she go? No job, no money. Sure, her boys were fifteen now and would soon be out of the house, but Linda was only ten, and Mary still needed to stay home for her sake. No. Leaving Johnny was not a realistic plan. Anna wasn't lying when she told Patrick she loved him. It was true. She didn't want to leave him, but having it both ways seemed unrealistic. It was a mess of their own making, with no reasonable solutions, except ending it with Mary. That was something she simply could not do. If forced to choose, she would have to choose Mary.

She jumped when the phone rang an hour later. Mary's voice, blissfully unaware of the impending storm, was a welcome sound to calm the voices in Anna's head.

"Good morning! How are you today?" Mary said, clearly in a good mood.

"Good morning. I'm okay. How are you?"

"I'm fine, but you don't sound good. What's wrong?"

Anna wasn't successfully hiding anything in her voice. "Nothing. Lynn is home sick from school today, and I guess I'm just tired. That's all."

"Do you want me to stop by?" Mary barely finished the sentence before Anna said, "No!" A bit too emphatically.

"Okay, okay. Seriously, what's wrong? Does she have some contagious disease or something?"

"No, no. That's not it. I just have a lot to do around here. Sorry. I didn't mean to jump down your throat."

"I'm not sure I believe you. It feels like something is very wrong. I know you too well."

"You're going to have to trust me," Anna said unconvincingly.

Ten minutes later came the knock on the door that Anna was expecting. She sighed, put down her coffee, and went to the door.

"I told you not to come over." She opened the door part way and stood in the space, preventing Mary from her usual abrupt and ebullient entrance into the foyer.

"Well, hello to you, too. Yes, I know you told me, but you also told me nothing is wrong, and I can see that's not true, so I decided to find out for myself. And obviously, I was right because you aren't even letting me in."

Anna reluctantly opened the door the remainder of the way, and Mary made her way to the kitchen for a cup of coffee, just as she did every other day. Mary moved about Anna's house as if it was her own. She filled her cup, grabbed a bit of the pastry on the counter, and sat down at the table. "Would you like to tell me what's happening here, Anna?"

Anna looked down the hallway to Lynn's bedroom, ensuring the door was fully closed. Then she sat down opposite Mary.

"We have to talk, but it can't be today while Lynn is here. Or while anyone is here. We need to be alone."

"You're scaring me, Anna. Please, tell me what the hell is happening, for Christ's sake!" Her voice started to get elevated, and Anna put her index finger to her lips and made a shushing motion to her.

Anna stood up and went down the hallway to Lynn's room. She quietly opened the door and found her sleeping soundly, her textbook still open in front of her and her reading glasses on her head. Anna turned and closed the door, confident she was asleep.

"Okay. I will tell you, but you mustn't raise your voice. We cannot allow Lynn to hear us, do you understand?" Mary nodded in agreement.

Anna took a deep breath and put her visibly shaking hands on the table. "He knows," she whispered.

Mary's face went white with a look of pure panic. She tried to speak but could only whisper, "What?"

"Yes. You heard me correctly. He knows. He saw us yesterday. He was here."

Mary's eyes widened. She stood and started to pace. She kicked off her shoes to muffle the sound of her footsteps. Her hand covered her mouth, still agape from the shock. Anna could see the sweat begin to form on her forehead. She motioned for Mary to come and sit back down.

"He saw us in bed? Oh my god, Anna! What did he say?" Mary asked.

"He asked me if we were having an affair and if I was in love with you. Of course, there's much more to it, but that's the bottom line."

"How did you answer him?"

"I answered honestly. Yes, and yes. He got angry, which I'm sure is no surprise, but the anger could have been much worse. But mostly, he's crushed. He says our whole marriage is a lie. I've broken his heart, Mary." She started to cry but held it back so as not to make any noise.

"What is he going to do? Do you think he'll tell Johnny?"

"I don't know. I don't think he even knows what he will do yet. He probably won't tell him right away. If I know Patrick, he will take his time to think about it before he reacts. He's pretty good about that. He's not impulsive, like me."

"What happened after you talked? Did you both sleep in the same bed last night?"

"Yes. He didn't want to make the girls suspicious, but he was out before I got up this morning, leaving a note to say he would be late tonight. I promised him I wouldn't talk to you about it while Lynn was home today. So that's why I didn't want you to come over. So now I feel like I've let him down again."

"I'm sorry, but I could hear it in your voice, and I had to know if you were okay. You're not, are you?"

"No, I'm not! But I have to pretend I am for the sake of my kids. We're experts at pretending, aren't we?"

Mary just nodded, the answer being obvious.

"Do you think he will ask you for a divorce?"

"I suppose it's possible, but he said the strangest thing that made me wonder. He said it wasn't like I cheated on him with a man. If it was another guy, he could fight for me, but he couldn't compete with you. He said, 'I've got two choices. Stay or go. That's it.' Don't you think that's an odd thing to say?"

"Honestly, I think it's the words of a pretty wise man. It's different, and he knows it. Not many men we know would recognize that. I know my Johnny wouldn't. He would either storm out or pack my things for me and kick me out."

"Well, wise or not, I'm still scared to death about what he is going to do." Anna stood and straightened her skirt. She took the coffee cups, put them in the sink, and said, "I'm sorry, Mary, but I need to ask you to leave. I've already gone against my word to him, and I don't want to make it worse if Lynn wakes up. We can talk more tomorrow when she goes back to school."

"Okay. I'll go. I don't know how I will hide this when I get home, though. I think there was a part of me that hoped we'd be able to keep this secret until the day we die. That was naïve, I guess." She walked to the doorway and Anna followed to walk her out. "Will you call me in the morning, please?"

"Yes, I will."

"I love you, Anna."

"I love you, too. Bye, Mary."

# Chapter Thirty-Two

## ANNA 1937

ANNA WAS STARING AT the pages of her book when Patrick came home after eleven p.m. that night. She was exhausted from crying most of the day, but she had to get a sense of what Patrick was thinking before she could sleep. He saw her as he was hanging his hat on the rack, and he gave her just a hint of a smile.

"Hi," she said.

"Hi."

"How are you? Can I get you something to eat or drink?"

"Maybe a beer would be nice if you wouldn't mind." Anna put the bookmark in the book and set it on the coffee table. She fetched the beer and handed it to him as he sat on the sofa. "Thanks." He hesitated. "I don't know what to say to you," he said awkwardly.

"I know. I don't, either, but I stayed up just in case you wanted to talk. I didn't know if you wanted me to sleep on the couch tonight."

"No, if anyone is going to sleep on the couch, it will be me. I won't have my wife doing that, no matter what our problems might be."

"You're a good husband, Patrick. I'm sorry I've been such a bad wife for you." She sat down in the chair next to the sofa.

"If you had asked me before yesterday, I would have said you've been a terrific wife, but clearly, our marriage is not what I thought it was. I just wish I knew what to do about it."

"What are the options in your mind?"

"One. We get a divorce, and I move out. Two. We get a divorce, and you move out." Anna made an audible gasp at that option. "Three. We stay together, and you promise to stop seeing her. Four. We stay together, and you don't stop seeing her. That's it. I think that covers all possible choices."

"None of them are good options, are they?"

"Depends on your perspective. You'd probably like option number four, but what about me? And I'd like option three, but then you will likely be unhappy, and we could end up divorced anyway. So where does that leave us?"

"I don't know, but I want to be honest and tell you that Mary did come over today because she didn't like how I sounded on the phone.

She was worried, but she only stayed for a few minutes, and I checked to make sure Lynn was asleep when we talked."

"Okay. Thank you for telling me. How did she take the news?"

"I think she's terrified you're going to tell Johnny."

"I'm not going to tell him. At least not now. I don't see what good can come of that. I'll tell you if I change my mind."

"Thank you, Patrick. Why are you being so nice to me about this? We both know I don't deserve it. I'm so ashamed of myself. I almost wish you would yell and scream because at least I would get what's coming to me." She broke down in tears again.

"I have a lot of things to think about, and getting angry isn't going to make that easier, but don't let my calmness fool you, Anna. You have broken my heart."

"I know, and I can't fix it, either. I can't help but think that I've ruined our lives." Her crying became more intense. Finally, he reached across and put his hand in her lap, palm side up, indicating he wanted her to take his hand. She did. He tugged at her arm to get her to leave the chair to sit next to him on the sofa. She did. He put his arm around her and her head on his shoulder as she cried. They sat there for a few minutes before either spoke.

"I think we should send the girls over to their friend's house this weekend so we can have some time alone to talk," he said.

"Okay." She wiped her eyes and nose with her tissue.

"As crazy as it sounds, I think I want to talk to Mary, too."

"You do?" Anna sounded shocked.

"Yes. I can't even explain why, but I feel like I need to."

"I'll tell her tomorrow. I'm sure she will come over again. You have my solemn word that nothing will happen with her until we figure this out. My word probably doesn't mean much right now, but it's all I've got."

* * * *

Patrick was gone again when Anna got up the following day. She got both girls off to school and impatiently waited for Mary to call. Instead, a knock at the door made Anna jump when she heard it. She answered it, pulled Mary into the house, and put her arms around her, weeping.

"Hey, hey...it's okay. Shhh. I'm here. It's okay. Shhh..." Mary held her and whispered into her ear.

"I'm so scared, Mary. I feel like everything is falling apart. What if he makes me stop seeing you? What if he says he will leave me if I don't? What if he takes the girls from me?"

"Shhh...one step at a time. He's not going to take the girls from you. He knows you're a good mother to them. He wouldn't do that."

"He said he wants to talk this weekend. He wants to talk to you, too!"

"Me? Why?"

"He said he feels like he has to. I don't know why."

"Wow. That's going to be one hell of a conversation. What am I going to say to him?"

"Be honest. That's what I've been doing these last two days."

"Okay. Let's back up a bit. You didn't give me any details yesterday. Tell me what he said to you when he told you he knew."

"The school called him at work to pick up Lynn because they couldn't reach me. Remember when the phone was ringing while we were making love?" Mary nodded. "I guess that was them. He figured I was just out at the market when they called, so maybe I would be home by the time he got here, and I could get her. So he came in and called my name, but I guess we were too involved. He saw us through the partially open door. It was, um...well, I guess it was afterward, and we were lying together kissing and whispering. He said he couldn't hear us, but could see what was between us and knew he didn't stand a chance. He knew we were in love, but he made me say it out loud anyway. He asked how long it had been going on, and I didn't lie. It made him very mad that I'd been deceiving him for so long.

"He told me to go to bed. He needed a drink and wanted to be alone. I was still awake when he came in because I had been crying. He just asked me whether I hated being with him...you know...in bed. I said no, which is true. I never *hated* it, but then he said he could tell it was different with you and wanted to know why."

"Was he angry when he was asking this?"

"No. He was very calm. We were just whispering."

"So, how did you answer that question?"

"I told him that it's a deeper connection with us. Emotionally. Physically. I'm sure that was like an arrow through his heart, but I couldn't lie to him anymore. I said, 'please don't hate me, Patrick,' but he didn't answer. He just rolled over and went to sleep.

"We talked again last night, and I asked if he would tell Johnny. He said no, not right now, but that could change. He said he would let me know if he planned to, so at least we will have some warning."

Mary let out an audible sigh of relief. "Oh, thank god. I've been petrified. I feared he had already done it because Johnny came home in a terrible mood yesterday."

"What are we going to do, Mary? I told him I expected him to ask me to stop seeing you, but I didn't think I could. I can't!"

"I can't imagine he's just going to be okay with us having an affair, do you?"

"No. That's what terrifies me. What will I do if he divorces me? Get a job? How could I take care of the girls and the house and still work enough to support us?"

"Well, he would have to pay alimony. He can't just walk away."

"What a mess I've made of our lives!" Anna turned away and sobbed.

"It's a mess *we've* made, and we did it because we love each other. Is that wrong?"

"It is when it hurts so many people."

# Chapter Thirty-Three

## PATRICK 1937

"GIRLS, DON'T FORGET YOUR toothbrushes. I don't want you to go a whole weekend without brushing," Anna said as she packed some snacks in a bag for them to take to their friend's house for the weekend.

"So, *why* exactly are you guys sending us away for the weekend?" Judy asked with typical teenage attitude.

"Because your dad and I want a weekend alone together. Is that too much to ask, Miss Nosy Body?"

"Hmph. It's sad when your parents kick you out for the weekend, isn't it, Lynn?" Judy smiled at her mother, letting her know she was not all that serious.

"I know. I feel so unwanted!" Lynn chimed in, also in a joking tone.

"Okay, smart alecks. Get a move on. I told Mrs. Harrington you would be there by ten. You're already running late."

"Bye, Dad," they both yelled down the hallway to Patrick, still shaving in the bathroom.

"Bye, girls! Have a great time!" he bellowed.

Patrick came out of the bedroom, wiping his face with a towel. He threw it in the laundry basket in the hallway and grabbed another cup of coffee from the pot. Anna was seated at the table, drinking hers and barely nibbling on a piece of toast.

"Well, here we are," she said nervously as she took a sip of her coffee. Finally, she put down her coffee cup and bit her lip.

"Yep. Here we are. Now what?"

"I didn't think I was in a position to decide the 'now what,'" she said, making air quotes with her fingers. "I'm not exactly in control of this situation."

"There are two people in this marriage, right?"

"That's true, but I'm not the injured party. I'm the one who committed the crime. So I don't think I have the right to decide what my sentence will be."

"Can you tell me how it all happened? I mean, how did you both come to realize you felt this way? How did you go from feeling something to doing something about it? And again, please, no graphics.

That's not what I want to hear. I just mean...how? What was I doing during this time? Being oblivious to you?"

"I think it started the very first day we met, to be honest. She told me how pretty my eyes were when we literally bumped into each other at the market."

"So, she flirted with you? The very first time?"

"No, no. She wasn't flirting. It was a spur-of-the-moment reaction to us accidentally being about two inches away from each other. She was probably even embarrassed that she said it at the time, and while I was flattered, I was also embarrassed. She told me that she hoped my husband complimented my pretty eyes often. I said I didn't think my husband even knew what color they were. Funnily enough, I asked you when I got home. You got it wrong."

"Strike one against me, huh?" He shook his head, mad at himself.

She ignored the comment and continued. "Then I started seeing her walking the kids to school, and we talked. Oh, I remember! It was a bake sale day, and she said she was a terrible baker. So, I volunteered to teach her. That's how we started spending time together. I knew I was feeling something almost immediately, but of course, I tried to ignore it. She was obviously feeling the same because she kissed me a few weeks later. I told her she was wrong—that I didn't feel the same—and I pretended I was horrified and sent her away, but she came back the next day, apologizing, and said she was sorry she misread my signals. That's when I told her she wasn't wrong at all. That I'd had a dream the previous night, and I knew when I woke up that the way I felt in the dream was how I felt when I woke up. But even after we admitted how we felt, we still didn't act on it. Neither one of us wanted to betray you and Johnny. We tried *so* hard to ignore it. I swear, Patrick!"

She started to cry and grabbed a tissue from the box on the table. "But it's like this force that takes over me. Nothing I can do can stop it. I've tried not talking to her. I've tried finding every fault I could about her. I've tried intentionally arguing with her so she would hate me, but nothing makes the feeling go away." The torment on her face was unmistakable.

"That feeling is what? Love, I assume? Or just lust and sexual attraction?"

"It's love. Yes." She lowered her eyes in shame.

"Did you ever consider leaving me?"

"No. I didn't. I swear. I was never unhappy here. I have always loved you. It never felt like I only had a certain quantity of love and what I felt for Mary had to take away from what I felt for you."

"But what about in the bedroom?" he asked, about as tentatively as possible.

"I will admit that when Mary and I started, I um...I was...I had trouble being with you. I was overwhelmed with what was happening and how I felt that I just...couldn't. So I put you off, feigned headaches, that kind of thing."

"We've been together hundreds of times in the past eight years. Did you think about her?" The hurt in his eyes was heartbreaking for Anna.

"Some...um..." She paused and took a deep breath. "Sometimes, I did. Yes."

Patrick stood and turned away. Anna thought she saw tears, but he hid his face from her.

"Does she...is...is she good to you? Does she treat you well?"

"She does. She is. She would never hurt me, Patrick."

"What would Johnny do if he found out?"

"Well, I know he wouldn't be as kind as you are right now, that's for sure. He's a bit more volatile. Not that I think he would hurt her. I don't think he's capable of that, but I don't think he'd be sitting down with her like this trying to understand. Mary said she thought you were a very wise man."

"Ha! Wise. That's funny. My wife has been sleeping with a woman for the last eight years, and she thinks I'm wise."

"You know what I mean. Just the way you are handling this, talking calmly instead of reacting in anger. I'm so overwhelmed by it. I keep waiting for you to tell me to get the hell out."

He sat back down again now that the tears had subsided. "Believe me. Those words have crossed my mind. I just can't seem to make them come out of my mouth. I want to, sort of. I feel like I should, sort of. But so far, it hasn't happened."

"Are you still going to talk to Mary?"

"Yes, I called and asked her to come over. She'll be here in a little while."

"Am I leaving or staying for this conversation?"

"I haven't figured that out yet. I just know I need to look her in the eyes and talk to her. I don't even know what I'm going to say, but she's stolen a piece of my wife's heart, hasn't she? So, I need to confront her about that."

"I don't know what I'm supposed to be doing now, Patrick. Should I just leave you be? Should I be trying to make it up to you?"

"How would you do that? You can't undo it, can you? You can't unfeel what you feel, no matter how much I want you to."

"I'm afraid you will take the girls away from me."

"Do you think your inclination or whatever you want to call it, hurts our daughters somehow?"

"No. How? They don't know anything about it."

"How do you know that one of them didn't do the same thing I did and come home early one day. They could have seen you just as I did."

"I know they haven't. Their attitude toward me has never changed, except for their teenage mood swings. It would be pretty traumatic if they had found out, and we would have seen a behavior change. Don't you think?"

"I guess you're right. Anyway, taking the girls away from you would hurt them and you, and that's not what I want to do. No, Anna. I'm not going to take the girls away from you."

Anna reached across the table and grabbed his hand as the tears she had been fighting all morning came spilling out. "Thank you. Oh my god, Patrick, thank you." She put her head down, sobbing uncontrollably. "I've been so frightened that I've ruined everything for all of us." Patrick reached over and put his hand on her shoulder. She lifted her head and looked at him as if asking permission to hold him. He put his arms around her and let her cry, caressing her hair.

"Shhh...shhh. It's gonna be okay." Her shoulders shook, releasing the anguish of the last few days. "I don't know how, but it's gonna be okay."

As he spoke, there was a knock on the door. Anna released herself from his embrace and grabbed another tissue. While she composed herself, Patrick answered the door.

Mary walked in and saw Anna at the table, clearly distraught. She looked to Patrick, reading the situation to see if this talk between him and Anna had gotten out of hand. He nodded as if to let Mary know that they were okay. Anna looked up and gave Mary a half-hearted smile.

Patrick spoke first. "Mary, have a seat. Can I get you something to drink?"

"No, thank you. Not just yet. Anna, are you all right?" She pulled up a chair next to Anna.

"I'm as all right as possible under the circumstances. Patrick, do you want me to leave?"

"In a minute. Let's talk for a bit." He sat down at the table across from Mary. "We've been discussing where we go from here. I'll be honest. I don't have any answers to that question yet, but I just told Anna I have no intention of taking the girls away from her."

"Oh, thank god."

"I know," Anna said, trying to hold back another flood of tears.

"Mary, I haven't decided exactly what I want to say to you, but I needed you to face me and talk to me about how and why this has happened. I think I've asked Anna a million questions so far. Now I need to hear from you."

"Okay. I'll tell you whatever you want to know."

"I'm just going to cut to the chase. Are you in love with my wife?"

Mary took a deep breath and looked him in the eye. "Yes, Patrick. I am."

"Does anyone know about this affair?"

"No. No one except you. We have been cautious. We both knew what was at stake if we got caught."

"Did you plan to seduce my wife when you met her?"

"Seduce her? What? No, Patrick. What reason would I have for doing that? I had no idea I could ever even be attracted to a woman. I think it surprised me just as much as it did Anna. I didn't plan this. I promise you. It scared the hell out of me, quite frankly."

"But not enough to keep it from happening, obviously."

"I'm not sure anything we could have done would have prevented it from happening, Patrick. We were powerless against our feelings. We still are. Well, I am. I guess I shouldn't speak for Anna."

Patrick looked over at his wife for a reaction. She was staring at the table, avoiding eye contact with both of them.

"Anna, are you feeling composed enough to leave Mary and me alone for a little while?"

She looked over at Mary, ensuring she was comfortable enough to be alone with him. Mary nodded in agreement. "Yes." She grabbed her keys and purse, hesitated for a moment, and then left.

Patrick sat back down and took the last gulp of his coffee. He tapped his fingers on the table, thinking about where to begin.

"Did you make the first move?"

"Yes, I think I did. It was a long time ago, as I think you know, but as I recall, I think I kissed her first. I tried to ignore what I had felt for her for a long time. It just became overwhelming. I'm sorry we betrayed you. I'm sorry I betrayed Johnny. You have no reason to believe me, but it's true."

"Do you still love Johnny?"

"I do. Not like I love Anna, though."

"And how do you love Anna?"

"Are you sure you want to know?"

"I'm sure."

"I love her completely. To the depths of my body and soul."

He took a deep breath and winced as if the words physically stung him. "Okay. I guess I asked for that, didn't I?"

"I tried to warn you." Mary looked at him and smiled, unsure how he would take it. He smiled back, sort of.

"Am I gonna get a direct answer like that to every question I ask?"

"Probably. You know me, Patrick. I don't beat around the bush."

"What kind of future did you imagine you two would have together? I mean, it's not like you could live together or anything like that."

"We didn't plan for a future. We didn't plan any of this. We knew that a future was outside the realm of possibility, so we just took it one day at a time. We tried to stop. We just never could, so we accepted what we had. Believe me. There was plenty of guilt and angst over the years."

"But again—not enough to stop you."

"I told you. It was like a train with no brakes. We couldn't stop it if we tried, which we did."

"So, what am I supposed to do here? Let you two continue sleeping together and pretend it doesn't bother me? I just don't know how I can do that. I love my wife and don't want to leave her, but I have my pride."

"I think we are in uncharted territory here. None of us know what to do. Anna and I have had this conversation a hundred times. 'What will happen if they find out? Will our husbands leave us? Will we lose our children?' I can't answer this for you, but let me ask you this. Has Anna been a good wife for you these past eight years?"

"Yes, she has."

"Did it seem like she didn't want to be around you?"

"No, I never got that feeling from her, but what if she's just acting? What if she has just been playing me for a fool?"

"Do you think she could act for eight years? I know for a fact that she loves you, Patrick. She has told me that countless times over the years. She wouldn't lie to me about that. If anything, she would lie to say the opposite if she thought I would be jealous that I wasn't the only person she loved, but it's a moot point. She loves you. Have you been unhappy with her this whole time?"

"No. In fact, I thought we were very happy."

"And do you think that, in general, Anna is also happy?"

"Yes. She seemed rather content, as far as I can tell. Not lately, obviously, but overall."

"That says a lot, don't you think?"

"Yes, but is she staying with me just because she has no other alternative but to do so?"

"If she were, you'd see it in her demeanor. She would be sullen or sad, but that's not the Anna I know, and I'm pretty sure that's not the Anna you know. She's a generally happy person, and she's raising your daughters to be happy and well-adjusted young adults. You've got a good wife, Patrick."

He nodded to concede the point, but countered with his own. "Are you okay with her having a relationship with you and me? If you are in love with her, how can that be okay with you?"

"In a different world, of course, I wish I didn't have to share her. Sometimes I lie awake at night and wonder if she's making love to you. It *kills* me. But she has to share me, too.

"I'm crazy about her and would love for us to live like any other couple, but that's not the world we live in. We've had to settle for what we *can* have versus what we want to have at some point. You are in a different position than I am, though. You could divorce her and find a new wife if you wanted to, but unfortunately, I don't have that luxury. You just need to ask yourself if you are happy enough to accept the wife you have for who she is."

"I don't know if I can do that." He stood up and walked into the living room, looking out the window and off in his thoughts. "I could just tell her that if she wants to stay married to me, she has to stop seeing you."

"Yes, you could."

"How would she react if I did that?"

"She would probably do it for you. That's how much she truly does love you, Patrick."

"But she would be heartbroken, right?"

"I can't speak for her. I can only speak for myself. I would be heartbroken. It would feel like I was losing a limb."

"All these years...how could I not know that you two felt this way about each other?"

"We did what we had to do to survive," she said matter-of-factly.

His expression softened as he thought about Anna. The anger of the past several days had abated some, and he looked at Mary with genuine concern for his wife's well-being. "Are you good to her, Mary? Do you treat her well?"

"I treat her as if each day with her is my last. Like she's a gift that can be taken away from me at any moment. This moment...this moment right here in your kitchen could easily be my last. The magnitude of that is not lost on me." She turned away from him to keep from crying.

# Chapter Thirty-Four

## ANNA 1937

ANNA WALKED THE TREE-LINED streets downtown, bustling as usual on a Saturday morning. The kids played stickball in the street, calling, '*Car!*' each time they had to pause the game to let the neighborhood vehicles pass them. On this cool but sunny day, it seemed as if there wasn't a care in the world for everyone in this town except Anna. Some of the children called out to her with a friendly 'hello,' and she responded with barely a nod. Her thoughts were spiraling out of control with fears of what was to come. What was he saying to Mary now? Were they arguing? Was he harsh with her? Would he tell Johnny and the children?

She sat on a bench on the outskirts of the park. A small dog roamed nearby, its owners nowhere in sight. He came to her and sniffed her legs. Nervous at first, not sure if he was friendly, Anna stiffened. He sat next to her and leaned on her legs, licking them, patiently waiting to be loved. She reached down to pat his head, and he closed his eyes. He lay at her feet for a time, comforting her in her fear. Finally, she began to cry—not for the dog, but because of the dog. He looked at her as if to say, 'It's okay. Spread the pain around. I'll take it.' So she let him and wept openly with him looking on. He jumped up onto the bench and licked the tears from her cheeks. She backed away at first, then gave in to the gesture. He lay down next to her and put his head on her lap. She ran her hands down his back with her nails, gently scratching the surface of his fur. His eyes looked up at her in gratitude and she stopped crying.

"What's your name, little man? Where's your family?" He wagged his tail at the sound of her voice. They sat for a short while, his head on her thigh while she stroked his head and back. Anna took a deep breath, willing herself the strength to bear what was to come when she returned home. The dog felt the change in her energy, and with her fears eased at least temporarily, he sat up, licked her once more, then jumped down and ran away.

\* \* \* \*

Anna turned the key in the lock and tentatively opened the door, unsure of what she was walking into. She took off her coat and went into the living room, where she found Patrick sitting in his chair and staring out the window. He looked sad but not angry, which eased her mind.

"Hi," she said, in barely a whisper.

He looked at her with barely a hint of a smile on his face, and Anna let out a breath she didn't realize she was holding.

"Hi," he said. "How are you?"

"I'm all right. I should be asking you that question. Are you okay? How did it go?"

"Okay, I guess. I think I understand a little better now. Of course, it doesn't solve the problem, but…"

"Really? What did she say to make you understand?"

"She said a lot. I didn't know the extent of what you feel for each other. I'm mad at myself for missing it all these years. I must have been oblivious."

"No, we were just very good at hiding it. Don't direct your anger at anyone else but me. You've done nothing wrong. I did this. Me and Mary."

"She said you tried to stop it in the beginning."

"We did. I desperately didn't want to betray you, and she felt the same about Johnny, but it was impossible. And I've carried so much guilt all these years."

"She asked me if I thought you were happy, overall, still being married to me. I said yes. Is that true?"

"Yes, I was. I am. What has happened with Mary is not a reflection of how I feel about you. They are two very separate things. I didn't go to her because I was unhappy with you. I went to her because I felt something for her that I couldn't explain, and I couldn't put her out of my mind and my heart."

"If I were to turn a blind eye, wouldn't that make me a coward? Too afraid to do what I should do and divorce you? Too afraid to lay down the law and tell you I don't want you to see her? I feel like my pride should make me leave you, but goddammit, I don't want to. I still love you so much, Anna. I feel so weak. How can I share you with her?" He lowered his head and started crying, his shoulders shuddering.

Anna put her arms around his shoulders to comfort him. "Patrick, you've been sharing me for the better part of eight years."

"Yes, but now I *know* it. Imagining you in bed with her!" he cried out. "How? How do I do that, Anna? Her touching you, kissing you. It's eating away at me!"

"I can't tell you what decision to make, Patrick. I can only tell you what I feel. I know you don't want to talk about this side of our relationship because it's uncomfortable, but you brought it up, so...what I get in bed from her is very different than what I get from you. It's like you said the other night – apples and oranges. My intimate relationship with Mary is more about our emotional connection, which is not something you have ever been all that attentive to. That's not to say you are cold. That's not what I mean. I just mean that when it comes to cuddling and talking and connecting—that's just not your thing. That's okay!"

"No, it's not my thing, but do you have um...do you, erm...do you get...*satisfied* with her?"

Anna blushed and turned her eyes downward before answering. "Um...yes."

"Do you with me?"

She hesitated. "Sometimes."

"Sometimes. Ouch." More tears fell onto his cheeks.

"I don't want to hurt you, Patrick. So, if you think turning a blind eye will torture you, then you shouldn't do it."

"My other options are not all that attractive."

"I know. I've destroyed our lives, haven't I? I'm so sorry, honey." She paused, then backtracked. "Oh...sorry. Do you want me to stop calling you that?"

"For now, at least, yes. I can't be your 'honey.'"

"Are you sure you don't want me to stay with my sister to give you time to think?"

"I am *so* tired of thinking. I feel like my brain is going to explode. I want things to go back to how they were a week ago. I think I'm the one who needs to go away for a little while. I need some time alone. I need to not be with you right now. Tell the girls I'm just going on a fishing trip or something."

"Are you leaving me?" Anna looked at him, dreading the answer.

He turned away from her. "I don't know."

# Chapter Thirty-Five

## ANNA 1937

ANNA WATCHED AS PATRICK carried his small suitcase down the stairs. He grabbed his fishing pole and tackle box to make a good show of it in front of the girls. Anna kept a smile on her face, knowing she wouldn't usually be crying if Patrick was going fishing. So she held it together for the sake of the charade.

"Dad, how come you never take us fishing with you?" Lynn asked.

"Because neither of you likes fishing. We tried that when you were little, remember? It was a disaster. You complained and cried the whole time."

"Not fair. I was probably about four at the time! I think I've matured a little in the last ten years, don't you?"

"Yeah, well, still. I go fishing for the peace and quiet."

"Geez Louise, Daddy. That's not very nice."

"I'm just kidding, Lynn. Where's your sister? Tell her I'm leaving."

"She's on the phone with her boyfriend, Jimmy. You'll never be able to get her off. They'll be on for another hour."

"Fine. Tell her I left. Be back in a few days unless I decide to stay longer, which I might. Love you, Lynn." He looked at Anna as he left, seeing the hurt in her expression. He paused for just a moment, then continued out the front door. Lynn returned to her bedroom, and Anna looked around at the empty space. A lifetime had taken place in this room. Was this the end of that era? Would they ever take another family photo at Christmas? She pictured the corner of the room where the tree would go. They would bicker about hanging the lights and ornaments, each wanting to do it their way. At Easter, when the girls were younger, she and Patrick would hide the eggs together after they went to bed. Two years ago, they found an egg from the previous Easter after it started to smell really bad in the corner by the front window. "We should count the eggs next time," Patrick had said, and they laughed together. She and Patrick might never laugh again, his anger and hurt likely beyond repair. This 'fishing trip' may be permanent, and how would she explain that to the girls? Telling them the truth didn't seem like an option. They would never speak to her again.

Finally, the bottom had dropped out of their marriage. Amidst the suffocating cloud of chaos, loss, and despair, Anna reached for her coat and keys and left to find the only lifeline she knew.

* * * *

Anna knocked on the door of Mary's house, praying Johnny wouldn't be the one to answer. Prayer answered. Mary smiled when she saw her, but her expression changed when she saw the anguish on Anna's face. She opened the door to let her in and ushered her into the living room, taking her coat and purse along the way.

"Is Johnny here?"

"No, he went down to see his buddy at the repair shop and took the boys with him. Why? What's wrong, Anna?"

Anna released a sigh that signaled so much angst. "Patrick left. Maybe for good, I don't know. He packed a bag. We lied and told the girls he went fishing, but I don't think he's coming back. I think I've finally hurt him enough to make him leave me." Her hands trembled as she reached for the cup of coffee Mary had poured.

Mary sat next to her, putting her arm around Anna's shoulder. "Do you think he's gone for good?"

"I don't know. I can't blame him if he has. What man is going to share his wife? Share her with another woman! No man can do that. It was foolish to think he would."

"Okay. Let me rephrase the question. Do you *want* him back? Or do you need him back because he provides for you, takes care of you, and keeps the neighbors from asking too many questions?"

Anna cringed at the inference, not because it was outrageous but because there was a hint of truth to it. "You know I love him."

"Yes, you love him. So you've said. I love my husband too, but in another life, is this how you would want it to be? Because it's not for me. If I had my druthers, I certainly wouldn't be living this double life and sharing you."

Anna turned to face Mary, putting her palm on top of Mary's folded hands. "Tell me about the life you would rather be living."

Mary lowered her head and sighed woefully. "Why? From experience, I can tell you that imagining it just makes it harder when reality hits and you realize it's just a fantasy. A dream that can never come true."

"Tell me anyway." She put her hand under Mary's chin. "Please? I'm a glutton for punishment."

Unable to resist Anna's request, Mary smiled and caressed her face. "I ask you to marry me, and you say yes." She kissed Anna gently, then continued. "We are allowed to get married legally. We live in a house with all our kids. We share a bedroom." They kissed again, and Mary brushed a tear from Anna's face. "We share *a life*. Everyone knows, and no one cares. There's no husband for you to go home to and crawl into bed with. There's no husband for me to pretend I want to have sex with. There's just you and me and our kids. We get to be our true selves, and the world knows we love each other. It's okay. Imagine that."

Anna smiled and stared at her with those eyes that had captivated Mary from the very first day. She put her hands on Mary's cheeks and leaned in to kiss her again, holding on to the kiss as long as possible. "You'd really marry me if you could?" she asked through her tears.

"Are you crazy? I'd marry you in a heartbeat. I'd marry you right now if they'd let me."

"It seems somewhat sacrilegious to have this conversation today–the day my husband has left me. But you're right. If I had my way, our life would be very different. I wouldn't have this split brain that is always with one person and thinking about the other. When I'm with him, I think of myself in your arms. When I'm with you, I think of how I'm betraying him."

"I think the answer to my original question is right there in that statement. Don't you?"

"Yes, but that doesn't change our reality, does it?"

"No, it doesn't," Mary agreed. "I warned you it makes it even harder when you dare yourself to dream about something that can never happen." Mary turned away as she spoke, as if physically separating herself from the fantasy.

"Our reality is I need him to come home. Because I have no idea what the hell I will do if he doesn't."

# Chapter Thirty-Six

## PATRICK 1937

PATRICK HESITATED A MINUTE before pushing the front door open. He took a deep breath, still unsure what he would say to Anna when he got inside. She saw him and gasped, completely caught off guard by his presence. She stopped herself from moving toward him to put her arms around him.

Tentatively, she asked, "Are you here to stay or just coming to pick up some more of your things?"

"To be honest, I'm not exactly sure why I'm here, but I woke up this morning and realized I needed to be here. So here I am. The bottom line is we still have things we need to work out, but we can't work them out if I run away from it all. How are the girls? Have they asked any questions?"

"You've been gone for two weeks. They started to get suspicious about a week ago. They asked if everything was okay, and I told them sometimes, couples need a little time apart. They seemed to accept that. I think they appreciated I didn't lie to keep up the fishing story façade, but they are very much aware that something is going on with us."

"I'll talk to them when they get home from school. I'm not sure what I will tell them, but I'll think of something."

"Is there any chance you will tell them the truth?"

"No, I don't think that's a good idea. Do you?"

"No, I don't, but this is happening to you too, so I guess you have the right to tell them if you choose. I had to ask, though, because that would require some preparation on my part if so. Not sure what I would do in that case. So thank you for not telling them."

"I think it would be too traumatic and, quite frankly, embarrassing for them. Having a mother who is the other way inclined is not news that will go over well."

"No, it wouldn't," she said meekly, unable to deny the harsh truth. "Did you come to any conclusions while you were gone?"

"I concluded that I still love you, foolish man that I am. I wish I didn't, but I do."

Anna held back a smile. "If it means anything to you, I still love you too."

"It does, and it doesn't, Anna. You loving me doesn't change the fact that you are having an affair with a woman and you are in love with her. How do I live with that?"

"Maybe the same way I live with it—one day at a time. That's the only way I've been able to keep my sanity and remain relatively happy all these years. Maybe you think this is just me having my cake and eating it too, but I promise you, this is not all fun and games for me. I wish I didn't feel this way. You have no idea how much I wish it not to be true. I denied it for a very long time, but it's part of me, Patrick. It's part of who I am, and I can't change it. There is a need in me that cannot be satisfied by anyone else, even though life would be much easier if it could." She turned away from him to hide the tears welling in her eyes.

"One day at a time, huh?"

"Yes. I wake up each day and say to myself, 'whatever the day brings today, I will handle it and be grateful for all that I have that is good.' It works because I *am* grateful. For *you*. For the girls. For our life. And yes, for Mary too."

"I don't want to be seen as being the weak man by staying."

"By whom? No one knows but the three of us. No one is saying that. If anything, I think it makes you the stronger man."

"How?"

"Because you are willing to stick by your family even though it is damned hard. That takes courage. Running away is easier."

"I'm not sure I agree with that logic, but if I'm honest with myself, I don't want to leave. I want to be here with you and the girls."

"I want you to stay. Will you?"

"One day at a time, but you have to promise me something. Please don't make a fool of me. Don't let anyone else find out about this, please. I'm begging you."

"I won't. I promise." She moved toward him. "Is it okay if I kiss you?" He answered the question by taking her into his arms and hugging her tightly. Then, he took her face into his hands and kissed her as gently and lovingly as possible.

# Chapter Thirty-Seven

## MARY 1937

"HE'S BACK?" MARY ASKED when she came over the next day.

"Yes, he came home yesterday."

"And is he staying?"

"For now, yes. We're taking it one day at a time."

"So that means you will be sleeping with him again?"

"Yes." She hesitated, knowing the answer was probably not what Mary wanted to hear. "Probably. I don't know. Does that upset you?"

"It doesn't matter if it upsets me because there is absolutely nothing I can do about it. Do I like the thought of him making love to you? No. But I never have."

"We agreed long ago that we would stay with our husbands. With all that that entails. Right?"

"Yes, we agreed, but it doesn't change how I feel about it. Johnny and I rarely have sex anymore. But Patrick is different, isn't he?"

"Yes, it seems so."

"So, did he take you to bed last night?"

"Yes," she said reluctantly.

"I see. And did you enjoy it?"

"Why do you ask me these questions? There's no way to answer it that doesn't cause some level of hurt. If I say yes, you take it as a betrayal, but if I say no, it's just another reminder that we both have to do things we may not want to for this to continue. It's a no-win situation for me. What do you want me to say, Mary?"

"I'm sorry. I get insecure sometimes. I'm afraid I'm going to lose you. The thought of not being with you is too painful to bear."

Anna moved closer to Mary and put her arms around her waist. "Don't be insecure. When it comes to making love, it's *you*. It's always been you. Just because I'm not completely miserable in bed with my husband doesn't mean I feel anything less about being in bed with you. No one—*no one*—does to me what you do to me. No one makes me beg for more. No one makes me cry after I've finished. No one reaches into my soul and touches me there. No one but you. Do you understand me?"

"Yes. My god, I do love you, Anna." She reached to push a lock of Anna's hair behind her ear.

"Good. You'd better love me. I'd hate to feel this way all by myself." She paused for a moment. "I did make him one promise, though."

"Uh-oh. What?"

"He asked me to promise not to make a fool out of him. We have to take every imaginable precaution to ensure that no one finds out about this. We can't take any chances."

"Well, that won't be hard. We do that anyway."

"Not well enough, obviously, since he found out. So we have to do better, be more careful."

"True. Okay. I promise. We owe him at least that much." They kissed tenderly, then more urgently. Mary's breathing became heavy. "So, what extra precaution do I have to take to make love to you right now? Because as wrong as I know it may be, this whole situation has made me realize how much I need you. I don't think I can wait any longer." She kissed Anna more passionately, pressing her hand to Anna's breast.

Anna continued kissing her while leading them closer to the front door to engage the deadbolt and chain lock. Then she grabbed her hand and took her to the spare bedroom.

# Chapter Thirty-Eight

## LYNN 1939

LYNN STOOD AT THE back of the wedding reception dining room, still stunned at the vision of her mother kissing Mary just an hour earlier. After the kissing incident, Anna and Mary returned to the reception hall as if nothing had happened, and Lynn watched them for the rest of the afternoon. With the benefit of her newfound knowledge, she realized their mannerisms and the way they interacted with each other were so personal, so truly intimate, that she couldn't believe she had never noticed it before. They stared more intently; they laughed more heartily; they spoke more deliberately. It should have been obvious.

Lynn moved across the room to find her father, drinking too much beer and talking loudly with his friends.

"Daddy, would you like to dance?"

"Sure, sweetheart." He slurred his speech just enough to let her know that talking to him right now might not be the best idea, but the band played 'Over the Rainbow,' and she wanted to get him away from his table, so she led him to the dance floor. He took her in his arms, and they floated out to the middle of the crowded floor.

"Is everything okay, Daddy? You seem upset today."

"Maybe just sad about losing one of my baby girls. You know me. I'm a sentimental bastard."

"Are you sure that's all it is? You and Mom haven't danced together all day. You aren't even sitting together. Are you two fighting?"

"Fighting? No. Pretending everything is okay? Maybe."

"Well, forgive me for saying so, but you are doing a lousy job of pretending. What happened?"

"Nothing happened. It's old news, honey. Don't worry yourself about it. Nothing we haven't dealt with a hundred times before."

"Can you tell me what it is?" Lynn feigned ignorance, knowing exactly what 'it' was. 'It' had a name. 'It' had been kissing her mother not one hour earlier.

"Your mother," he slurred, "is making a f..." He stopped himself mid-sentence.

"Making what, Daddy?"

"No. Never mind, sweetie. It will be fine. Let's talk about something else, okay? Today is a happy occasion. We will work it out. We always do."

"But I hate seeing you so upset. You only drink this much when something is bothering you."

"Well, as I said—old news. I'll get over it. That's what I do. Hey, where's your sister? Let's see if she's ready to leave for the honeymoon yet. Did you catch her bouquet? You'll be getting married before we know it." He broke away from the dance floor, grabbed her hand, and led her out of the main reception room.

Judy and Jimmy came down from their room at the hotel with their bags packed, ready to be driven in their "Just Married" car away to the airport on the way to their honeymoon. The guests clapped as they made their way down the long staircase.

Judy glided through the crowd, saying her goodbyes and gracious words of thanks. When she reached Lynn, she pulled her off to the side and leaned in close to speak privately.

"Are you okay, Lynn? You aren't going to do anything foolish while I'm gone, are you?"

"Why do you assume I'm going to be foolish?"

"Well, you aren't exactly great under stress. Your track record precedes you."

"Gee, thanks, Jude. I talked to Daddy while we were dancing. He almost told me what was wrong, but he stopped himself. He just said that he would get over it like he always does. Do you think that means he already knew about this?"

"Maybe. They haven't exactly been like love birds these last couple of years. Remember when Daddy left for a little while about two years ago? I'll bet this was the cause."

"I remember, but I can't imagine he would have stayed all this time and let this happen behind his back. If he does know, it's no wonder he's miserable. Are you going to ask Mom about it when you get back?"

"I don't know. Maybe. I don't want to make it worse. Daddy might be even more upset if he knew that we know. Do you plan to talk to her?"

"No! I'd be mortified! It's too awful even to discuss. I wouldn't even be able to get the words out. Have you been watching them? Do you *see* the way they look at each other? It's sickening."

"They look to me like two people in love."

"In love! Have you lost your mind?" Lynn looked and sounded outraged.

"What, you don't think two women can be in love?"

"No. They can't!"

"Of course they can, Lynn. Don't be naïve. I'll talk to Mom when I get back."

"Well, I don't even want to think about it, much less discuss it. So leave me out of it, please."

"Suit yourself, little sister. In the meantime, I need to find my new husband and get the *real* party started. Can you believe I'm a married lady?" She flashed the ring on her left hand and broke into a cheek-to-cheek grin.

"No, I can't. What am I going to do without you?" Lynn made a fake frowny face.

"Well, to start with, try to play peacemaker between them, okay? You're Daddy's little girl. If anyone can cheer him up, you can."

"I'm not even sure I'm going to be able to *face* Mom, much less be her go-between."

"Try. Please? For me."

"Fine. I hate that you know I'll do anything for you."

"You hate it, and I take full advantage of it." She pinched Lynn's cheek lovingly, hugged her, then grabbed her husband's hand and led him out the door.

# Chapter Thirty-Nine

## ANNA 1939

LYNN UNLOCKED THEIR FRONT door and held it open for her parents before entering. She hung up her coat and kicked off her shoes, sighing in relief that her toes were finally getting a break. Anna did the same, then headed to the kitchen to put up a pot of coffee. Patrick went straight to the refrigerator and pulled out a beer.

Anna turned away from the sink and said, "Don't you think you've had enough to drink today, dear? Give me a few minutes, and the coffee will be ready."

"Coffee isn't going to cut it for me this evening, *dear*." He made his way to the living room, kicked off his shoes, pulled off his tie, and plopped on the couch.

"Is something bothering you, Patrick?" Anna asked.

"Who me? Nooo. What could possibly be bothering me?"

Lynn quickly made her way to her bedroom, being conflict-averse. The evening was about to go downhill fast, and she wanted no part of this conversation. But, when she closed her door, she listened to see if she could hear their conversation. It was like a traffic accident that she could not turn away from, no matter how disturbing it may be.

"Are you just going to make snide comments at me all evening, or would you like to tell me what's bothering you?" Anna asked.

"Snide comments seem like a good approach to me. How about you?"

She put her hands on her hips and sighed. "No, not really. What's going on?"

"You must know. You can't possibly be that naïve, Anna."

"Well, apparently I am, because I have no idea what you are talking about."

"I saw you. You and Mary. I saw you before the wedding and again during the reception. It's bad enough that you continue to see her, but you could at least be more discreet. There were a hundred people there, Anna! Are you trying to make a complete fool of me?"

She walked over to the chair next to the couch and sat down, facing him. "No, Patrick. I'm not. I'm sorry. I thought we were out of everyone's sight. Apparently not."

"No, apparently not. Anyone could have seen you. Anyone *may* have seen you. What were you thinking?"

"We hadn't seen each other in a little while. I got carried away."

"After all these years, you still react that way about each other after just a few days?"

"Well...yes."

"You sure as hell don't react that way with me when I come back from my fishing trips."

"We don't need to go over this again, do we, Patrick? It's different with her. You know this already. This is well-worn territory we're covering here."

"I guess when you flash it in my face, I get just a little bit more upset about it. How do you not understand that?" His voice got louder and louder with each response.

Anna lowered her voice in reply. "Please, Patrick. Lynn is going to hear you." She reached across to grab his hand. He pulled it away.

"I don't care. I've been silent about this for far too long, Anna. You don't seem to consider my feelings on this subject at all. Maybe it's better if our daughters know about this. The truth about their mother would certainly be enlightening, don't you think?"

"You promised me years ago you wouldn't do that!"

"You promised me you would be discreet. Promises break sometimes. Maybe the promise of this marriage is what needs to be broken."

"Is that what you want?"

"I didn't use to want that, but now I'm not sure. We've slipped farther apart while you and Mary have gotten closer. I'm swimming against the tide, Anna. Johnny left Mary a year ago, but I hung in there, thinking we could still do this, but I'm not so sure we can, at least not if you are going to pull stunts like today."

The phone rang, and Patrick answered with an irritated and angry, "Hello!"

"My, my...someone is in a foul mood," Mary responded from the other end of the phone line.

"Not now, Mary. Anna is busy. She can't talk to you."

"What's wrong, Patrick?"

"I'm sure your *lover* will fill you in as soon as I leave the house. Goodbye, Mary!" He hung up, making sure they all heard the slamming of the receiver.

"Was that necessary, Patrick? There's no need to be rude."

"I disagree. I think I have plenty of reasons to be rude. I'm sick of being the one who always has to make the sacrifice."

"Sacrifice? You think *you* have to make sacrifices? You have no idea what it's like to be in my shoes. I have to put on a show every single day for every single person in my life *except* for Mary. There's not another soul with whom I can let down my guard. I spend every moment of every day making sure your needs are met and the kids' needs are met, but my needs are rarely met because the real me has to hide. So yeah, occasionally, it gets the better of me and I slip. I'm sorry for that, but I swear, Patrick, you have no idea what goes on in my head. You are free to leave me if you've had enough of this. I've never shackled you to this marriage. You've known for ages this is who I am. So spare me the 'I always have to make sacrifices' speech, okay?" Anna stormed out of the room, grabbed her coat and keys, and slammed the front door behind her.

Lynn crouched on her bedroom floor with her ear against the door. The cold hard facts had come to light. Yes, her mother was having an affair with Mary. A long-term affair, from the sound of it. Her father knew. For years, he'd known. Lynn got off the floor and collapsed face down onto her bed as the tears took over.

# Chapter Forty

## LYNN 1939

LYNN CAME OUT of her bedroom, the house was deathly quiet, the clock on the wall providing the only sound with its otherwise imperceptible rhythmic ticking. She found her father with a beer in his hand, staring off into the ether. She made some noise to let him know she was coming into the room, then sat next to him on the sofa.

"Penny for your thoughts?" she asked tentatively.

"You're gonna need a lot of pennies."

"I can tell." She leaned into him and he put his arm around her. "I heard what happened, Daddy. I didn't mean to eavesdrop. I couldn't help but hear."

"I'm sorry, sweetheart. You shouldn't have been subjected to that conversation. We got a little heated, I guess."

"Do you want to talk about this?"

"It's not easy to talk about. Besides, it's between your mother and me. It has nothing to do with you and Judy. So like I said this afternoon, it's old news, but sometimes the old news gets dragged back up to the top of the front page."

"Are you and Mom going to get a divorce?"

"I don't know, sweetie. I hope not."

"Does this mean that Mom is a, um...a hom...a lesbian?"

"I think you should ask *her* that question."

"I don't think I could. It's too embarrassing. Too mortifying!"

"In your mother's defense, let me say that this is not some sordid, perverted affair. On the contrary, she and Mrs. Monahan love each other. I know it's hard to understand, but it's true. It took me a very long time to accept it. I thought I had. But today, I saw them, and I just got so angry and humiliated." Patrick could hear Lynn whimpering into his chest as he spoke. "I'm very sorry you found out this way, honey."

"You aren't the one who should be apologizing. How could she do this to you? To all of us? If people find out, our whole family will be shamed. I'll be the laughingstock of the school!"

"No one will find out. And in one more year, you will be out of that school anyway, so there's no need to fret over that. You are almost an adult, Lynn. You will soon find out that the world is made up of *all* kinds of people. Some can't help but fall in love with someone they shouldn't. That's your mother. She can't help it."

"Are they really in love?" Lynn asked.

"Yes. They are. Much to my dismay."

"I didn't know that was possible."

"It is. As I said, it takes all kinds, but if you need more clarity, you will have to ask your mother to explain it to you."

"I'm not asking her. I don't want to know anything about it. I'd rather just pretend it isn't happening. Head in the sand is a good strategy, don't you think?"

"I've tried that. It doesn't always work, but you're a big girl now. You can make your own decisions about what conversations you do and do not want to have with your mother."

# Chapter Forty-One

## JOSIE AND TRISH 1999

THE CARDINAL BALANCED ON the feeder outside Josie's kitchen window chirped its fluent mating call to the cherry red male in the nearby tree. He landed next to her on the branch, then both faced the window to meet Josie's glance. Legend has it that a cardinal is the spirit of a loved one lost, and she thought of her parents, long gone from her world.  What would they think of her now, in this phase of her life? Would they still harbor old feelings of disappointment, or would they recognize her personal growth to be true to herself? The birds flew off as if answering, perhaps in the negative. It wasn't a mystery she would solve today, or any day, for that matter. In the meantime, another parent waited across town for Josie and Trish to arrive for Thanksgiving dinner. Trish was still upstairs putting on her make-up, so Josie took Max for a walk. He must have sensed Josie was leaving for the day because he moped and meandered down the street, prolonging the inevitable. Josie let him, knowing that Trish was probably not ready to go to Marilyn's house yet anyway.

When Trish came downstairs, she didn't realize Josie was out with Max, and she chattered as she walked around the kitchen. "Josie, honey. Let's not forget everything we need to bring with us today. I hope my mother is in a good mood. I don't think I can take an afternoon of criticism." Trish looked around, realizing Josie was nowhere to be found. "Hmmm. I guess I'm talking to myself. Well, in any case, don't forget the pie and the green bean casserole." Josie reappeared, coming in through the back door with Max slowly following.

"I was having a conversation with you, and since you weren't here to reciprocate, I played your part," Trish said.

"Oh? And what did I say during this little chat?"

"You reminded me to grab the pie from behind the milk carton. While you were at it, you told me how nice I look."

"That was very smart of me. I was right. You look beautiful. Your mother will approve."

"For your part, you've done your usual nice job of not looking too gay. So I think we will pass inspection."

"Oh, good. I need to make sure I stay on Marilyn's good side. I might need her as an ally someday." Josie smirked and leaned over to kiss Trish.

Trish put her arms around Josie. "You and my mother teamed against me would be a force to be reckoned with. No, thank you." She kissed Josie passionately, reminding her which team she belonged on.

"Mmm. Okay! Message received. I'm on your side!"

"Let's go. You know how my mother hates it when we're late."

"Sure, now that you've got me all hot and bothered, you want me to go see your mother. Thanks a lot."

"You're welcome!" She laughed on the way out the door.

* * * *

They arrived at Marilyn's house a few minutes later and knocked on the door. No answer. Trish gave Josie a 'what the hell?' look and tried again. Maybe she was upstairs and didn't hear the knock, so she tried yet again. Still no answer. Trish took out her key, which she only used for emergencies, and unlocked the door. They were met with the smell of burning food and a layer of smoke near the ceiling, not enough to signal a house on fire but enough to indicate something was wrong.

"Oh my god. What is happening here?" she said in a panic. They both ran toward the kitchen to find smoke billowing out of the oven door. Trish turned it off, then did the same for the two burners on the stove that were simmering away.

"She's not down here," Josie said, rushing toward the staircase. They bolted up the stairs, taking two steps at a time, and hurried to Marilyn's bedroom. They found her face down on the bathroom floor, unconscious with a cut bleeding from her head.

Trish was frozen in place, unable to move in any direction, so Josie took charge. "Go call nine-one-one!" she yelled, snapping Trish out of her trance. When she left the room, Josie knelt and felt Marilyn's neck for a pulse. Faint, but at least it was something. She didn't want to move her neck in case of a traumatic head injury, so she just made sure her airway was clear. Next, she grabbed a towel off the vanity and pressed it against the head wound to slow the bleeding. Trish returned to the bathroom; her face had lost all color and expression.

"She's alive. The pulse is faint, but it's there. There's a lot of blood, but I think maybe it looks like more than it is because just pressing a little with this towel seems to be holding it back. How long did they say they would be?"

No answer from Trish. Just pure panic.

"Trish! Stay with me! How long until they get here?"

"They said five minutes."

"Okay, go make sure the front door is unlocked, and there is a wide enough pathway from the stairs to the door for a gurney. She's gonna be okay, but you gotta stay calm, okay?"

Trish nodded, barely comprehending. They could hear the sound of sirens coming closer and closer.

"Go meet them downstairs, babe. Tell them to hurry."

Josie held the towel in place until the first paramedic arrived in the bathroom to take over. The blood from the floor soaked Josie's pants, and her hands were covered in it. She stepped back to let the paramedics do their work and went looking for Trish.

Josie found her standing in the middle of the kitchen, staring blankly at the food. Josie washed the blood off her hands, guided Trish to a chair at the table, and poured a glass of water.

"Here, honey." She handed the glass to Trish. She opened the oven, grabbed the oven mitts with Thanksgiving turkey prints on them and pulled out the badly charred bird. "I'm afraid this must have happened a while ago," Josie said reluctantly. "This bird is pretty badly burnt. The implication of what that meant was unspoken but obvious. A long period of time lying on her bathroom floor did not bode well for Marilyn's recovery.

Josie could hear the paramedics making their way down the stairs, so she took Trish's hand and went to meet them at the door. Marilyn was still not conscious. She had an IV in her arm and an oxygen mask over her mouth. There was a bandage on the head wound, halting the excessive blood loss for now, at least until she got to the hospital. The head EMT stopped to brief them while the other two rushed her to the ambulance.

"She's breathing, but it's critical. Based on what we can tell, she appears to have lost consciousness and hit her head on the sink as she fell. It is, unfortunately, a rather common occurrence for older folks. We're taking her to South Nassau Hospital, and the trauma unit is awaiting our arrival. You can follow us."

"Why can't I go in the ambulance?" Trish pleaded.

"We need the room to maneuver in there, so we'd prefer that you didn't, but you can if you insist."

"No, I understand. Please do what you need to do. Is she at least stable for now?"

"For now." He sounded tentative.

Josie took charge and grabbed their keys, coats, and Marilyn's purse and ushered them both out the door behind the paramedics. Once in the car, she took a breath and looked over at Trish. Her face was ashen, her eyes wet with tears, and her blank stare was heartbreaking.

"Take a deep breath, Trish. We'll get through this. We'll be right behind them and talk to the doctor as soon as possible. I know you're terrified. I'm right here with you. I've got you, whatever happens." With that, she started the car and trailed behind the ambulance. Since they used lights and sirens, it took only a minute for them to get far ahead of the car. Josie was relieved to see just how quickly they disappeared out of sight. It meant Marilyn would be getting to the hospital in just a few minutes. In the meantime, Josie reached for Trish's hand and held it tight, willing her to stay hopeful and strong.

* * * *

They sat in the hard plastic chairs in the emergency room for two hours before a doctor came out to brief them. It was the longest two hours of Trish's life. She barely spoke, just stared straight ahead. Josie took charge as much as possible, finding Marilyn's medical information in her purse, but with Trish zoned out, there were many questions that Josie simply could not answer.

Finally, the double doors opened, and a woman called out Marilyn's name. Josie responded and shook Trish to get her attention.

"Ms. McCann, I'm Dr. Anne Arthur, the neurologist on call. We've done an initial workup on your mother and found that she has suffered a stroke, likely followed by a fall. The damage from the fall is treatable and doesn't appear to have caused any significant damage, but I'm afraid the stroke is rather more serious. We suspect she was probably without oxygen to the right side of her brain for some time, long enough to have potentially significant ramifications. The next twenty-four hours will be critical in determining her long-term prognosis."

"Is she going to live?" Trish asked, the tears steadily streaming down her cheeks.

"It's difficult to say at this point. If she survives the night, I'll have a better idea of what we are dealing with in the morning. We are doing everything we can for her, but it just depends on how much damage there is in the brain."

"Can we see her?" Josie asked.

"Not yet, I'm afraid. First, we need to get her settled in the ICU. Once she is situated, I'll send the nurse to come and get you, but it will likely be at least another hour. So you may want to take this opportunity to get some food or coffee. Also, if there are other family members you need to contact, now might be a good time to make those calls." Josie and Trish looked at each other, digesting the not-so-subtle message the doctor conveyed with that last sentence.

Josie thanked the doctor and helped Trish back to their seats. She pulled one of the chairs around to face Trish, grabbing her hand. "I know this looks bad, but we've got to keep the faith. Your mother is a strong, stubborn woman. She's not going to leave this world without a fight."

Trish let out a short giggle through her tears. "That's true. She'll live just to spite the doctors who say she won't." They both smiled at each other.

"She can't die now. I can't live with knowing that I've disappointed her. All she wanted was for me to meet a nice man, get married, and have kids. I've done none of that for her!"

"Trish, listen to me. What she *wants* is for you to be happy. She never asked you to live your life for her. She knows you've found your path, and she made peace with it. In your heart, I know you know this to be true. She was not disappointed in you. How could she be?"

"I can't help but think back to everything she said when I first told her."

"Yes, but she explained all that. It was baggage from the past. It wasn't how she really felt about you. She made that clear when she came for dinner, remember? Please, Trish. You will eat yourself alive with guilt if you keep thinking this way. Besides, she's still in there fighting, and we've got to stay focused on that, okay?"

"Will you please try to call Aunt Judy again? She needs to be here."

"Sure." Josie went to the payphone to make the call. As she was dialing, she wondered how many heartbreaking conversations had taken place on this phone. Family calling family, breaking tragic news to the person on the other end of the line. This drab, sterile, cold concrete and hard plastic space was the scene for so much human emotion. As she dialed, she wished she wasn't adding another chapter to the story of this room.

"Hi, Judy? This is Josie. Trish's girlfriend?"

"Yes, of course. Hi, Josie. Happy Thanksgiving. What can I do for you? Is everything okay?"

"I'm afraid not. Your sister has had a stroke. Trish and I are here with her at South Nassau. You should probably come if you can."

"What? Oh my god! Is it serious? What a stupid thing for me to say. It's a stroke. Of course, it's serious. I'm sorry, Josie. I'm just in shock. How is Trish?"

"Also in shock. She's physically here but barely functioning. I could use some help calming her down."

"I'm on my way. I'll be there in fifteen minutes."

"Thanks, Judy."

* * * *

Another two hours passed before a nurse came out and informed Trish that her mother was settled into ICU, and Trish could see her briefly. The hospital room was a sensory overload. Machines beeping, lights flashing, the smell of disinfectant. Trish stepped in, then immediately took a step backward when she saw Marilyn. Josie grabbed her hand and led her back into the room and to the side of the bed. "Talk to her," Josie said. "She can probably hear you. She needs to know you are by her side."

Trish tentatively reached for her mother's hand, careful not to disturb the IV lines in her veins.

"Do you want me to leave you alone with her?" Josie asked.

"No, please stay. I think I'll faint without you." Josie shook her head, but stepped back to let Trish have her moment with Marilyn.

"Mom. It's me. I'm here, and I'm holding your hand. Maybe you can feel it? The doctor says you've had a stroke, and it's serious, so pay attention, okay? I'm scared, Mom. Please fight your way through this. You know as well as I do that you aren't ready to leave this earth. You have too much left to do. Who will judge my food and fashion choices? Who will people watch with me and comment on all the crazy things folks do when we go to a restaurant? Who will tell and retell all those embarrassing stories about my childhood?

"Maybe you are tired right now and don't feel like fighting. I get that. You probably feel like shit right about now. If it helps, I feel like shit, too, just in a different way. Josie is here with me. Josie, do you feel like shit?"

"I do. Believe me, I do."

"See? Oh, and Judy is out in the waiting room. She probably would tell me to stop because you don't like it when I curse, but yeah, she feels like shit too. So you're not alone. We are all here feeling miserable in solidarity with you. The only way for us to feel better is for you to fight this, okay?

"They will kick me out of here in a minute, and Judy will come to see you. I'll come back as soon as they let me, but in the meantime, please, Mom. Please don't leave. Please? I love you."

They sat quietly in silent prayer until the nurse ushered them back to the waiting room. Trish fell into Judy's arms in tears, her shoulders shuddering as she cried out loud. Judy held her tight until the sobbing subsided. She took her thumbs and wiped the tears from both sides of her face, kissing her forehead. Then she transferred Trish into Josie's embrace and went to see her sister.

# Chapter Forty-Two

## TRISH 1999

JUDY REJOINED TRISH AND Josie in the ICU waiting room. The look in her eyes betrayed the attempt at putting on a brave face for Trish's sake. They sat in silence, waiting for news from someone—anyone. Josie brought them coffee from the cafeteria, and they took turns taking cat naps in the only waiting room chair that was even semi-comfortable enough to do so. As Judy slept, Trish put her head in Josie's lap, hoping to find some respite from the wheels spinning in her brain. Josie caressed her hair with one hand and rubbed her arm with the other.

"Do you think she's going to die?" Trish whispered.

"No, babe. I don't. And you need to focus your mind on thinking the same. Make her feel your positive energy. She's not going to go yet. Okay?"

"But what if she lives and is incapacitated?"

"Then we will deal with it and make sure she has the best care possible."

"My mother isn't easy at the best of times."

"Perhaps now is not the time to focus on her quirks and your mother/daughter personality differences. How about we stick to making sure she stays alive, shall we?"

"Do you think she has accepted us and our lifestyle? Or was she just negotiating a fragile peace?"

"She doesn't strike me as the kind of person who tones down her feelings to make someone happy, even if that person is you. On the contrary, she is nothing if not blunt, which, by the way, is a trait she passed along to her daughter."

"Are you saying I'm like my mother?"

"Ha! Really? Do you not know this about yourself? C'mon. I thought you were a little more self-aware than that. By the way, it's not a derogatory statement. On the contrary, I like knowing exactly where I stand with her and with you. Especially you."

"Oh? And where do you think you stand, smarty-pants?"

"Well, I'm here, aren't I? I get to be the one to help you through this. I don't see you letting anyone else into your inner circle. I mean, I hate that we have to be here, but I'm happy to be the one to hold your hand right now. Maybe I'm over-confident, but I think your mom would be happy I'm here with you."

A voice quietly chimed in from the semi-comfy chair on the other side of the room. "She would be," said Judy. "She likes you, Josie. She respects you. She thinks you make her daughter happy, which is all she ever wanted, despite her initial bluster."

"Good thing we weren't talking about our sex life, Aunt Judy. Welcome to the conversation." Trish smiled as she spoke.

"If you were, I would have tuned you right out. Love you girls, but nah...no desire to listen to you whispering your sweet nothings."

"Sweet nothings? Who still uses that phrase?" Trish mocked.

"I do. I'm old, remember?" She shifted to her other side in the chair, making groaning noises. "Did I miss anything? Any news?"

"Nothing. But since the sun is finally rising on this interminably long night, it means the doctors should be starting their rounds soon." As she spoke, the machines inside Marilyn's room started to beep loudly, and the nurses came out of their respective patients' rooms to hurry in to see what was happening. Trish sat up, blood rushing from her face. The door closed behind each person running in and out of the room, impeding any view they might have had from the waiting area. All three of them stood, Josie holding Trish's hand. Judy's hands came up to her face to hide the expression of terror. All three were crying.

Doctors and nurses continued to go in and out of the room. Finally, a young physician came out and motioned for them to have a seat so they could talk.

"As I'm sure you've seen, we've been attending to your mother for about twenty minutes now. Her heart rate and blood pressure dropped suddenly, and she stopped breathing. We were able to resuscitate her, but she is very unstable. Unfortunately, her vitals indicate she may be shutting down. The damage to her brain is extensive, and while she's putting up a good fight, I'm afraid her current prognosis is rather poor. I wish I had better news for you. I'm very sorry. If you have things you would like to say to her, now would be the time. You can stay in her room as long as you like."

Trish fell into Judy's arms, and they cried together uncontrollably. Josie followed the doctor back to the nurse's station.

"Doctor, can I have a moment, please?"

"Of course."

"For Trish's sake, and so I know how to support her and her aunt...is there nothing else you can do at this point? Is she dying?"

"Yes, I believe she is. She's shutting down rather quickly, I'm afraid. You should prepare them for the worst. It would take a miracle at this point to bring her back."

"How long do they have to say goodbye?"

"Well, it's impossible to say for sure, but I would say it's probably a matter of an hour or two at most."

"Thank you, Doctor."

"You're very welcome. And again, I'm so sorry."

Josie turned and watched as Trish and Judy spoke softly, drying each other's tears and trying to find words. Josie returned to their sides and pointed them toward Marilyn's room, but she stayed behind.

"I'm going to wait out here. You guys go. Talk to her. Tell her how you feel," Josie urged.

"Honey, please come with me. I need you," Trish begged through her tears. Josie reluctantly followed, but again, she stepped back to let them have their spot at her bedside. They each grabbed Marilyn's hands and leaned in to whisper to her. As Josie watched from the back of the room, her heart broke as she observed the grief in her love's eyes. Complete and utter helplessness overcame her, and tears ran down her cheeks.

"Mom, I love you. I'm sorry if I've disappointed you. I know I didn't turn out the way you wanted me to. Thank you for trying to understand me. I hope you know I only ever wanted to make you proud. I don't think I've been able to do that most of the time, but I've tried to be the person you've raised me to be. If you need to be with daddy now, I understand. He will be so happy to see you." The words were nearly unintelligible through the tears. "Do you promise to watch over me? I may need your strength from time to time." As she said the words, Marilyn squeezed her hand ever so lightly.

"She hears me. She squeezed my hand! As soon as I asked her to watch over me, she squeezed! Thank you, Mom. Thank you for that gift." Trish caressed Marilyn's face and pushed the hair off her forehead while Josie and Judy smiled at them through their tears. Then, for a fraction of a moment, Marilyn opened her eyes. She looked at Trish then at Judy. Then she closed her eyes and took her last breath.

# Chapter Forty-Three

## TRISH 1999

JOSIE TOOK TRISH'S HAND to steady her as they walked into her mother's house for the first time since Thanksgiving Day. It was December 22nd. Josie was torn between putting this off until after the holidays or bringing Trish to her mother's beforehand so she would get it over with before Christmas. In the end, they decided that either way, this simply wasn't going to be a very happy holiday, so better to take the first step at least. As they walked into the kitchen, Josie said a silent thank you to Judy, who'd arranged to have a cleaning crew come in to deal with the mess in the upstairs bathroom and the kitchen.

They moved about the house, with Josie attempting to take a practical approach by discussing what needed to happen going forward. What should they do with her clothes? When should Trish think about selling the house? What did she want to do with all her personal belongings? When it became clear Trish was not quite ready to discuss these things, Josie simply listened and consoled her.

"How am I supposed to decide what she would have wanted me to do with all of her things? She didn't expect to die this young. I don't even know if she had a will!"

"She probably did. Your mother seemed very organized. Judy will know, I'm sure. I'll talk to her about it, okay? We don't need to answer any of these questions now, but it's good that we are here because you can take a good look around and start to formulate a plan for whenever you think you might be ready. This is, sadly, all part of the grieving process, Trish. Everyone does it in their own way and in their own time. I'm here to help you take each step as you go."

"I'm sorry our first Christmas is going to be ruined."

"Do you honestly think I'm worried about that? I would give up *all* my remaining happy Christmases if I could take away your pain right now. Seeing this look in your eyes is tearing my heart in two." Josie put her arms around Trish and let her go limp, releasing yet another round of tears. "For today, how about we just look at your mom's desk and see if any urgent paperwork needs to be handled?"

Trish nodded, and they moved into Marilyn's den, where she had an antique roll-top desk. Bills and papers were neatly organized in the slots, with post-it note reminders of who to call and what to pay. Josie took the late and overdue statements and put them in a pile to take with them. When she got home, she would call each of the companies to let them know what had happened. The electric and gas bills needed to be paid to keep the lights and the heat on while deciding what to do going forward.

As they rummaged through the papers, they found three sealed envelopes. One for Trish, one for Judy, and one for Josie. They looked at each other quizzically. "Maybe they are Christmas cards that she had purchased early in the season, but the envelopes don't feel like cards."

"Well, aren't you going to open it?" Josie said.

"I'm almost afraid to. What if she wrote me a letter in anger?"

"You have to get past this notion that she died angry with you. It just isn't true, honey, and it's causing you so much heartache."

"Well, you open yours, then."

"No, I feel like this is something you need to do first, but whatever this is, it's a moment you have to have with her."

They took the letters to the kitchen table. Trish opened her envelope first. When she unfolded the letter inside, a pressed red rose flower fell out.

"What's that from?" Josie asked.

"I have no idea."

*My dearest Patricia,*

*I am writing this letter shortly after returning from dinner at your house when I met Josie. Well, perhaps I should say when I met Josie properly because I acted like a petulant child the first time I met her at the restaurant. I wish that hadn't been her first impression of me. On the other hand, I had no impression of her that night because I was too wrapped up in my righteous indignation. So tonight was really my first opportunity to get to know her. Even though I sat you both down after dinner and told you that I was sorry for my behavior, I feel like there is more to say, so here I am, writing you a good old-fashioned letter.*

*Inside this envelope, you will find a pressed rose. After you left the restaurant that night, but before they came to clean off your table, I noticed one of the buds had fallen off the flowers Josie gave you. So I went over to the table and I took the bud. I wasn't sure why I did it at the time, but it was an impulse, I guess. I watched you that night much as I watched you tonight. I watched you look at her across the table, and I'll be damned if I didn't see two people who are madly in love with each other. You look at her with such clarity of purpose, like you finally know what you want. She makes you laugh in a way I've never heard you laugh before. There is a confidence about you that I've never seen in you in the past. It occurred to me as I was driving home that I had seen that look and that confidence somewhere else before. I saw it on my mother's face when she was with Mary. You are so much like her, my darling girl. I spent many years angry with my mother for loving Mary. All these years later, I'm embarrassed to admit I was ashamed of her. I never talked to her about one of the most important things in her life. Looking back on it, I now know she was as in love with Mary as you are with Josie. I wish I had the courage and strength to talk to her back then because I'm sure it was very hard for her. I made it even harder. I don't want to do that with you, Patricia. I will not turn away from you because of who you love. Instead, I want to turn toward you and tell you that I'm proud of you for being true to yourself.*

*I now know there was a reason I took that rosebud from the table. It was symbolic of what I saw in you and Josie that night. I'm glad I kept it, and now I want to give it back to you.*

*I love you with all my heart,*
*Mom*

Trish finished reading, looked at Josie, and just sobbed. Josie held her tight, comforting her and whispering into her ear. When the tears finally subsided, she wiped her eyes with the tissue Josie had given her.

"It's time for you to read yours."

"Based on your reaction, I'm not sure I want to. I still can't tell if your letter was good or bad."

"Just read."

Josie nodded and opened her letter.

*Dear Josie,*

*I've already written a similar letter to Patricia, so I'll tell you what I told her. I am writing this shortly after returning from the dinner at Patricia's house where you and I met properly. Thank you again for giving me a second chance to change your opinion of me. After the restaurant incident, I'm sure you thought I was quite a bitch. You weren't wrong, but as I told Patricia in her letter, I saw a different side to my daughter that night. And I saw it again tonight. There is something extraordinary about you and Patricia. You complement each other. Her smile is broader and more genuine than I've ever seen. You look at her with love, and she looks right back at you the same way. It's quite breathtaking.*

*I want to thank you for making her so happy. I think you two have what it takes to make it through the long haul. My daughter is very special to me, as you can imagine. There is almost no one that I think would be good enough for her, but of all the five billion people on this planet, I think she may have found the only one. So take good care of her, okay?*

*With love,*

*Marilyn*

She read it again. And again. Just like Trish, she wept without holding anything back.

"This is so oddly beautiful. It's almost as if she knew she was going to die. She asked me to take good care of you." She handed her letter to Trish for her to read, and Trish did the same.

"Now do you believe me that you have been beating yourself up for nothing?" Josie said.

"I can't believe she said all of this. I'm just...stunned. She was proud of me."

"Of course, she was. She had every reason to be. You're an amazing woman, and she knew it."

"I thought she was ashamed of me. I thought I had broken her heart."

"I knew that night that she had had a change of heart. It was obvious in the way she spoke to both of us. No one goes out of their way to say something like that unless they mean it."

"I'm not ready to do anything with her stuff yet, okay? I have to sit with this for a little while. Plus, I have to find out if she had a will and made provisions for anything."

"I'm quite sure her will has set aside some sentimental things for Judy and the rest to you to do with as you wish, but none of that has to be decided today. So let's go home, okay? It's been an emotional day and I think you need time to absorb it all."

"I hate that her last moments in this house were so frightening for her. She loved this place."

"All of the good memories will outweigh the bad over time."

"I hope you're right, because all I can see right now is that blood on the floor and the sight of the paramedics carting her away on that gurney." Trish started to cry again, and Josie embraced her and held her close.

"Try to put your focus on that letter she wrote to you. Let that be the last memory of her. She was writing to you with love, pouring it all out over the page for you. That's what you should remember."

Trish sniffled and faced Josie. "And as it turns out, she loved you too! Who knew?"

Josie's eyes filled with tears again. "I still can't believe she left us both these amazing gifts. Your mother may not have been perfect, but she sure knew how to leave an impression. I will treasure that letter for the rest of my life." Josie looked up as if speaking to the heavens. "Thank you, Marilyn. I will take care of her. Don't you worry."

# Chapter Forty-Four

## ANNA 1939

ANNA RETURNED TO THE house a couple of hours after storming out in anger. Patrick was sitting in the dark, a glass of scotch and a cigarette in his hand. Anna could see him by the dim light of the hallway. Rather than turn on the lamp, she let her eyes adjust to the darkness for a moment, then spoke.

"I see you've graduated from beer to the hard stuff, huh?"

"Don't start again, Anna. Please. Your daughter heard our argument. She knows everything."

"What?"

"You heard me."

"I told you to keep your voice down earlier. What did she say to you? Oh my god. What are we going to do?"

"*I'm* not going to do anything, but you probably have some explaining to do. She asked if you were a lesbian. I told her she needed to ask you that question herself, but that yes, you were having an affair with Mary, and you are in love with her. She said she was too embarrassed to discuss it with you, and she's afraid of being shamed out of school."

"Oh, god. Oh, god, no." Anna's heart was racing and she needed to catch her breath. "Is she asleep?"

"I doubt it. She was crying when she went back into her room. It would be best if you talked to her. She wants to pretend it didn't happen, but you can't do that. You need to talk to her."

"Okay. What on earth am I going to tell her?"

"Try the truth. You've been lying to them for so many years. Maybe it's finally time they know who their mother really is."

Anna went back into the kitchen, grabbed a shot glass from the cabinet, and downed a glass of scotch from the bottle Patrick had left on the table. She hated scotch, but she needed something to calm her nerves, and coffee wasn't going to do it this time.

She tentatively knocked on Lynn's bedroom door, then let herself in without waiting for an answer. She found Lynn face down on her bed, whimpering into her pillow. She sat down on the edge of the bed and put her hand on Lynn's back. Lynn immediately brushed her away with a 'don't touch me!' gesture.

"Lynn, your father told me what happened. We need to talk about this, okay?"

"I don't want to talk about it. There's nothing to discuss."

"Oh, I think that's about as far from the truth as we could get, don't you? I know this is uncomfortable. Believe me. It's just as uncomfortable for me, but we can't just pretend it hasn't happened."

"Why not? I can."

"No, you can't, and you know it. Now come on. Look at me. Please?"

Lynn slowly turned over, her eyes bloodshot red and her cheeks wet with tears. Anna reached to dry them, but Lynn again pulled away.

"Okay, listen to me. I know you don't understand what's happening, and I can't blame you for that. This is some very adult stuff, and you're too young to understand it yet."

"I'm not a kid anymore, Mom. I'm sixteen."

"Yes, well, you may think that means you are all grown up, but you're wrong. Until you fall in love yourself, you will not be able to understand what is going on here."

"Well, when I fall in love, I can guarantee you it won't be with a girl!"

"For your sake, I hope that's true, sweetheart. Because you have no idea how hard this is for me."

"I don't want to hear about it, Mom! It's just too embarrassing to discuss."

"Yes, it's embarrassing. For me. All you have to do is listen, okay? Now look, the first thing I need to make sure you understand is that I love your father and both of you girls with all my heart. Nothing I'm about to tell you changes that, okay?"

Lynn nodded and wiped her eyes again.

"Sometimes, people develop feelings different from what most people think is the right way to feel. And no matter how much we wish those feelings would go away, they just don't, so we accept them and find some way to deal with it all. That is what happened to me with Mary. I know you probably have all sorts of thoughts running through your head, and you are ashamed and embarrassed, but the truth is I love Mary in the same way that I love your father. Well, sort of the same. It's not some perverted affair, and I'm not the depraved person you probably think I am. I spent a long time denying what I felt, and I made myself very unhappy in the process. I didn't want to feel this way. I didn't want to put everything I have on the line just to do as I pleased. I've cried about this more times than I can count. I never wanted to hurt you or your sister or your father, but I know I have. Well, maybe not your sister because she probably doesn't know."

"She knows."

"What? How?"

"We saw you today. Out in the hallway during the reception. We saw you and Mrs. Monahan kissing."

"Oh, no. I'm so sorry, Lynn. I never meant for that to happen." She put her head down, furious with herself for ruining everything by being so careless earlier at the wedding. "Was Judy upset?"

"Yes, but she refused to let it spoil her wedding. So instead, she said she would talk to you when she returns from her honeymoon."

"Okay. So, now that we've established that I have hurt *everyone* in this family, let me just say that if I could make this all go away, I would. But I can't. I have tried and tried. And your father and I have talked about it many times. My days of lying to him are over, and they have been for a long time now. So I hope I can be honest with you too, and you can accept me for the very flawed human being I am. I'm your mother, and I love you. I hope you can forgive me."

She got up to leave, then paused, hoping Lynn would say something to stop her. Instead, Lynn lay back down and rolled over, turning her face away from the door. Anna left, quietly closing the bedroom door behind her.

"How did it go?" Patrick asked.

"Not well. Judy knows too, by the way."

"What?"

"Yes. They saw us at the wedding today, too. I don't know what to say except that I am so very sorry, Patrick. I really messed up this time. I don't know if Lynn is ever going to get over this. She's so angry with me."

"That makes two of us." He shook his head in exasperation.

"I know. I just hope nobody else saw. It was a huge lapse in judgment. I know that now. I hope you all can forgive me at some point."

"Time. That's the only thing that heals. Time and space. They will forgive you. Their generation is different from ours. They aren't as set in their ways. Just give them time."

"I don't deserve you, Patrick."

"You're right. You don't." He got up, left the room, and went to bed.

# Chapter Forty-Five

## ANNA 1939

PATRICK HAD MADE HIMSELF for most of the next day, making excuses about errands he needed to run. Anna typically handled all of the errands for the household, so it was obviously a ruse to get out of the house, but she didn't question him, instead allowing him some space to think. For her part, Anna took time alone after lunch to walk the neighborhood, searching for answers to an unanswerable problem. Mary had called earlier in the morning while Anna was washing the breakfast dishes, asking to come over, but Anna said no. If either Patrick or Lynn saw Mary right now, it would only worsen things. As she wandered around town, deserted on a Sunday afternoon when all the shops were closed, Anna found herself in front of the Our Lady of Lourdes cemetery. As she wandered through it, she read the names in stone and said a silent prayer. She made her way to her mother's headstone for the first time in a dozen years. She had died of the Spanish flu when Anna was nineteen. She sat on a bench under the oak tree in front of Ellen Sullivan's headstone. The stems of flowers likely left by a visitor months ago lay bare at the foot of the stone. Anna stared at the marble slab, then wept and put her head in her hands.

"Oh, Momma, I've made such a mess of things. I think you would be mortified if you could see me now. Maybe you can, and maybe you are. I know you'd be just as ashamed of me as the rest of my family is. My husband will probably leave me, and at least one of your grandchildren hates me, if not both. I don't know how to make it right anymore. If I do what everyone wants me to, I deny myself the greatest love I've ever known. I'm sure you wish my husband filled that role, but that's not how it is. I don't know what I did to deserve this...this...curse! How can it be that the thing that everyone finds so appalling and disgusting about me is the thing that makes me feel the most alive? What am I supposed to do about that? I wish I could talk to you again to see if you've ever felt what I'm feeling. Probably not. I know I'm just the deviant of the family. Did you know this about me before you died, Momma? Did you know I would be such a disappointment to you? I'm sorry, Momma. I wish I could make Patrick understand how sorry I am. I never meant to hurt him. He's such a good man, and he got so unlucky the day he met me. Everyone in my life would be better off if I didn't exist." The soft weeping was now full-on sobbing, and she reached into her purse for a tissue.

"I hope you didn't mean what I just heard you say," a voice said from behind her.

Anna turned and gasped in surprise that someone had heard her confession. "Oh, my. I'm sorry. I had no idea there was anyone else here."

"Don't be sorry, dear. I shouldn't have interrupted you. I wouldn't have if not for that thing you just said. I'm Tildy Franklin. I live around the block from here and visit my husband's grave every week. He's right over there." She pointed to a headstone three plots away. She got up from her seat and came around to sit next to Anna. "Do you want to talk about it, dear?"

Anna hid her face behind her tissue, afraid to let Tildy see her. "No, thank you, Mrs. Franklin, but…"

"Please, call me Tildy. Everyone does. You're Anna, right? I saw you talking to Ellen and realized you must be her daughter. I met Ellen many years ago when we were young. I remember when you were born. Oh! She was so thrilled with you, her little Anna."

"Yes, I'm Anna, and I don't think she would be thrilled anymore."

"Oh, I find that hard to believe. Once you become a mother, there is nothing your child can do to change that sense of joy and pride."

"If you only knew, Tildy."

"Would you like to tell me?"

"No, I can't. It's too shameful. My mother would hate me if she were alive right now."

"Now, hush, Anna! I know that's not true. She would be furious to hear you say that. She could never hate you. Whatever it is, she would be loving and understanding. Maybe she died too young for you to know what a good-hearted soul she was. Nothing, I mean nothing, could make her hate you, dear."

Anna looked into Tildy's eyes, wanting to unload the burden of her troubles but holding back out of fear.

"I know you don't know me from Adam, but I can promise you that if you wanted to tell me what's bothering you, I would listen and understand just like Ellen would have done. There's absolutely nothing you could say to make me think otherwise." Tildy reached over and put her hand over Anna's. "I've got no reason to share your secret with anyone. I promise. Please, dear. It will make you feel better."

"I'm in love with someone who isn't my husband," she whispered.

"I see. Tell me more."

"It's not...it's not, er, another man. It's a woman."

Tildy nodded, taking it in. "Ah. Yes, that is a predicament. Okay, dear. Is there more?"

"Yes, but isn't that enough?"

"That's up to you, my dear. I don't know the whole story, but here's one thing I do know. You aren't the first woman in history to fall in love with another woman, and you certainly won't be the last. So let's put aside the fact that you are married for just a minute because that's a whole different ball of wax. But trust me, sweetheart. You may think you are alone in the world, but you aren't."

"Have you ever felt that way about a woman?"

"No, but that's really beside the point. I can still empathize, even if it's never happened to me. We fall in love for all sorts of reasons. Some are just more complicated than others. Let me ask you, Anna. Does this other woman know that you are in love with her?"

"Oh, yes. She feels the same. We've been...we have...we've felt this way for a very long time. Years."

"So, you've had a...uh...well, for lack of a better term, a relationship all these years?"

"Yes. I love her so. This just feels like such a curse!"

"Love is never a curse, dear. Do you think she feels like her family would be better off if she didn't exist either?"

"No. I think she's stronger than I am. She's not married, so maybe it's a little easier for her. Well, she's not married anymore, I should say. They're divorced."

"Is your relationship the reason they got divorced?"

"Mostly, yes."

"Your husband. Does he know?"

"Yes, he does. He's known for a long time now, but our daughters just found out, and that was all my fault. I was selfish and careless, and now I've ruined our whole lives."

"I see. So, I'm guessing, based on what I heard before we started talking, that they have not taken the news very well?"

"That's an understatement. My husband, bless his heart, has tolerated this for years because he knew it was something I couldn't change and he wanted me to be happy, but I think he's had just about enough of tolerating it by now. And my daughter, well...she just hates me. She's embarrassed, ashamed, disgusted, mortified...pick an adjective along those lines. I'm sure it will fit."

"How old is your daughter, dear?"

"Sixteen."

"Young still. Doesn't know the ways of the world yet. She's got a lot to learn, but she thinks she knows everything, am I right?"

"Yes, that about sums it up." Anna nodded with a slight hint of a smile.

"Well, here's something I've found after many years of living and most of those years being married. Marriage is damned hard under the best of circumstances. When we're teenagers, we're expected to choose a partner to spend the rest of our lives with, and we haven't even figured out who *we* are yet. On top of that, society imposes all these rules upon us. People can be so cruel and judgmental when they think we aren't following their rules. Just imagine if we really did 'live and let live.' Wouldn't most people be so much happier?" They both shook their heads in agreement. "Now, tell me this, Anna. In a perfect world—one that wasn't judgmental and cruel—would you and your lady friend be together?"

"Yes. We would. Happily."

"But, of course, we don't live in a perfect world, do we?"

"No, we sure don't, Tildy."

"Okay, so my advice, not that you asked for it..."

"I'm asking for it. I'll take any advice I can get."

"My advice, then, is to try to balance your happiness with the happiness of those around you. It sounds like there isn't a scenario where everyone involved will be happy. Am I right?"

"That's true."

"So, there has to be a compromise that allows each of you to get a little bit of happiness. That might not even mean happiness *right now*. If your husband, as you say, has tolerated this long enough, maybe it's time to set him free. He won't be happy about it now, but maybe this will allow him to have some happiness in the future. The same goes for you. Maybe you don't want to divorce him now, but will that give you both the freedom to be fulfilled down the road? Your daughter is angry with you now, but eventually, she will realize you can't live for her just as she can't live for you. She will likely be off and married soon. Would she want you and her dad to be unhappy for the rest of your lives? Probably not."

"Not her dad. Me? I'm not so sure. I think she wishes a lifetime of misery upon me right now."

"That's because she's hurt and doesn't understand love yet. She doesn't understand we can't control who we fall in love with. Love doesn't really care; it just happens where it is supposed to happen."

"Maybe you're right," Anna said.

"Now, I'm not saying you should get divorced just because old Tildy told you to. Not by any means. Marriage and divorce are very personal decisions. Only you can make that choice. But I think you might be stuck in the 'fix it right now' mindset. Sometimes, you have to break the bone completely before you can reset it to heal."

Anna's eyes welled again, and she dabbed at them with the tissue. "Tildy, I don't know who you are, but I think you are a very wise woman."

"No, not wise, dear. Just old. I've been through it all. My Freddy and I didn't have the perfect marriage. Not by a long shot. But we compromised, and we figured it out. I do know this, though. You aren't going to solve any problem by disappearing from this earth. Your family needs you, even if they don't realize it. A mother is the heart and soul of a family. You are Ellen Sullivan's daughter. If you are even a little bit like she was, I'm sure you are the heart and soul of *your* family."

# Chapter Forty-Six

## ANNA 1939

ANNA PREPARED A LOVELY dinner that evening, hoping to get a chance to talk to Patrick alone to see what, if anything, he wanted to do about their situation. She took Tildy's advice to heart, but wasn't sure if she could go through with it. She had to see where Patrick's head was before she made any decisions. The thought of him leaving for good filled her with dread, but maybe Tildy was right. Maybe there needed to be some sadness before any happiness could be found for them. There wasn't much joy for them in the current situation, so perhaps it was time for a drastic change.

As they sat down to dinner, Anna poured him a beer and handed him a healthy helping of his favorite meal. He didn't seem overly angry, but he was much quieter than usual. Lynn was absent, having spent the day at her friend's house, as far away from Anna as possible. Usually, that would upset Anna even more, but she needed this time to be alone with Patrick, so it was better that she stayed away. As the dinner finished, Anna cleared the plates, then broached the conversation.

"Did you talk to Lynn before she went out today, Patrick?"

"Briefly, yes."

"How is she? Is she still upset?"

"Yes. She's hurt. She's confused, and she doesn't understand any of this. I can't say I do either, but I've just had a lot more time to get used to it."

"It seems you've reached the point where you no longer want to be with me. Your days of tolerating this situation appear to be over. Am I right?"

"Well, I'd be lying if I said no. Let's face it. Things are not as they used to be. At least we still had some intimacy in the past, but now that's gone too. It feels as if all your affection goes to Mary. There is very little left over for me."

"I can see how you might feel that way. From my perspective, I guess I feel like you are so upset and disappointed with me that you don't want my affection. So maybe it's a bit of a vicious cycle. I withdraw, you get angry, I see your anger, so I withdraw even more."

"I think you may be right." Patrick folded his hands in front of him and lowered his head in sadness.

Anna reached over and put her hand on his. "Patrick, do you want a divorce? I know you aren't happy. Maybe if we cut the cord, you will find happiness with someone else in the future—a woman who isn't a complete failure as a wife. You certainly deserve that. I won't hold you back if that's what you want to do."

"Are you saying that just so you will have more time to be with Mary without worrying about me?"

"If that were the case, I would have asked you for a divorce years ago."

"Okay. Point taken. The truth is that I've been thinking maybe we should try a separation. I don't know if I'll ever be interested in another woman, so a divorce might not be necessary."

"Never say never, Patrick. Another woman might come along and sweep you off your feet." She looked at him, and he noticed she was crying, which caught him off guard.

"Why are you crying, Anna?"

"The thought of you with another woman makes me sad, but that's an extremely hypocritical and selfish point of view on my part, isn't it? I have no right, but my tears don't seem to care if I have the right or not. They have a mind of their own. I remember when we fell in love all those years ago. You made me feel so special. You've been a good husband, Patrick. Better than I deserved, but I think it's time I set you free."

"If I leave, Lynn will be even more upset with you. You realize that, don't you?"

"Yes. I do. I'm sure that, in some way, I deserve her wrath. So consider it my punishment."

"I don't want you to be punished, Anna. I want you to be happy. Why do you think I've put up with this for so long? It was because I love you, and I know that, in your way, you love me too. But I'm not her, and I never will be. So maybe we do need to separate, for both of our sakes."

Anna's tears came on stronger, and she buried her face in her hands. He reached over and put one hand on her shoulder while wiping away his tears with the other. At that moment, they both realized Lynn was standing just outside the entrance to the kitchen. Neither of them heard her come in, so there was no telling how much of the conversation she heard.

"What's going on?" she asked, with a mixture of anger and concern.

"Your mother and I are just talking about our situation."

"Oh. Well, since that's a subject I want no part of, I will leave you to it. Good ni..."

"Lynn, come in here. This impacts all of us," Patrick said forcefully.

She sighed in exasperation, then sat down next to him, staring downward to avoid Anna's gaze. "I don't want to talk about this," she snarled.

"Well then, just listen. I want you to know your mother and I love you very much. Even though I know you are angry with her, I expect you to treat your mother with the respect she deserves."

"But she doesn't..."

"That is non-negotiable, young lady. Is that understood?"

"Yes, sir."

"Good. We are working together to decide what will be best for all of us. You may not like whatever that decision may be, but it's not yours to make. Our job is to make sure you have two parents who love and care for you and will do what's best for you, regardless of whether or not you agree. And when you are out of the house in a couple of years, you can make your own decisions. Okay?"

"Yes, sir."

"And?"

"Yes, ma'am."

"Okay. You may go to your room now. Good night."

Lynn stormed out without reciprocating the good night wish.

"Thanks for not saying anything about the separation yet, Patrick."

"We will tell them when Judy gets back from her honeymoon. In the meantime, I'll start looking for a place."

# Chapter Forty-Seven

## TRISH 2000

IN JANUARY, TRISH FINALLY returned to work, having opted to take a short leave of absence between her mom's death at Thanksgiving and the New Year. Her students were so sweet upon her return. They created handmade cards for her, telling her they missed her and were sorry she was sad. She opened the cards on her lunch break and cried as she read each one. Cassie entered the teacher's lounge. Trish saw her headed her way so she dried her eyes with her lunch napkin, trying to hide her grief. It was the first time Cassie had seen her since before Thanksgiving break. Cassie looked at Trish and saw the tears in her eyes. She bent down and gave her a hug, whispering condolences. After a moment or two, Cassie was crying along with her, and they hugged each other tightly. Trish held on for as long as Cassie would have her, feeling yet another round of vulnerability. The grieving process was exhausting for Trish. Until now, Josie had been her strength, but she was on her own again at school and felt overwhelmed with sadness.

"Trish, maybe it was too soon for you to come back. You look so tired. Why don't you go home and give it another week or so?"

"I can't. Josie is back at work, so I am alone all day anyway. I'll just sit there and think and feel sad. At least here, the kids are somewhat of a distraction."

"You and Josie are very close, aren't you?"

"Yes, we are. Very close." Trish hoped Cassie was starting to see the complete picture where Josie was concerned. They had never talked about it, but Trish often alluded to their relationship in terms that made the intent clear. She just wasn't sure if the message was getting through. She was uncomfortable saying it outright at school. Cassie would probably be okay with it, but could she take that chance? In an attempt to feel her out, Trish added, "I've never been closer to anyone in my life."

"Trish, I hope you know you can trust me."

"I do, Cass. What makes you say that?"

"Because I want you to know that if there's ever anything you need to talk about, I'm here for you."

"Are you giving me a hint, Cass?"

"I'm trying to. Is it working? It's been like a year, and you haven't told me yet."

Trish smiled, then broke out into a laugh. "Do you have class now, or is this a free period?"

"I'm free. Would you like to take a walk? It's not too cold out there today. If we bundle up, it might be nice."

"I'd like that." Trish immediately became nervous. Coming out to people was not easy, no matter who it was. Telling her mother was disastrous, but telling Aunt Judy went fine. She wasn't sure which reaction she would get from Cassie. As if Cassie was reading her mind, she put her hand on Trish's arm and smiled at her. They put on their coats, hats, and scarves, and went outside to walk through the schoolyard.

"Is it safe to say you've figured this out, Cass?" Trish asked tentatively.

"I think so, but I'd still like you to tell me just in case I'm wrong."

"Okay. Here's the thing. I'm in a relationship with Josie. I haven't told anyone even remotely connected to my work life because I'm afraid of getting fired."

"They would be crazy to fire you. You're one of the best teachers we have. Those kids are lucky to have you."

"Is that your only reaction?"

"Well, since I figured it out about six months ago, this isn't news for me, but I'm still glad you told me. Does it feel good to say it out loud?"

"It does. It's quite liberating, but it's terrifying too."

"I wish you didn't feel like you needed to be scared to tell me. I'm your friend, Trish. Did you think I was going to have a problem with it?"

"I don't know. I didn't think so, but it's a risk."

"Well, there's no risk with me. With the expected exception of the last month or so, you've been happier than I've ever seen you. It's obvious you are in love."

"Really? Obvious?"

"Yes! Remember after spring break when I told you that you must have been having sex? It was written all over your face."

"Oh, I remember, all right. I was terrified you could see right through me. How could I be so transparent?"

"So, are you gonna tell me about it, or will I have to pry it out of you?"

"What would you like to know?"

"Everything! How did you meet? When did you know you had feelings? Is she the first woman you've been with? How's the sex?"

"I'll tell you what. Since it's about thirty degrees out here, how about we meet for drinks after work tonight, and I will fill you in. I'm freezing my ass off out here."

* * * *

"Bartender, can I have two shots of tequila, please?" Cassie asked when they sat down at the bar. "Stand-by. We may need you to keep 'em coming."

"Getting drunk may not be the best idea."

"Sure, it is. You're more open when you've had a few. I'll call you a cab to get you home. Or maybe we can have Josie pick you up and then I can meet her."

"Fine." Trish gulped the shot and signaled to the bartender for another. "Okay, so here's the thing. I'm in love. I mean, seriously, head over heels, I wish I could marry her, in love. It's like she's the thing I've been looking for my whole life, but I didn't know it. Now that I know, oh my god. It's fucking amazing. Why did I wait all these years? Why didn't anyone tell me it could be like this?"

"Wow, that's a lot to digest. Where did you meet her?"

"In our school! She came on career day to talk to the kids. I was immediately attracted to her, but I denied it. We went out for drinks, got to know each other, and even flirted with each other, and I still refused to see what was right in front of my face. She finally asked me to dinner, and I asked her if it would be a date. She said that was up to me. At the end of that night, she kissed me. One thing led to another, and I haven't stopped falling in love with her since."

"How romantic! I'm so happy for you. Now tell me about the sex."

"What? You want details about that?"

"Sure, of course I do."

"Well, to be honest, it's amazing. Best ever. It's nothing at all like being with a guy. She's attentive and sexy and...and...it's just incredibly erotic."

"You look like you are about to have an orgasm right here talking about it. This is so great for you, Trish. You deserve this. Are you going to move in together?"

"Eventually. We're trying not to rush it, but I'm ready. I already asked her to marry me." Trish smiled from ear to ear as she said it.

"What! Seriously? What did she say?"

"She was far too rational, and said since I was just coming out, I needed to take time to make sure this was what I wanted. So, the answer was 'not yet.' How dare she be so logical."

"Sounds like she's a smart woman." Cassie signaled for the bartender to pour two more shots. "How did your mother take the news?"

"It was a disaster at first. She was shocked and mortified. We went through a rough period, but she came around eventually, thank goodness. It would have been awful if she had died before we got a chance to reconcile. I'm grateful for the last couple of conversations I had with her about it. It gave me some peace. In the process, I discovered my grandmother was a lesbian!"

"What?" Cassie asked, shocked.

"Yep. Can you believe that? She had an affair with a woman for years that started in nineteen twenty-nine! Josie and I now call her Badass Grandma Anna."

"Maybe it's all in the genes."

"I think so. I feel like I was born this way, and now I'm finally, after fifty-four years, being honest with myself. If it weren't for being afraid to be out at school, I'd be shouting it to anyone who would listen. I'm in love with Josie Molina."

"Do you think Principal Armstrong would care? I tend to doubt it."

"It's not her I'm worried about. It's the parents. After all, I'm corrupting their children, right?"

"That's such bullshit."

"I know, but I don't think I can take the chance. I have a couple of very vocal parents in my class."

"What do you think about telling Armstrong...you know, proactively?"

"That might not be a bad idea, but is there some buried clause in the code of conduct manual that would force her to fire me if I did?"

"I guess maybe we should read that thing and find out." They both laughed.

"I'll take a look tomorrow. I think I have it buried in my desk somewhere. If there's nothing specific, I may go ahead and tell her. If nothing else, I will either get fired or feel more comfortable and less afraid of being found out." Trish reached for her fourth shot of tequila. As she put the glass back down on the bar she suddenly realized she was officially drunk. Cassie kept up with her but seemed to be holding it together better.

"Why can't I stand up on this bar and tell everyone I'm in love with Josie? Can I do that? I think I'm gonna do that." She started to get up on her chair, and Cassie pulled her back down.

"Whoa. Easy there, my friend. That's not a good idea. You'll end up falling and breaking your neck, and Josie will kill me. I hope she thinks you're cute when you're drunk."

"Why aren't you drunk, Cass? I suddenly can't feel my feet. That last one just hit me like a ton of bricks."

"I'm a bit more solid than you. What are you, a hundred pounds?"

"A hundred and twenty, smart ass. Am I slurring my words?"

"You're starting to. We need to call Josie to come and pick you up. Gimme your cell phone." Cassie scrolled through the preset numbers and found Josie's name.

"Hi, Josie. This is Trish's friend, Cassie." Trish leaned in toward her and the phone and loudly said, "Hi, baby!"

"Hi, Cassie. Is everything all right? Is Trish okay? She sounds kind of funny," Josie said.

"Yeah, well...the thing is, she's a little tipsy. Well, maybe more than a little. We've been doing some shots, and the last one seems to have thrown her over the edge."

Again, from the background, "I love you!"

"Oh, boy. That must have been a helluva shot. She sounds completely wasted. I hope you ladies are at least having fun."

"We are. She's very entertaining when she's drunk, but obviously, she can't drive home, so can you come and pick her up? I'm going to call a cab for myself. Otherwise, I would drive her."

"Sure. I'll be happy to take you home as well. Where are you?"

"We're at Mulcahy's down by the water."

"Okay, give me about twenty minutes. Maybe you should get her a cup of coffee in the meantime."

"I will, Josie. Thanks!" She hung up. "Okay, my inebriated friend. Your chauffeur is on her way. We're going to ply you with coffee while we wait. Bartender!"

"Coffee! No, I want another shot."

"No way. You're done. Four seems to be your limit. Actually three. Four is over your limit."

"I wanna marry her, Cass. I really do. Why can't I?" she said, in a whining, pleading kind of way, like a five-year-old who had been told she couldn't do something.

"Maybe someday you will be able to marry her, why don't you have a commitment ceremony for now? I know it's not the same, but at least it's something."

"I wanna go back thirty years, meet her when I'm twenty-five, and have a slew of babies with her. I never wanted to have babies before. I do now! We should adopt! Thass it! Thass what we'll do." She slurred every word and barely held her head up on the table. The bartender came over with the coffee and smiled at Cassie, entertained by the situation.

"Trish, here...drink this. You're a little old to adopt, don't you think? I hate to be the one who has to bring this to your attention, but even thirty years ago, you weren't having babies with her. That's just not how it works." Cassie laughed at her, clearly finding drunk Trish highly amusing.

Trish took a sip of the coffee, then looked at it, clearly disappointed it wasn't tequila. "Cass, have ya eva been in love? I don't think I ever have been until now."

"Yes. I have. You're right. Sometimes you think you are in love until the real thing comes along. Then you realize you had no idea."

Trish saw Josie walking toward the bar. "Speaking of the real thing, here she comes now! Hi, baby. I love you!" She threw her arms around Josie's neck, and they nearly fell over from the force of it. Josie looked at Cassie and smiled.

"Hi, hon. I see you are having a good old time, huh? Hi, Cassie. It's nice to finally meet you. I've heard a lot about you." Josie reached to shake Cassie's hand.

"I have heard tons about you, especially tonight! But, beware, she wants to go off and have babies with you."

"Babies, huh? Hmm...I think we are just a little bit past child-bearing years, sweetie. I think we need to get you home and put you to bed."

"Bed! Yesss, please take me to bed! I want you!"

Josie and Cassie burst out laughing. "Okay, missy. Now I know it's time to get you out of here. Has the check been paid, Cassie?" She nodded yes. "Great, can you grab her things, please?" Josie put her arm around Trish's waist and led her to the car. It took considerable effort from Josie and Cassie to hoist her into the backseat.

As they drove, Trish fell asleep as soon as the car started moving. Cassie and Josie took advantage of the opportunity to get to know each other a bit.

"Is this the first time you've seen her drunk, Josie?" Cassie asked.

"*This* drunk, yes. She's gotten tipsy before, but this is a first. She's going to feel like hell in the morning."

"I wish I had a tape recorder going the last thirty minutes. She was so funny. She's crazy about you, you know."

"The feeling is entirely mutual, Cassie."

"I'm glad she has you. I've never seen her this happy. It seems you two are perfect for each other. It's adorable."

"I got lucky the day I met her. She's pretty much rocked my world."

They heard a soft groan from the back seat, and Trish lifted her head. "I think I'm gonna be sick." Josie quickly pulled the car to the side of the road and helped Trish get out. She bent Trish forward at the waist and held her long blond hair back while her body took care of expelling the alcohol from her system.

"Maybe tequila isn't your drink, honey."

"Ya think?"

Cassie and Josie continued to laugh while Trish suffered the first of what was sure to be a series of consequences for her night of revelry.

* * * *

Trish rolled over and squinted at the clock, quarter after eleven. She lifted her head, then immediately put it back down again, pain piercing through her temples. She shielded her eyes from the bright sunshine beaming through the window and moaned with a mournful cry of agony and regret. Josie tiptoed into the room and sat down on the edge of the bed. She put a large mug of coffee and a bottle of aspirin on the nightstand.

"Good morning, beautiful."

"Who said it was good?" Trish growled.

"Well, the sun is shining, there is coffee and aspirin by your bedside, and the good news is that you probably won't feel any worse than you do right now. Exactly how much did you have to drink?"

"I don't remember much. It was shots, so it didn't seem like a lot until it suddenly hit me. How did I get home?"

"Wow. I didn't realize you were that far gone. I came to get you. You don't remember?" Trish shook her head. "Well, apparently, you were very entertaining. Cassie said you had a lot to say about us."

"Uh-oh. What did I say?"

"Well, you said you wanted to stand on the bar and tell everyone you were in love. You wished it was thirty years ago so you and I could have, and I quote, 'a slew of babies.'"

"Babies! What?"

"Yep."

"Did I do anything foolish?"

"Well, unless you consider puking on the side of the road foolish, then no, not really. You were adorably harmless."

"To say that I don't exactly feel adorable right now would be the understatement of the year."

"But the good news is you came out to Cassie. You've wanted to do that for a while."

"She told me she had figured it out six months ago. She was waiting for me to tell her. I guess I'm not very good at hiding it."

"Well, we knew that already." Josie leaned over and kissed her on the cheek.

Trish propped herself up to a sitting position and took a few sips of coffee. "I remember her saying she thinks I should come out to our principal in order to be proactive. What do you think about that?"

"What kind of person is she?"

"She is a good person. I think she would be fine. I just wonder if ignorance is bliss, in this case. She might have to do something about it if she knows, whereas I get to keep my job if she is clueless. You know—plausible deniability." She took another gulp, willing the coffee to make the headache disappear. "On the other hand, I just hate having to pretend you don't exist."

"Well then, if you hate it that much, I think you should tell her. If she is a good person, she will find some way to do the right thing."

Trish rolled over onto the bed and groaned miserably again. "It won't matter anyway because I'm pretty sure I'll be dead before Monday."

"I'm afraid you will just have to suffer through this. Hangovers are the gift that comes on the back end of the fun."

# Chapter Forty-Eight

## ANNA 1942

MARY KNOCKED ON ANNA'S front door, holding her umbrella close in a feeble attempt to keep away the driving rain that pelted against her raincoat. Anna ushered her in, armed with a towel to help dry her off. She removed her drenched raincoat, her galoshes, and her kerchief and left them to drip in the hallway.

"Come in, come in. You are soaked to the skin. My goodness. This is one heck of a storm. There must be three inches of rain out there!"

Mary shivered from the dampness, and Anna put her arms around her to warm her. They kissed softly, and Anna leaned in again, hoping for something more passionate. Instead, Mary pushed back, clearly not in the same mindset as Anna.

"What's wrong? You look upset."

"I'm sorry. It's not you. I'm just worried. Michael and Kevin went to the Army offices this morning to enlist. Since Pearl Harbor, they have been anxious to get overseas to join the fight. They leave for basic training in about a week, and to be honest, I'm terrified for them. I'm not sure who is worse between Japan and Germany, and the thought of my boys fighting in a war is frightening."

The sky started to crash, and the rain on the roof was drumming ominously. "I'm sorry, hon. I can't imagine how upsetting it is for you. I can't believe we are at war again. My girls are both talking about volunteering with the USO. It seems everyone wants to do their part, which is great, but it doesn't make it any less scary. I wish I could ease your fears."

"I know. The only thing that can ease any of our fears is for this nightmare to end quickly, but based on what I read in the *Times* today, that doesn't seem likely. Roosevelt thinks it's going to be a long haul with Hitler."

They made their way into the kitchen, and Anna poured some coffee and put out a pastry to go with it. Mary was still shivering, so Anna reached for her cold hands to warm them between hers. She brought them up to her lips and kissed them, and Mary closed her eyes to hold back the tears lingering at the surface. Anna moved closer to cup Mary's cheeks in her hands and leaned in for a tender kiss to comfort her.

"Let's change the subject," Mary said. "How are things with Patrick?"

"He called yesterday to say he still doesn't want to get a divorce, even though we've been separated for a while now. He said he doesn't plan to get re-married, so what's the point of divorcing. I told him that was all right with me if that's what he wanted. I think the 'til death do us part' thing is significant for him. I'm not sure what the distinction is for him, given we aren't together as husband and wife, but that's his choice. Since you and I can't get married, it doesn't matter, I suppose."

Mary asked, "And how is Lynn doing? Still got her head in the sand about you and me?"

"Yes. I've tried to talk to her about it at least a dozen times. She wants to pretend it isn't happening. She and Judy are so different! I can say practically anything to Judy, and it doesn't upset her. She just wants me to be happy. Not my Marilyn. Nope. She would rather I was miserable as long as I wasn't inflicting this shame upon her."

"I'm so happy my kids never found out. I don't think any one of them would take it well. Linda might be okay, but not my boys. Johnny did me a huge favor when he promised not to tell them."

"Oh, I forgot to tell you! Lynn and her fiancé, William, have finally set a date! They want to be married before he gets shipped overseas. He finishes his basic training next week, and they will have a small ceremony with a justice of the peace after that. I'm happy for her. It's true, she's not the easiest child in the world, but I think William is good for her. Maybe he will get her to ease up on me a bit. One can hope, at least."

"Oh, that's good news! Do you realize what else that means in the way of a nice little side benefit?" Mary winked at Anna.

"What?"

"With Patrick in his apartment and the girls married, you will have your house to yourself. We'll be able to spend more time together. Maybe we could even spend the night together whenever Linda goes off to one of her sleepovers with her friends. Can you imagine that? In all these years, I have never been able to wake up next to you."

"That seems almost too good to be true. Since Patrick left, I look over at the space beside me in the bed, and I want you to be there with me. To fall asleep with you without having to set the alarm in order to ensure someone doesn't come home to find us. That would be bliss."

Anna's gaze trailed off into the distance, and her expression changed to one of sadness.

"What is it, love?" Mary asked.

"I just get tired of this always being so hard!"

"We knew when we started this that we were destined for a life of secrets and hiding. I'm surprised Patrick put up with us for as long as he did, quite frankly."

"Do you think in a hundred years from now, things will have changed?" Anna asked.

"I doubt it, sadly. I don't think we will ever be accepted, but remember that in three years, Linda will have graduated and will probably be out of the house. Would it be a pipe dream to think that we could live together after that? We could move to a new town and tell people we are sisters. No one needs to know the truth. I've heard about some women doing that."

"Where would you have heard something like that?"

"I was sitting in the beauty parlor a few months ago, and these ladies were gossiping about a couple of women they knew who lived together. One of them said they were sisters, but the other said, 'I'll bet they are just a couple of those lesbian types who are pretending!' Of course, they said it in this awful, derogatory tone and the other women looked horrified at the thought, but in a new town, that could work, don't you think?"

"Yes, but that means moving away from our kids and grandkids," Anna replied.

"Well, we could either make sure it's only a train stop away, or one of us could learn to drive. Oh, wouldn't that be fun!" Mary exclaimed, with a look of both excitement and determination on her face.

"You realize, of course, that you would have to tell your kids if we did that. They would never understand why we are living together otherwise."

"Why not? Two single women trying to combine expenses to save money. I think it makes total sense. Can you imagine how wonderful it would be to finally live the life we've wanted all these years?"

"Maybe I'm just not as optimistic as you are. There has not been one day of our lives together where I thought we would be able to live openly and honestly. I think I will always feel like an abnormal freak in the eyes of the world."

"Well, I'm not ready to give up on our dreams just yet. I can't. It makes this life too hard, and I have to have something to hold onto.

Anna, I've been in love with you for over thirteen years. I feel the same, if not more now than I did back then. I have to believe you and I will have some kind of a life together one way or another. A happy ending."

"I know, honey. We *do* have a life. A beautiful life, and I don't regret a minute of it. It's just not the same as the life everyone else gets to live, and that weighs on me sometimes." She let go of Mary's hand when she heard the key in the front door lock. Lynn shook off the rain and made her way into the kitchen.

"Oh, hello, Mrs. Monahan," she said rather coldly.

"Hello, Lynn. So lovely to see you! I heard you and William have set a date. That's terrific news. Where are you going to live after the wedding?"

"The army will house us at Fort Hamilton when he gets shipped out."

"Lynn, have you made your guest list for the wedding yet?" Anna asked.

"Mom, are you fishing for information about whether I'll be inviting Mrs. Monahan?" She pointed across the table at Mary. "The answer is no."

"Lynn! How dare you be so rude."

"Rude? You think I'm rude? What about what you two have done to both of our families? Now that's rude!"

"Go to your room, Lynn. Your insolence is appalling."

"Mom, I'm eighteen years old. I don't have to do what you tell me anymore. I don't have to be nice to anyone if I don't want to. My opinion doesn't seem to matter to you, so your opinion doesn't matter to me anymore." Lynn stormed out of the kitchen, put her rain gear back on, and left in a huff.

"Ouch," said Mary. "She's cold! That kid can hold a grudge like nobody's business. She's never going to forgive us, is she?"

"Well, it's me she won't forgive. You only get the attitude when you happen to be here. I get it all day, every day. I never thought she and I would have such a contentious relationship. It breaks my heart. I'm so sorry she treated you that way."

"It's all right. You didn't expect her to invite me, did you?"

"Maybe I was holding out hope that she was coming around, but clearly, I was mistaken. So now do you see why I don't think we could ever live openly and honestly? If I can't get my daughter to accept me, how on earth do we expect anyone else will?"

# Chapter Forty-Nine

## PATRICK 1944

PATRICK LEFT WORK AT the warehouse and slowly walked the crowded street. Even at his unhurried pace, he made his way down the avenue faster than the cars stuck in traffic. Construction crews worked on a water leak in the middle of the roadway, prompting car horns and hot tempers. He wasn't ready to shut himself into his lonely apartment for the weekend, so he went into the local pub, hoping for someone to talk to besides himself. The place was bustling with harried laborers blowing off steam from a hard day's work. His eyes needed time to adjust to the dark and smoky atmosphere, so glaringly unlike the bright sunlight on the street. As he made his way to the only available seat at the bar, he signaled to the barkeep for a beer. Sitting down, he looked to his right and noticed the fellow next to him. Possibly the only man on earth who knew what he had endured, he tapped Johnny on the shoulder and reached out to shake his hand. Johnny smiled the kind of smile that betrayed his actual state of mind—an 'I'm happy to see you but not so happy overall' type of grin.

"Johnny, my friend. How are you? Geez, it's been forever since I've seen you."

"Hey, Patrick. Good to see you. Yeah, it has been a long time. Probably since I left Mary, which is what, four years now? How've you been? Are you still with Anna?"

"We've been separated for a long time, but not divorced. Guess I don't want to sever the tie completely for some reason. Don't ask me why. It's silly, right?"

"If you are holding out hope, I think you're gonna waste a lot of precious time. Those two will not change, no matter how much heartache they cause."

"I know, I know. Maybe I just don't like the idea of being divorced."

"You need to find yourself another woman, Patrick. Our wives didn't hesitate to do that, did they?"

"Did you find another woman?"

"I've found a few. Just none that I want to marry. Maybe I'm better off alone. I've lost my desire to invest my heart into a relationship. She knocked the wind out of me long ago, ya know?"

"Your boys are overseas in the war now, right?"

"Yes. The last I heard, Michael was somewhere in Italy, and Kevin was in Germany. It's been a while since I've gotten a letter from either of them and that weighs pretty heavily on me these days." The bartender took away his empty beer mug and replaced it with another.

"I can't imagine. My girls are volunteering for the USO, and Judy's husband is also in Europe. Everyone I know is worried about someone who may never come back home. Strange times we live in. I'll be praying for your boy's safe return."

"Thanks. Do you see much of Anna and Mary these days?"

"I stop by when something needs fixing, or we need to talk about the girls, but other than that, I stay away. Mary is almost always there when I come over. They are practically living together now."

"It's so sickening. I don't understand them at all."

"They can't help it, Johnny. It's like a disease."

"I don't believe that for a minute." Johnny swigged the rest of his beer and signaled to the bartender for another. His voice was rising, the alcohol getting the better of him. "I think they are just perverted, and they've got you believing it's some epic love affair. It's bullshit if you ask me. Bartender, gimme a shot of whiskey with a beer chaser, will ya?"

"We probably just need to agree to disagree on this point." Patrick studied him, watching his demeanor change. "Hey, Johnny, maybe you've had enough. How about we get you home?"

"I'm fine. I don't need any help. As I said, I'm perfectly happy on my own."

"Well, if you don't mind me saying so, you don't seem fine." Patrick signaled to the bartender to hold off on any more drinks.

"Actually, I do mind, Patrick. It's none of your business. Just leave me alone, okay? You and our dyke wives can fuck off, as far as I'm concerned!" Heads turned in their direction, the crowd's attention now focused on them.

"Okay, Johnny."

Johnny lowered his head, immediately regretting the outburst. "Hey, Patrick. I'm sorry."

"Don't worry about it, okay? How about you let me help you home." He stood up, threw a dollar bill on the bar, and helped Johnny up from his stool. They left the smoke-filled room and stepped outside, their eyes readjusting again, this time to the sunlight. "Where do you live, Johnny?"

"Just down this street. It's not far." Patrick held his arm steady, ensuring Johnny didn't stumble in front of all the neighbors on his block. As they approached the apartment building, Patrick noticed two military officers standing out front, waiting for someone to come in or out of the building. He and Johnny ascended the steps about halfway when one of the officers spoke.

"Sir, excuse me. Are you John Monahan?"

Johnny turned around, noticing them for the first time. Uniformed officers at the door during wartime meant only one thing. So Johnny kept going up the stairs, refusing to acknowledge them. If he didn't answer, then it couldn't happen.

Patrick grabbed him by the arm, preventing him from walking into his building for a moment.

"Officers, can we do this inside, please?" Patrick asked.

"Yes, sir. Is this Mr. Monahan?"

Patrick nodded in the affirmative and released his grip on Johnny so he could enter the building. As he fumbled for the keys, Patrick took them from his trembling hands and opened the door, escorting them inside. One of the officers reached into the inside pocket of his uniform and pulled out a telegram. He held it out to Johnny, who refused to take it. Instead, he turned his back on the officers and sat on his sofa, head in his hands.

"Patrick, read it, please," he said.

Patrick took the paper, read it to himself, then sat down next to Johnny, a hand on his shoulder.

"It's Michael. I'm so sorry, Johnny."

"Read it!"

"Okay.

'The Secretary of War expresses his deepest regret that your son, Second Lieutenant Michael Monahan, was killed in action on the 15th of February 1944 in Italy in the performance of his duty and service to his country.'

Patrick folded the telegram and set it on the table in front of Johnny. "Officers, is there anything else you need from us?"

"No, sir. We are deeply sorry for your loss. We will inform you of the return of his body via another telegram in a few days." And with that, they turned and left the building.

Patrick stood up and paced the floor, unsure what to do to console him. He knew they needed to inform Mary, but didn't know how to broach that subject. So even though Johnny was still somewhat drunk, Patrick went to the liquor cart and poured him a shot of whiskey.

"Here." He held the glass out to Johnny, who grabbed it and downed it immediately. "Johnny, we need to go tell Mary."

"I know. I'd rather die myself than give her this news. It is going to destroy her. I know I act as though I hate her, but despite everything, she was a good mother to the kids, and they love her so much. Loved. Michael. Loved. Oh my god." He put his head in his hands and sobbed uncontrollably. Patrick sat next to him, wrapped his arms around him, and let Johnny's head fall onto his shoulders. Patrick allowed him to release all the anger, disbelief, and grief into him as if he could take some of it from him—for him. He thought of his daughters and the anguish he would feel if his world had just fallen out from under him as it had for Johnny on this day. An hour ago, they shared a beer, bemoaning their wives and ex-wives. Johnny's entire family structure had been irrevocably altered until the end of his days.

He lifted his head off Patrick's shoulder and wiped his eyes and nose with his sleeve. Patrick searched the room for tissues but found none, so he pulled a clean handkerchief from his pocket. "I'm going to call Anna to see if Mary is there, okay? I'll walk you over, and we will tell them together, okay?"

"Okay. I don't think I can get the words to come out, Patrick. How can I tell her that her little boy is gone?"

"If you can't, I will do it for you." Patrick went to the phone and dialed his former home phone number.

"Hi, Anna. It's me. Yes, I'm okay, thanks...actually, not really. Is Mary there with you? Okay, good. Stay put, all right? I'm on my way over." He hung up before Anna could ask any more questions. "Do you need a few more minutes? Maybe another drink?"

"No more whiskey. It's not helping. Let's go."

* * * *

Patrick walked slowly with Johnny, letting him set the pace. The slow walk was a delaying tactic, even though the events to come were inevitable. Johnny kept his head low, avoiding eye contact with the neighbors on the avenue. It was the first warm spring day, and the streets were crowded with folks tired of being confined in their homes for the winter. Patrick thought about the peculiar way things happen in life. Why would he run into Johnny today, of all days? Years had passed since they last spoke. Was he meant to be there by some twist of fate?

He was forever bound to Johnny like no other man on this earth could ever be. Of course, both would argue that it is not a bond they wished to share, but nevertheless, there it was. Was it destiny that brought them together today?

Patrick was about to knock on the door when Anna opened it to greet them. She saw Johnny with him, and the look of shock on her face was profound. Mary stepped from behind Anna with the same incredulous face, seeing Johnny with tears in his eyes.

"Johnny, what's happened?" Mary practically whispered, afraid to hear the answer. Johnny pushed through the doorway and pulled Mary into him, crying out Michael's name.

"Michael! Oh God, how could you take Michael from us? He's gone, Mary. Our boy is gone." They held each other so tightly, weeping in unison and calling his name. Patrick and Anna hugged and cried, too, feeling grief through osmosis. Words failed. Johnny had to hold Mary up and carry her inside to the sofa. Her body simply refused to participate. Anna feared she had fainted and ran for a glass of water and a cool rag. Johnny knelt by her side, his head buried in her chest. Anna returned and put the rag on Mary's head while Patrick had a hand on Johnny's shoulder for support. He quietly wept while Mary drifted off into a state of shock. Her crying had stopped for the moment, her eyes blearily focused on the ceiling, and she did not—could not—speak. Her breathing was inconsistent, her lungs unsure when to interrupt to ask her to inhale. Anna tried to offer her the water, but she had drifted onto another plane, not seeing or hearing anyone in the room.

Anna reached for Patrick's arm and led him into the kitchen. She whispered, "How did Johnny find out about Michael? Why are you with him? Did he call you? Don't get me wrong, I'm glad you were, but I'm bewildered."

"Believe it or not, I ran into him in the bar where he was in the process of getting drunk and mean. So, I walked him home. The officers met us at his door and gave us the telegram. He was killed in Italy about a month ago. Johnny has the telegram in his pocket. It was just pure luck that I happened to be with him. He could barely walk, so it was fortuitous I was there to help him get over here. It almost seems like someone was watching over him."

"Oh my. Divine intervention, maybe?"

"If there is such a thing, then yes, I would say so. But still, I feel so incredibly helpless. If all I can do for them is walk him over here, that's not very much. My god, the agony they must be feeling especially knowing that Kevin is still over there!" Patrick started to weep again, and Anna put her arms around him in a feeble consolation attempt.

Mary suddenly sat up, regaining a measure of self-control, and spoke to Johnny. "We have to tell Linda. She went over to her friend Dorothy's house after school today. How are we going to tell her, Johnny?" The desperation in her voice broke the other three hearts in the room. "What will we say? She idolizes Michael. I saw her writing to him again just last night."

Johnny wiped his eyes and nose with the handkerchief that Patrick had given him earlier. He got up off his knees and sat next to Mary on the sofa. His arms enveloped her while he tried to find the words. "We will find some way, Mar. She's not a little girl anymore. Every time she writes him a letter, she says she knows he may never read it, but it will certainly crush her, as it is crushing us. We have to be ready for that." He rocked her gently in his arms and kissed her forehead as he spoke.

\* \* \* \*

Johnny and Mary left together for Mary's house to break the news to Linda. Patrick and Anna sat stunned, unable to comprehend what this meant for Mary and Johnny. Anna did not even get to speak to Mary, much less console her before they left. Instead, she intentionally stepped back to let her and Johnny grieve together first. In time, their shared experience as parents would be healing for them. For today, though, there was nothing but pain.

As Patrick and Anna sat on their sofa with Anna's head on his shoulder, the front door opened, and Lynn came in, shuffling along with her very pregnant belly. She stopped in surprise as she entered the living room, first at seeing her father, who would not usually be there, and second at seeing her parents embracing.

"Hi, Daddy. I didn't expect to see you here. What's going on? Are you two getting back together or something?" She smiled in hopefulness.

"No, Lynn. I'm afraid not. We got some bad news today. Mary and Johnny's son Michael was killed in action. I was with Johnny when he got the news, so we came over here together."

"Oh, my god. That's so awful. I always liked Michael. He was nicer to me than Kevin was when we were kids. I even had a crush on him when I was about twelve. What a tragedy! Isn't Kevin still overseas?"

"Yes, he is. I can't even imagine what they will do if he dies too."

"How are Mr. and Mrs. Monahan doing? My goodness, they must be absolutely brokenhearted."

"That they are, kiddo. That they are," Patrick responded.

"Does Linda know yet?"

"They left a little while ago to tell her."

Lynn sat on the chair next to the sofa and looked closer at her mother. "Mom, are you okay?"

Anna looked up, genuinely shocked that Lynn was suddenly interested in her well-being. She gave the question due consideration to encourage more dialogue with Lynn. "Well, if I'm completely truthful, I'm quite upset about it. All I can think of is my reaction—our reaction," she pointed back and forth between Patrick and herself, "if we were to get news like this about you or Judy. I'm not sure I could go on, truth be told. I know that's what Mary and Johnny are feeling right now, and I just feel so helpless."

"Is there anything I can do for you?" Lynn asked with obvious concern.

"No, sweetheart, but thank you for asking." Anna thought about saying something like, 'it's nice to have you caring about my well-being again,' but she thought better of it. *Let's let that sleeping dog lie,* she thought to herself. Maybe the ice was melting thanks to Lynn's impending motherhood.

Patrick put his arm around Anna again, and she returned her head to his shoulder. "Anna, do you want me to stay over tonight? You might not want to be alone. I can stay in the spare room. I just thought you might like the company. This is not the time to be alone and sad."

"I think I would like that. I can make us some dinner." She raised her voice to get the attention of Lynn, who had gone into the other room. "Lynn, can you stay and eat, or do you need to get home to William?"

"I can't stay. I just came to pick up that baby stuff from the attic, but if you need me, I suppose I could call him."

"No, honey. We will be fine. You go be with your husband."

# Chapter Fifty

## MARY 1944

MARY KNELT ON THE small kneeling bench in the pew in Our Lady of Lourdes church, staring off into space. It was deserted, except for an altar boy who was tidying up after Sunday service. She tried to pray, but no words came to her. She inhaled the smell of the burning candles and listened to the echo of the altar boy's movement while her fingers fumbled with the edges of the paper from the telegram that she clutched.

*The Secretary of War expresses his deepest regret...*

The words tumbled in her mind as she tried, yet again, to absorb them. The subsequent telegram they'd received days later informed them of Michael's homecoming. He would be buried with full military honors the following Friday. Kevin had been granted several days' leave to return home to say goodbye to his twin. He would arrive on Thursday. If not for the details that needed to be handled, Mary would have been unable to get out of bed. Johnny had been staying at the house in Michael's bed, his attempt at feeling closer to his son in those first few days of crippling grief. His company both soothed and saddened her. Michael and Kevin looked so much like their father. Each time Johnny came into the room, she saw her son with a face that would have been his in twenty years if he hadn't been taken from them.

She thought of this and so many other things as she knelt in the church. The sound of the massive cathedral doors opening and high-heeled footsteps approaching brought her focus back into the present. Without even looking back, she knew the footsteps were Anna's. Mary sat back up and lifted the kneeling bench out of Anna's way. Anna crossed herself, kissed her rosary beads, and entered the pew next to her. It was the first time they had been alone since they got the news. Anna reached for Mary's hand and clutched it tightly, hoping the gesture would convey what words could not.

Mary and Anna sat together in silence. There was no longer any noise in the church except for the bells tolling on the half-hour. The tears came and went on Mary's face, and Anna wished she could say something—anything at all—to stop them.

Mary spoke first. "I've missed you."

"I've missed you so much, Mary. I can't imagine what you are going through. I wish I could be the one to comfort you through this. Has Johnny been helping you?"

"Yes, he's been great. Surprisingly great. It's just terrible that it took something so tragic to get us to be civil to each other, but it's not the same as leaning on you. I want to just fold myself into you and cry until there is nothing left. When can I do that, Anna? Ever?"

"Yes, I promise. Soon. After the funeral, we will find some time to be alone, and you can cry on me for as long as you need to. In the meantime, so many people want to help you through this. Take comfort from them. Kevin will be home in a few days, right?"

"Yes, on Thursday. I don't even know how to help him through this. It's like he's lost a limb. He and Michael would finish each other's sentences. He's going to be inconsolable." Mary stood and left the church pew from the opposite side of Anna. She walked up to the altar and stared at the statue of the Virgin Mary with baby Jesus in her arms. Anna remained seated, unsure whether to follow her or let her be, but Mary answered the question for her by looking back and signaling she wanted Anna to join her. She put her arms around Mary's shoulders and led her to the candles, where they put their hands together on the long matchstick and lit the very first votive in the top row. Anna looked at Mary and said, "To Michael. May he rest in eternal peace. Amen."

A door from behind the altar opened, and the priest walked down the steps to meet them. He motioned for them to sit in the pew just in front of the candles. He turned toward the votive they'd lit, bowed his head in prayer, then turned back toward them in the pew.

"Mary, on behalf of the entire congregation, please let me offer my condolences for the terrible loss you've suffered. God is surely watching over him and your family during this time."

"Forgive me, Father, but I'm not sure God is here right now," Mary said rather sharply. "I've been a believer all my life, but at this dark moment, there is no God for me."

"Mary, it's completely normal for you to feel angry at God, but..."

"I'm not angry, Father. I'm just alone. There are no prayers that will console me, no masses or sermons that can give me the answers I need. I will find them on my own, somehow. Or I won't, but either way, God is not here. God is not anywhere. Please, spare me the 'only God knows why He has chosen to take Michael from us' speech. It doesn't help, and it's just something you say to placate those that are grieving." She turned to leave the church. Anna followed, but looked back at the priest and mouthed an 'I'm sorry' to him.

Outside the church doors, Mary stood stock still as the bells overhead chimed to announce the noon hour. She squinted her eyes and pointed them toward the sun, allowing the intensity of the light to envelope her and blur her vision. As Anna exited the building, she stood behind Mary, unsure where to go from here—literally and figuratively. Again, Mary decided for her by turning back toward her.

"I'm going home, Anna. I will see you soon. Good-bye." Mary walked toward the street to hail a taxicab.

# Chapter Fifty-One

## MARY 1944

A MOURNFUL WHISTLE SOUNDED in the distance as Mary and Johnny stood on the station platform waiting for Kevin's train to arrive. They held each other's hands as if to prevent each other from falling over. There was a sense of relief for his impending arrival, but the reason for his return drastically overshadowed it. Kevin's face, identical to Michael's, stepped out of the train car and caught Mary's eye. She held tighter to Johnny's strong hand, caught off guard by the contrasting levels of sorrow and joy that overcame her. Kevin bear hugged her, holding her as close as possible as they cried together. When Mary finally released him, he repeated the process with his father. No words had been spoken yet, as none were needed. Sorrow and joy.

They left the station quickly, the happy homecomings of the other soldiers too much for any of them to bear. The previous day, Johnny had gone to the station to see the coffin off the train and to the mortuary. That experience made him just as eager to leave the station on this day as it did the day before. His face was pale, almost gray. His eyes were bloodshot from lack of sleep and too many tears. Kevin put his arm around him as they walked from the platform, offering strength to his heartbroken father. Finally, in the car on the way home, Mary broke the silence.

"The neighbors have been taking care of the food for us these last couple of days. I hope you are hungry because there is so much of it. And more will come tomorrow."

"I haven't had much of an appetite, Mom. I feel sort of detached from my body, so things like food and sleep are of no consequence to me right now, but still, it's nice of the neighbors to think of us. How is everyone? How's my baby sister? How is Anna, Mom?"

Johnny flinched briefly at the mention of her name, but made a good show of hiding it for Kevin's sake.

"She's fine, dear. Thanks for asking. She's upset for all of us and wishes she could do something." She took a breath and sighed before continuing. "But there's nothing to be done, is there? This is just something we must find some way to live through for the sake of our family. As for Linda, she is at the house and anxious to see you. We've been getting so many deliveries of food and flowers that she decided to stay home to receive them."

"I have some good news among all this heartache. I'm being transferred stateside and out of combat. Since our family has already lost a son, the Army says they want to get me out of harm's way, so I will report to Fort Hamilton on Monday."

Johnny pulled the car over to the side of the road. Mary's mouth dropped open, but she was unable to say anything in response.

"I was thinking on the train that I'm so happy I will never have to look another Nazi in the eye again, but then I started thinking. Why did my brother have to die to make that happen? He's my fucking twin! So how could I possibly be happy about that? What's wrong with me? What would Michael think? He'd be ashamed of me!" Finally, he broke down crying, his head lowered to his knees in uncontrolled grief.

Mary listened to her firstborn son bawling like a child, blaming himself for the shred of happiness that had come his way in the middle of unthinkable turmoil. Finally, she turned in her seat, put her hand on his shoulder, and thought about what she needed to say to him.

"Kevin James Monahan, look at me!" The increased volume in her voice startled both of them. He looked up at her sheepishly. "Your brother would be thrilled that you have been pulled from combat duty. If you think for even a second that he would be ashamed of you, then all of that twin intuition that you two claimed you had all these years was just a bunch of bullshit. If you know your brother at all, then you'd know he could never be ashamed of you. He would want you home and safe! The news that you are stateside is fantastic. It's the best thing I've heard in a very long time, and it's a tiny sliver of light in this dark place that we have found ourselves in. I don't ever want to hear you talk like that again. Do you hear me?"

Kevin was so startled, so utterly shocked that not only had she raised her voice to him, but she even *cursed* at him, he started laughing. He looked at Johnny, who also started laughing. Eventually, Mary joined them, willing to poke fun at herself for her uncharacteristic outburst. The laughter through their tears was the ultimate microcosm of everything they were feeling and thinking. Sorrow and joy.

# Chapter Fifty Two

## MARY 1944

MARY OPENED HER EYES in the darkened bedroom and looked at the clock. Three-thirty in the morning. She tossed for a few minutes, trying to resettle, but realized sleep was not in the cards in the small hours of this Saturday morning. The funeral on the previous day had been a celebration of Michael's short life, and she thought, *well, that's what he would have wanted.* The prospect of going on without her son was daunting, but for his sake—and for Kevin and Linda's—she had no choice. Then she thought of Anna. Her dear Anna, who had tried so desperately to be of comfort to Mary in these last few days, but who had to remain on the outside looking in for obvious reasons. She longed for Anna's arms around her, whispering in her ear that everything would be okay. Not today, but someday.

As she lay in bed, she heard the sound of rustling in the kitchen. She threw on her robe and slippers and made her way to see what was happening. Kevin stood at the sink holding the coffee pot under the faucet as if to clean it, but he seemed frozen in thought, his hands and the pot under the running water but not moving. She waited for him to snap out of it so as not to startle him. She made an exaggerated shuffling sound upon nearing the sink. She gently guided him out of the way and took the coffee pot from his hands to clean it for him. He smiled and sat down.

"Why are you up so early, honey?" she asked.

"Same reason you are, I'll bet. I don't sleep much. It feels like part of me is missing, and I won't sleep until I find it. I hope that passes soon, or I'll be catatonic before long. What about you?"

"I guess it's the same, but I hadn't been wise enough to give it a name like you just did. A part of me is missing. There's nothing I can do to fix that. It's like, I close my eyes, wishing I'm fine, even though I know I'm not this time." She got up to lower the flame on the percolating coffee pot. "Do you want to talk about him?"

"No."

"Do you want to tell me about the war? Or is that too painful too?"

"I don't know if I can yet. I think I need to make more sense of it before discussing it in any detail. Otherwise, I will sound like a madman. These kids who are lining up so enthusiastically to enlist, just like Mike and I did...they have no idea what they are in for. Sure, we all want to serve our country, but it's not anything like we all think it is. It's twenty-four hours a day of destruction and loss and fear and anger and...it's just...everything. Everything horrible all rolled up into one experience. I'm trying not to think about what it was like during Michael's last moments. I just hope it was quick."

"They told me it was, but they probably say that to all the families. So we're better off not knowing. It can't change the outcome, can it?"

"Unfortunately, not." He fidgeted in his seat. "Hey, can we change the subject, please? How are things with you and Dad? You seem to be getting along okay."

"We're helping each other through this. We have a common goal. You and Linda are our mutual priority."

"What about Anna?"

Mary suddenly got nervous. "Um...what...what about her?"

"Mom." He tilted his head toward her in an 'I'm not as naïve as you think' kind of way. "Do you think I didn't know Anna is the reason you and Dad got divorced?"

"What? What are you talking about?" She lowered her gaze and her hands began to shake.

"Mom, c'mon. I'm not a kid anymore. Can you be honest with me, please?"

Mary stood up, hoping stepping away from the table would give her a moment to think. She was entirely unprepared to come out to Kevin, and she wasn't even sure he was telling her that he knew. Sweat began to form on her upper lip, and she shuddered as she paced.

"Mom. Come sit down and talk to me. You look like you've seen a ghost. It's me. I'm your son, and I love you. I know what's happening."

"What...what is it that you...um, that you think you know?" She sat back down, still refusing to look him in the eye.

"Okay. Do you need me to say it? Maybe it's too hard for you to say the words. I know it's a very personal thing to talk about."

"Um..."

She could see he was staring her in the eyes, but she was too embarrassed to meet his gaze.

"I know that you and Anna are lovers."

Mary gasped. "Oh my god, Kevin. Do you? How? How did you find out?" Her breathing became ragged, and her hands began to shake in fear.

"It's obvious. I'd have to be blind not to see it. It's in the way you look at each other, how you speak to each other. You have a language with your eyes. Dad gets visibly twitchy whenever he hears her name. I've never seen two people more in sync with each other than you and Anna."

"How...how long have you known?"

"Years. Several years. Michael knew too. We discussed it. I'm not saying we weren't a bit confused and taken aback when we first figured it out, but we both decided that in the end, we just wanted you to be happy. It's obvious she does that for you. I'm not stupid. I know how people can be, so it's no great mystery why you've had to keep it a secret. Folks in this neighborhood would have a field day with this, so I get it, but don't you think it's time we were at least honest with each other?"

"I'm just...stunned. Speechless. I thought you would hate me if you knew."

He reached across the table and took her hands in his. "Hate you? How could I hate you?"

"Oh, believe me, sweetheart. People in my 'situation' are hated by their families more often than not. There's not much acceptance for people like me. Most people think we are depraved, horrible human beings. We could even be arrested for it. Did you know that?"

"Yes, I do know that, and I don't understand it. You aren't hurting anyone. Why would you belong in jail? I've been off fighting a war. A war that's all about hatred. I just don't have the energy to fight against love, Mom. In perspective, with what I've been through, it's just not worthy of a fight."

"That's a very mature way of looking at it, dear, but I think your father and Patrick and Lynn would argue differently about who we are hurting."

"Well, Dad and Mr. O'Brien, I can understand, because it was their marriage that was impacted, but Lynn too?"

"Yes. She has given Anna so much trouble over it. She refuses to accept it. Instead, she's rude and nasty to both Anna and me. It's causing Anna such heartache. Now maybe you can see why I never told you kids. The thought of you feeling that way about me was unbearable."

"Well, that surprises me, but I'm not Lynn, Mom. And I love you no matter what."

"Does your father know that you know about this?"

"I don't think so. We've never discussed it. Maybe Mike did, but I doubt it. He would have told me because it's probably not a conversation that would have been an easy one. Dad's pretty set in his ways. I think I know how he feels about it."

"To say that he is unhappy about it is an understatement."

"Yeah, I figured as much, but putting him aside for a moment. Do you want to tell me about you and Anna?" He stood up to grab the coffee pot and filled both of their cups. When he finished, he leaned against the counter and waited for Mary to respond.

"I'm a little embarrassed, I guess. I never expected to be discussing this with you. Is there something specific that you would like to know?"

"Well, for one thing...when did it start?"

"I'm ashamed to say that it was a very long time ago. We were both still married and living with our husbands and you kids. I'm not proud of that fact. I want you to know that, Kevin. I just didn't know any other way. We tried for a long time to ignore what we felt, but it was no use."

"Okay, so when? Define 'a very long time ago.'"

"Almost fifteen years ago."

"Wow. You weren't kidding. That must have been a tough time for you."

She lowered her head, recalling those first few months and the anguish she and Anna went through, trying to ignore the intensity of what they were feeling for each other. "It was. But it was also..." She paused.

"What, Mom?"

"I'm not sure if I should say. It might be uncomfortable for you."

"I'm a big boy. I think I can handle just about anything that doesn't involve losing my twin brother."

"I was going to say it was also...lovely. I felt something for her that I had never felt before, and it was lovely. It still is. I'm sorry if that's upsetting for you, Kevin. It's not lost on me that it is hard for you to hear your mom talk about her love for someone that isn't your dad."

"It's okay. And for what it's worth, I think Dad has finally started to move on. So maybe there is someone out there in his future who can make him happy too."

"I hope so. I honestly never intended to hurt him. I know I have, but I never meant to."

"So, what does the future hold for you and Anna?"

"Probably no different than the present. We hide our true selves from everyone in our lives, and we try to find time to be alone when it doesn't make anyone suspicious. It's what we've done since day one, and I don't see that changing any time soon."

"Have you thought about moving to a different town and living together as sisters? No one would need to know, and in a new place, no one knows your history."

"I suggested the very same thing to Anna, but the idea of moving away from you and Linda is very difficult for me."

"Who knows where I will end up living once I get out of the army? With any luck, I'll get married, then anything could happen. The same goes for Linda. Mom, you can't live your life for us."

"Sweetheart, I've been doing that for fifteen years. I don't know how to do anything else."

"Well, maybe you should try. Sooner or later, Linda and I are going to have to break away from you and Dad. So I wouldn't blame you if you took that opportunity to do something for yourself that would make you happy." His sincerity was evident, and it touched Mary deeply.

"You are a wonderful son, Kevin. Your brother is watching over you, and he is proud. I'm certain of it." Mary's eyes watered.

"Well, you raised me. If I'm a good son, it's because of you. And Dad. He had a tiny bit to do with it." He smiled at the joke made at his father's expense.

\* \* \* \*

Anna browsed Marconi's Market aisles, searching for a spice she needed for a recipe she was planning to try the next time she cooked for her and Mary. Standing in front of the herbs, she heard a voice calling her name. She turned to see Kevin approaching her with a smile on his face. He looked tired and skinny, and his hair was closely cropped in his Army buzz cut. She smiled a knowing smile at him—one that said sorrow and joy. He came close to her and wrapped his arms tightly around her, feeling her warmth and love.

She put her hands on his cheeks and said, "Kevin, I'm so glad to see you. I didn't want to interrupt when I saw you at the funeral. My goodness, the Army sure has made a man out of you, I see. You look so much older than the last time you were home. I won't bother asking how you are because that's a stupid question and I already know the answer, but I want you to know that I'm so sorry for your loss. I loved Michael, and I love you too. If there is anything at all I can do to ease your pain, please tell me, and I will do it."

His eyes welled up with moisture as he responded. "Actually, I think maybe there is something you can do. Do you mind if we take a walk and talk in private for a bit?"

"Of course, dear." She finished the purchase of her spices, and they walked outside onto the busy sidewalk. Anna could tell that he wasn't kidding when he said 'private' because he didn't start talking until they were in the park, away from the crowd. The cherry trees were just beginning to bloom, and their pink flowers were blowing in the breeze as they sat on a bench.

"How are you, Kevin...really?" she said once they were settled.

"I am...coping, I guess. That's probably the best word for it. I'm just taking it one minute at a time. Some are good, and most are not so good."

"That's to be expected, I suppose. Your mother told me you are stateside now. She is so relieved; I can't even tell you!"

"So am I, Anna. So am I. If I never see Germany again, that will be perfectly fine with me."

"I'm sure. So, tell me, what did you want to talk to me about?"

"It's about my mom. She and I had a long talk this morning. I told her I know about you and her. I've known for a long time. Michael knew too. And I also told her that it's okay. I'm good. I want her to be happy. She's happy when she's with you; I can see that."

Her voice quivered as she responded. "Oh, my, Kevin. Forgive me. You've caught me completely off guard. I...I had no idea you knew. I don't think she did either."

"She didn't," he said.

"How did you find out?"

"We just figured it out. All the signs are there if you're paying attention. It's obvious...well, to me at least. And then I started seeing the way you both had to plan things so carefully. You were always very deliberate about arranging your time together, and especially your time alone. I once walked into the room when you didn't realize I was coming in, and the look in your eyes was so...connected. I told my mom this morning that I don't think I've ever seen two people more in sync than you two. I'm sure it's been challenging for you."

"At times, yes. It has. Unfortunately, there is a lot of deception we must engage in. It makes me feel very guilty, like I'm a terrible person for lying to so many people."

"But you haven't had much choice, have you?"

"No, we had no choice at all. We simply couldn't be discovered, and that meant deceiving our husbands, which I regret most of all."

"I know. My mom said the same thing, but that's all in the past now, and soon, all of us kids will be gone from the house. So you will be a little freer, I should think."

"To some extent, maybe."

"Well, that's actually what I wanted to talk to you about. I suggested something that Mom said she had already tried to get you to agree to. I think you should go live in another town and tell people you are sisters. No one needs to know anything. No nosy neighbors will be around to spill your secrets."

"Oh, my goodness, Kevin! I can't believe this."

"Can't believe what?"

"Well, first, that you are so understanding and supportive about this. That's not the typical family response, trust me. Second, that you would try to help us and even encourage us to find a way to be together. I'm just floored!"

"Well, like I said. I just want her to be happy. I know that's what Michael wanted too." He hesitated as he looked up and saw her tears. "Anna, why are you crying?"

"I'm just amazed that you could be worrying about us at a time like this. It's so unselfish."

"I'm sorry if other members of our families have not been as kind. Maybe someday, things will be different, and people won't care as much."

"Maybe. Unlikely, though."

"You do love her, don't you, Anna?"

"Oh, Kevin. If I could only find the words to tell you how much I love her. I haven't been able to be there for her since your brother passed, and it's killing me that I can't help her through this. Next to my children, she is the most important thing in the world to me. Please know that. I try very hard to make sure she knows it whenever I have the opportunity."

"She knows." He smiled and kissed her on the cheek. "Now that the funeral is over, it will start to sink in for her. She will need you then. Promise me you will be there for her."

"I promise, Kevin."

"And promise me that once Linda moves out, you two will think about having your own life, even if it means going to a place where no one knows you. We will come to find you, wherever you are. So you needn't worry about that."

"I promise that, too."

"Can I walk you home, Anna?"

"I would love that, Kevin."

# Chapter Fifty-Three

## TRISH 2000

TRISH SAT ON A bench in St. Charles cemetery, her coat wrapped tight around her to shield her from the cold November breeze. One year. One whole year since Marilyn McCann drew breath on this earth. A year of holidays, anniversaries, birthdays, all celebrated without her. Trish spoke aloud to her mother, recounting some of the events of the past three hundred sixty-five days.

"Josie and I moved in together about a month ago, Mom. I hope you would have been happy about that. I think you would. I sold my house and moved into hers, but we may want to get a place that we both pick out together at some point. I came out to both Cassie and my principal at school a few months ago. They both were great about it. Mrs. Armstrong said if she heard any complaints from the parents, she would shut them up immediately by showing them my students' progress all these years. It was such a relief knowing I didn't have to fear getting fired. Of course, I'm still cautious with what I share at school, but it's a huge weight lifted off my shoulders."

The wind picked up, and Trish imagined it was her mother, sending the message that she heard her and was happy.

"Aunt Judy and I have seen a lot of each other this year. She misses you terribly. Does she come to see you? Probably. I'll bet these are her flowers on your gravestone. Did you know she has a boyfriend? She told me when I saw her last week. I was shocked! Happy, but shocked. She says he's a nice little man she met down at the senior center. Who knows? Maybe there will be a wedding in her future." She paused, thinking long and hard about her next thought.

"Um…speaking of weddings. I know you probably wouldn't be thrilled about this, but I'll say it anyway. I'm going to ask Josie to marry me. I know it won't be legal, but I still want us to make that commitment to each other. Did you know I asked her once already? It was only a month or so after we started dating. She turned me down. Well, she didn't turn me down, exactly, she delayed me. She said it was too soon, and I needed to make sure this was what I wanted. I'll never forget what she said because it made so much sense. She said, 'you think you are going to feel this bliss forever, but at some point, real life is going to kick in. There is no getting around it, but I can't imagine the joy I will feel when you are on the *other side* of Mount Blissful, and you *still* want to marry me. I want you to ask me again when that happens.' Well, guess what, Mom? I'm on the other side. I know who she is, and I've seen all her annoying habits. I just want to *be* with her. I hope you can be okay with that. Because I sure am." Trish got up from the bench and knelt in front of the headstone. She traced the outline of Marilyn's name with her finger. Marilyn 'Lynn' O'Brien McCann. Then she put her fingers to her lips, kissed them, and put them back on the stone over her mother's name.

"I love you, Mom."

# Chapter Fifty-Four

## JOSIE AND TRISH 2000

JOSIE PARKED HER CAR in the driveway. She saw Trish was already home, and she smiled. She had expected her to stay later at school today, so it was a pleasant surprise to see her home. Maybe they would order a pizza or something. Friday night was the perfect pizza and movie night. She opened the front door and found a post-it note next to the lock. It said:

*Proceed to the dining room, please.*

She smiled, expecting a romantic dinner waiting for her on the dining table, so she took a moment to give Max a belly rub and did as instructed. But there was no smell of food, so she thought maybe she had jumped to the wrong conclusion. In the dining room, there was an eight by ten piece of loose-leaf paper—the kind only a teacher or student would have—taped to the light fixture hanging over the table. It said:

*Well done! You've completed your first assignment. I just wanted to make sure you could follow instructions. Now, go to the living room and press the power button on the stereo. Then press play on the CD player. Then take three steps to the left.*

Josie chuckled out loud at the theatrics of it all. She made her way into the living room and turned on the CD player. A soft, romantic song played, but at a rather loud level. She turned it down a bit, then took her three steps to the left. Another note awaited.

*Okay, so now that you turned it down, turn it back up again, please! Then do an about-face and go to the other side of the room.*

Josie laughed again. Trish knew her too well. She returned the volume to its original level, then turned around and followed the next instruction. Max followed her every step of the way, excited to be part of the process. On the sofa against the wall, another note said:

*Much better. You should know by now that I had the volume set precisely where I wanted it. Proceed to the kitchen and open the refrigerator.*

Josie did as she was told. In the fridge, there was a bottle of champagne and two champagne flutes. She looked at the bottle. Dom Perignon.

*Very nice.*

*Take these and proceed up the stairs, please.*

When she got to the staircase, she noticed there were letters on the rungs of the banister, but she was so anxious to get to the top, she didn't take the time to see what they spelled out. At the top of the stairs, another note said:

*In your impatience, I couldn't help but notice that you didn't give any consideration to the name of the peak you were ascending.*

*So please go back and pay attention. Then continue to the bedroom.*

Josie grunted in feigned frustration and went back down the stairs. The letters on each rung of the banister said:

*M O U N T   B L I S S F U L*

Josie grinned from ear to ear, remembering what that name meant. She took the rest of the steps two at a time and ran to the bedroom. Upon opening the door, she saw Trish, dressed to the nines and down on one bended knee, holding the open ring box in her hand.

"Oh my god," Josie whispered, bringing her hands up to cover her mouth.

"Josephine Molina, as you can see, I am officially on the other side of Mount Blissful. I have never been happier in my life than I am right now, thanks to you. Will you *please* marry me?"

"Patricia Marie McCann, it would be the supreme honor of my life to marry you."

Josie bent down to meet Trish's face. She kissed Trish passionately, then got on her knees and threw her arms around her. They fell over onto the floor, nearly breaking the champagne flutes as they rolled around, kissing and laughing. Max wanted in on the excitement and plowed into them, licking and pawing at them. When they finally sat up, Trish took the sapphire ring out of the box and placed it on Josie's left hand. Perfect fit. Two lives, one heart.

# About Barbara Lynn Murphy

Barbara Lynn Murphy is originally from Long Island, New York, but currently lives in suburban Atlanta, Georgia with her wife and five dogs. She is a late bloomer to writing, having only started doing so in earnest during the Covid years. What was once a passing fancy has morphed into a second chapter in her professional life (although she still maintains her day job in Technology—for now.)

Connect with Barbara:
Email: barbaralynnmurphyauthor@gmail.com

Facebook: Barbara Lynn Murphy

Twitter: https://twitter.com/BLMurphyAuthor

Instagram: https://www.instagram.com/barbaralynnmurphy/

## Note to Readers:

Thank you for reading a book from Desert Palm Press. We appreciate you as a reader and want to ensure you enjoy the reading process. We would like you to consider posting a review on your preferred media sites and/or your blog or website.

For more information on upcoming releases, author interviews, contest, giveaways and more, please sign up for our newsletter and visit us as at Desert Palm Press: www.desertpalmpress.com and "Like" us on Facebook: Desert Palm Press.

Bright Blessings

www.ingramcontent.com/pod-product-compliance
Lightning Source LLC
Chambersburg PA
CBHW051339020726
47501CB00007B/2180